FoRGet-me-Not BLue

FORGET-ME-NOT BLUE

Sharelle Byars Moranville

HOLIDAY HOUSE   NEW YORK

HOLIDAY HOUSE is registered in the U.S. Patent and Trademark Office.

Printed and bound in June 2023 at Maple Press, York, PA, USA.

First Edition

1 2 3 4 5 6 7 8 9 10

Library of Congress Cataloging-in-Publication Data is available
from the Library of Congress.

ISBN: 978-0-8234-5359-7 (hardcover)

To Con and Sofie

chapter 1

"Sof!"

She tried to wake up, but the blanket of sleep was so comfy.

"Sof, open the door."

Why didn't her brother open it himself?

Then she remembered.

Connie had put a deadbolt on the inside of her door.

A couple of nights ago, one of her mom's friends had stumbled into the kitchen where Con and Sofie were making sandwiches. He'd caught up a handful of Sofie's hair and stuck his face in it, making weird noises. She'd tried to twist away, but he didn't turn loose.

Con had planted his open hand in the guy's face and shoved him. "You touch my sister again, you'll be sorry!"

The man sneered as he staggered into the backyard where their mom and her friends were partying. Sofie glared at him.

"You okay?" Con asked, smoothing Sofie's hair.

She nodded, but her heart was racing.

And it was racing now. What if Con hadn't been there?

But now, she could lock herself in her room anytime their mom was partying or that guy came around.

She unlocked the door.

"Swim lessons," Con said.

"I know."

"You need to pee before I shower?"

She nodded.

She heard Con throwing beer cans into the recycle bin. All the clanging and banging might wake her mom—which was probably the idea. Connie was angry about the party. But it hadn't been *all* that bad. People had mainly stayed outside because the weather was nice.

Still, Sofie hadn't been able to sleep because of the pounding music and people laughing and arguing. Sofie knew the regulars, like Lili with the big beautiful eyes. Lili had been around ever since Sofie could remember. Last night, she'd worn so many eyelashes she looked like a llama.

"Bet she shoplifted them on the way here," Con had muttered to Sofie.

But Lili had a big heart, like their mom. Lili stole stuff and gave it to people she liked. Sometimes it was a pretty T-shirt or fancy underwear or sunglasses. Once it had been pills. When Con understood what was happening, he'd taken Sofie to the attic and for the first time in a long time they'd slept side by side on the floor. She had felt safe, even though Connie said what Lili was giving away downstairs could kill a person.

"Does mom know the pills could kill her?"

"Yeah. She knows."

That was good. Their mom would never take pills like that, because her kids needed her.

When they saw Lili a few days after the night of the pills, she'd been beat up so bad she could hardly see and her arm was in a cast. Sofie was sorry, because Lili was nice.

"She stole from the wrong person," Con said.

When Sofie came out of the bathroom, she crossed the hall to her mom's room. Sofie opened the door a teeny crack to make sure she wouldn't see anything she didn't want to see, like a boyfriend without any clothes on.

But there was only her mom, asleep with her feet sticking out from under the cover, a streak of sunshine across them.

The room was painted her favorite color—forget-me-not blue. Sofie crept in, feeling the cool from the air conditioner in the window.

The T-shirts and scarves and her mom's shorts and sundresses on the floor were soft under her feet. Some came from the rich lady her mom cleaned for, but most were thrifting treasures. Sofie stood beside the bed, watching the way her mom's nose moved a tiny bit with each breath.

She was beautiful. Her silvery blond hair matched the hair of the girl in the photo on the table. That girl was Summer Jones, Sofie's grandmother, who had been a teen movie star. Sofie might be a movie star someday. She could make a lot of money and help her mom.

In the kitchen, Con reminded her they needed to leave in fifteen minutes.

"I know."

He had grown another foot in the night; his shoulders had gotten wider and his feet bigger. Soon he wouldn't fit in the tiny attic—the space he staked a claim on when they moved into this house two years ago. They had never lived anyplace for that long before. But before, they always slept in the same room. Or the same car, that time they were homeless. Which she didn't remember, but Connie did. She didn't understand why he wanted to be in the attic alone when together was better.

She put on her swimsuit, then a pair of blue-and-white-striped shorts with red stars—which she loved so much she wore them anytime they were clean. She topped it off with a white T-shirt with a sparkly red star on the front they'd found at the clothing pantry. Red was her favorite color. The shirt had a stain near the bottom, but most things from the clothing pantry had stains. She tucked in that part.

The pipes clanged as Con turned off the shower.

She couldn't find her flip-flops in her room. She looked in the living room and the kitchen.

The Uno deck was on the kitchen table exactly where it belonged, thank goodness. Since her mom was having parties, maybe they should put the cards where they wouldn't get damaged. But moving them could be bad luck.

Playing Uno was their ritual. *Uno* meant *one* in Spanish. And there were three of them. A triangle had three corners and could fit inside a circle, and circles were safe.

Once, when Sofie was in first grade, Social Services had almost taken her and Con away because their mom had left them alone in the trailer for a week. She'd gone to a New Year's Eve party and not come home. Con had called her and begged, but she was with friends in Texas. Sofie had tried to be brave and not cry, but Connie really had been brave. And they'd almost kept it a secret.

When their mom came back, she'd been so, so sorry, and they had to forgive her. She promised on her life she would never do it again. She loved them and they loved her so much. They'd bundled up and gone outside in snow and sunshine and a forget-me-not-blue sky. They'd held hands and marched in a circle singing a silly song until it ended with *Ashes, ashes, we all fall down.* And then they crumpled into the snow laughing.

They did that over and over until the trees spun. Sofie remembered the cold on her cheeks. The shadows on the snow. The birds fighting at the feeder in front of the trailer-park office.

Sofie took a deep breath and let it out. The danger of being taken away by Social Services was in the past, but it felt as close as the breeze stirring her hair.

Where were her flip-flops?

She finally found one under the steps, a crumpled beer can beside it.

Connie was going to be so mad about the mess. A pile of clothing was tangled in a broken folding chair. A turned-over cooler gaped open, and cigarette butts and cans were everywhere.

She searched for the other flip-flop, walking through the wet grass. When she found it inside the overturned cooler, her heart beat a dance of relief. The flip-flops were her only shoes.

Inside, she gathered up her towel, swim cap, and *The Higher Power of Lucky* as Con called, "Ready."

She'd snatched up the book at the Community Center library yesterday, sure it was the perfect summer book. The girl on the cover looked a little like Sofie, and the yellow and orange colors cried *Fun!* And it had the word *lucky* in the title. *And* it had a gold sticker. Books with stickers were the best.

"I wish school wasn't out," she said as they walked to the bus stop.

She liked everything about school. The books. The tests. Especially the tests. The free breakfasts and lunches that helped their mom. The teachers. The field trips. The media center with all the books. And her best friend, AnaMaria, who was in Arizona staying with grandparents for the summer.

"I'm going to be in Mr. Bloom's class next year," she told Con.

"You might get the other fifth-grade teacher."

"I'll get Mr. Bloom."

At the end of each year, he gave the Student Explorer Award—a big beautiful globe of the world that hummed when it spun on its axis. Con had won it when he was in fifth grade. When their mom sold it on eBay because they needed money, Sofie had seen the hurt in Connie's eyes. She would win the globe next year and she and Con would share it. A week in her room, a week in the attic with him. They would not let their mom sell it.

The Y was downtown, so any bus that came along on Southeast 16 would get them close. They shouldn't have long to wait on the shady bench. Sofie scrunched and twisted her towel into shapes. A mountain. A deadly cobra. The Very Hungry Caterpillar.

When the bus didn't come quickly, Sofie opened *The Higher Power of Lucky*. It was shabby, with a bent corner. Most of the books from the Community Center library were beat up. But they were still good.

On page one, she discovered both she and Lucky had too much curly hair. Ha! And like Lucky, she also loved eavesdropping even though it was wrong.

As she read, Sofie felt the dry desert heat as Lucky tidied up around the Found Object Wind Chime Museum and Visitor Center in a tiny town called Hard Pan in the Mojave Desert. *The Higher Power of Lucky* was going to be a wonderful book. And she knew the story would end happily because that was a Rule.

Con was beside her listening to music. He used to read all the time too. She had been excited when he got the phone for his thirteenth birthday last week. But she was beginning to hate it. Maybe he would drop it crossing the street and a bus would crush it.

When the bus came, it was packed but Con nudged her on. She showed her pass and grabbed the same pole as Con. As they neared downtown, the gold dome of the capitol glistened on the skyline.

At the Y, a big building with lots of glass and shiny tiles, they watched little kids finish their lessons and climb out of the pool and be wrapped in towels. Sofie's group was next.

She wouldn't be here if Con hadn't discovered there were scholarships for swimming lessons at the Y. Their mom could never afford them.

She turned to see what Con was staring at over her shoulder.

There was a swimmer who hadn't been here last week. She was about Sofie's age, with goggles around her neck and a towel over her shoulder. An older girl was with her. Why was Con staring?

She bumped against his side. "Do you know them?"

He shook his head.

When the instructor blew her whistle to call swimmers into the water, Sofie hurried to get in. She ended up in a lane next to the new girl, who had BETH written in black marker on her swim cap. Sofie's cap had her full name, SOFIA, on it because that sounded more like the name of a librarian—which was what she really wanted to be.

chapter 2

A few days later, Sofie stood in the free-lunch line at the Community Center with Connie and her mom. Sofie and Con came here anytime there was no school. Their mom came on the days Tommy's Place, the restaurant where she worked, was closed.

Sofie's mouth began to water when the smell of tuna casserole with cornflake topping floated down the line. She and her mom loved that casserole, but Connie hated it. He mumbled something about cat food.

She turned around to say, "Sorry, Connie. But there's cherry pie."

At the same time, their mom said, "Look, Con, cherry pie!"

He looked like he didn't know whether to roll his eyes or wag his tail. He was so confusing these days.

Her mom brushed Sofie's hair out of her eyes, then refastened a barrette. Sofie loved having her mom mess with her hair. She always wondered where her mom's straight hair came from. The movie star Summer Jones had curly hair, as did Sofie. Maybe her mom's dad had straight hair.

Once Sofie had asked her mom, and her mom said she had no idea. She didn't even know if he had hair. He was just some dumb kid from California who'd left teenage Summer Jones stranded and pregnant in Des Moines, Iowa, a long time ago. "And here we all are," her mom would say, smiling.

Today her mom looked extra beautiful. She wore a blue T-shirt with a splash of color on one shoulder that made Sofie think of a giant flower, or maybe a melted rainbow. The blue was kind of purply and turned her mom's eyes the same color.

New people who didn't know better were in their regular spot, so they found a place at a long table by the windows. There were usually new people at the free lunch, but a lot of the same people, like the mom with the sweet baby in a stroller who'd started coming a few weeks ago. And the tall guy with the piercings and tattoos. He'd been around forever. He came all the time for weeks and then disappeared. But after a while he'd show up again, and Sofie always felt a wave of relief.

Today a guy who wasn't a regular stared at her mom. When people did that, Sofie wondered if it was because her mom was so pretty, or because she was so tall. Connie was tall like her.

Her mom smiled at the new guy, showing the dimple in her right cheek. Sofie so wanted a dimple. When she was little she'd tried to sleep with her finger poking into her cheek, hoping she'd wake up with a dimple too.

Her mom's dangle earring sparkled in the sun. Her signature look was a dangle in one ear and a little stud in the other. Sofie wanted a signature look. She was too young for dangles, but she always wore sparkly little studs. What if she wore only one? Would that be a signature look, or just kind of weird?

Her mom slid her cherry pie across to Connie so he had two pieces. "Because you hate the casserole," she said.

"Thanks," Con said, in a deep voice that came now and then and startled them.

Since her mom really liked cherry pie too, Sofie slid her own across to share.

After lunch, while Con went to shoot hoops, Sofie and her mom went to check out the clothing pantry and the library at the other end of the building. She linked hands with her mom, not in a babyish way but like friends, until her mom turned left to the clothing pantry and Sofie turned right to the library.

In this library you didn't need a card, and you could keep a book as long as you wanted. Actually, forever. This was where her books came from. They were her most precious possessions.

When she was holding a book she felt safe. They were bolt holes for escaping. Sometimes Con called her Meerkat because meerkats—which Sofie thought looked kind of like very hairy humans when they stood on their back legs—were famous for their bolt holes.

The lady in charge waved Sofie over to a table. "You want to help, Sofie? We got in three boxes of kids' books this morning."

"Sure."

Sofie could put them on the kids' shelves in any old order since this wasn't a real library. But she pretended it was. She sometimes dropped in and alphabetized the books by author's last name just for fun.

Now and then she glanced at her mom, who was looking at boys' stuff even though Con didn't want her picking out his clothes anymore.

As she shelved books, Sofie decided for sure to be a movie star like Summer Jones and make a lot of money so Con could go to college and become a doctor. And then she would become a librarian because she didn't really want to be a movie star. She would be the head librarian downtown in the building with the murals and stained glass. And she would have the keys so she and Connie could stay all night sometimes.

After a while, her mom gave up looking for clothing. "Nothing," she said. "Let's find Con and go home."

They hadn't been home long. Con and her mom were trying to start the lawn mower. Every time they yanked the cord, the mower coughed. Then quit. Sofie was sitting on the steps looking at a dragon book she'd brought home from the library.

She'd ditched *The Higher Power of Lucky* when she discovered Lucky's mom was dead and her dad was very weird and not around, so Lucky became a ward. A *ward* was someone guarded by a *guardian*—which did not sound good to Sofie. Sofie did not believe a story with a dead mom could end happily. Probably the sticker on the front had been a mistake.

But her new book was wonderful. She'd never seen a book where the pages folded out to be three pages wide so the dragon threatening the village looked bigger than the sky. It was called *The Paper Dragon* and it didn't have a lot of words, but they all felt very important. The book was beat up and two of the fold-our pages were crumpled, but she smoothed them. She couldn't wait to show it to AnaMaria because of the big, beautiful illustrations. Actually, she might give it to AnaMaria as a welcome-home present.

AnaMaria could draw like a wizard, and she drew herself and Sofie in all kinds of clothes with all kinds of hairdos. Often, they were dancing. Sofie missed AnaMaria even though she'd only been gone two days.

The sound of an old truck rattling down the alley made her look up. The truck stopped, a rusty door screeched open, and an old man got out—a very tall, skinny, shabby old man.

"Gunner!" her mom cried, running to hug him. "It's so good to see you."

"Con and Sofie," she called. She gestured like she was presenting royalty. "Meet your great-granddad!"

In Sofie's whole life, she had never once heard of him. She looked at Con, who shrugged with his eyes.

And why did their mom call him Gunner? That couldn't be anybody's name.

A wild bush of shaggy gray hair, white whisker stubble, and faded clothing made him look like a street person. And he stared at her so long she wondered if he was frozen. Then he came to life and went back to the truck for something, which he offered to her mom with a grin.

"Have you ever seen finer strawberries?" he asked.

Her mom laughed and kissed him on the cheek and said thanks. She didn't seem a bit surprised. Almost like she'd been expecting him and the strawberries.

He grinned at Con. "You don't remember me."

Con shook his head.

"You were a little guy when I was here before."

Then his eyes came back to Sofie.

She looked at her dragon book until the scarecrow and her mom walked past her into the house. He smelled moldy.

"He's really our great-granddad?" she said to Con.

Con shrugged. "I guess. Mom sure seems glad to see him."

Later, when the scarecrow left to run an errand, her mom told Con and Sofie he would be staying with them for a while. "Until he gets on his feet."

"Why isn't he on his feet?" Con asked.

Her mom's neck turned pink. "Why isn't anybody? Gunner is a good man. You kids will love him." She touched Sofie's hair. "For now, Sofie, would you let him use your room?"

What was wrong with her mom? "No. Where would I sleep?"

"I was hoping you could share the attic with Connie. It won't be for long."

"No way." Con was shaking his head. "I need my privacy."

Their mom sighed. "I know it's asking a lot. But Gunner saved my life once. When you were a baby, Con. And I think I saved him too."

If things had been so great, why had he left?

Her mom was looking at her, reading her mind. "We don't need to bother him with a lot of questions," she said. "He's family."

No. He was not. Family was the three of them. Her. Her mom. And Con. Her mom had always said Sofie and Con didn't have dads because they didn't need them. The three of them stuck together and life was fine. And there was no room for a smelly old man. What was her mom thinking?

chapter 3

A wave of thunder rattled the house. Dim morning light came through the attic window. Sofie sensed Con stirring on the other side of the sheet he'd strung down the middle of the attic for privacy. The attic was very hot and stuffy, but Sofie had loved falling asleep the last five nights close enough to touch her brother. But she still didn't want that scarecrow in her room, because it was just wrong.

She sat up. "What time is it?"

"Ten forty."

Her mom would have left for work because she had the early shift.

Wind slammed rain against the window. Probably her mom was getting soaked on the way to work.

Con headed downstairs, pulling on a T-shirt. With every big rain, water leaked through the kitchen ceiling, even though their mom had told the landlord about it a hundred thousand times. Sofie hurried to follow. She knew the drill.

While Con used ragged towels and his feet to mop up puddles, she found two pans to catch the worst drips. A drop landed in her hair and tickled its way through to her scalp.

Out the back door she saw that the old scarecrow's truck wasn't parked in its place in the alley.

"Where do you think he goes all the time?"

Con shrugged. "He could be taking Mom to work."

Maybe he *could* be. This time. But what about the other times when he jumped up and went off without a word? And why was Connie always pointing out good things about the old guy?

"But don't you wonder why he acts so weird sometimes? And why he just appeared out of nowhere?"

And why the scarecrow man and her mom were so close. That was what really annoyed Sofie. The way they told stories about people Sofie didn't know. The way they made each other laugh. The way her mom cried and leaned against him for comfort. Sofie really didn't like that. He needed to get out of their life before he broke something.

She knew Connie had his doubts too. She saw how watchful he was when the scarecrow was around. But the scarecrow was watchful too. Actually, Sofie thought they were kind of alike that way. Yesterday, Con had told her he'd seen the scarecrow without his shirt and realized he was really tan on his face, neck, and arms. And he had a lot of muscles for an old guy.

As if thinking about him had conjured him, the truck shuddered to a stop in the alley. She sighed.

He came in dripping, putting down bags and brushing rain off his clothes.

"What's up?" he said, looking from one to the other.

Con shrugged, finishing his mopping. "Not much. What's up with you?"

"Took your mom to work."

"Thanks, man."

Sofie shot Con a look. He shouldn't be so nice. It encouraged the scarecrow to stay.

He began unpacking bread and cheese, cans of tomato soup, a box of tea bags, and fresh fruit. Today it was strawberries and apples. He ate more fresh fruit than anybody Sofie had ever known, and was always offering it to her and Connie and their mom as if grapes were precious rubies and bananas were bars of gold.

He set a sack of doughnuts on the table. "For you kids."

The smell curling out of the bag almost made her reach for it. The doughnuts were from the place downtown. She loved to stand outside the front window and watch them ride along on the belt until they tumbled into the bubbling oil, then came out all plump and golden and got showered with cinnamon and sugar.

Her jaws ached for a bite.

"I thought Sofie liked doughnuts," the scarecrow said as she went to her mom's room where she could eavesdrop without having to see the doughnut bag.

"She'll probably eat one later. She's crabby in the morning."

She was not. He talked about her like she was a baby.

Through the thin wall, she heard the rattle of the sack. She wiped the corner of her mouth. This was not fair.

Could she hear them chewing, or was it her imagination? It was probably the rain, which had almost quit.

"What's that you're reading?"

"A book my old fifth-grade teacher gave me. He works at the Community Center in the summer. He liked it when he was my age."

Sofie knew Con was talking about Mr. Bloom. She heard the scarecrow man laugh.

"What?" Con said

"The title of the book is *Holes* and we're eating doughnuts."

After a beat, Con said, "Yeah."

At least he hadn't laughed. Sofie was glad for that.

"My ex-wife Donna was a reader. You and Sofie remind me of her with all your books."

Donna was the great-grandmother who sent a big box of presents from California every year. Sofie and Con had never met her. Their mom had never met her either, but they all knew she was mean.

There was money in the Christmas boxes, but the rest was a lot of fancy useless stuff, according to their mom. Sofie remembered the year Donna sent a beautiful, soft little blanket for each of them. Sofie had rubbed hers against her cheeks, eager to curl up on the couch and read, wrapped comfily in its softness. But their mom had snorted at the silliness of something so fancy it had to be dry-cleaned. Like they could *ever* afford dry-cleaning. That would be like throwing money in the fire and watching it burn. Sofie had hated putting her wonderful blanket back in its wrapping.

And one year, Donna sent cheese and crackers. Con and Sofie could see through the clear plastic window on the box that the crackers inside had mouse turds on them. Their mom said those weren't actually mouse turds, but who could be sure? They shoved them in the sell-online pile, but Sofie knew no one would buy them.

Then there was the three-thousand-piece Harry Potter Hogwarts puzzle that they got all excited about until Con noticed it would be 45 inches wide and 32 inches long when it was put together. Their table didn't have room. Sold online.

Even though her mom insisted Donna was mean, Sofie thought the things in the Christmas boxes were wonderful—not the crackers with the mouse turds, those must have been a mistake. But the gifts just weren't for their family.

Then last Christmas came the chess set, which she and Connie had hidden, and he was teaching her how to play.

"Our older kids were like Donna," the scarecrow was saying. "Like you and Sofie. Born holding books. But when Summer came along, she was like me. Donna and I said she was our Indian Summer."

Sofie's eyes flashed to the framed photo of sixteen-year-old Summer, so beautiful and famous, that sat on a small table against the wall. A candle in a pretty green glass container sat beside the photo. When her mom lit the candle, light flickered like sunshine through trees. Summer had died when Con was a baby.

Sofie took the velvet keepsake box off her mom's dresser and sat cross-legged on the silky sheets that smelled like her mom. The keepsake box had belonged to Summer.

Con and Sofie and their mom had looked through the keepsake box so often their fingers had worn away the velvet in places. Sofie picked through the jumble of old photos, matchbooks, charms. A diary Sofie had given her mom that her mom never wrote in. A necklace with a broken chain. Her and Connie's hospital bracelets were near the top, and further down was their mom's, cracked and yellowed. Sofie rubbed her fingers over the smooth brown nut that made her think of a petrified eyeball. There was a menu from a fancy restaurant where Summer Jones had eaten with movie people. A sparkly clip-on earring in the shape of a starfish.

She still heard Con and the scarecrow talking, but she couldn't make out what they were saying. Maybe they were sitting on the porch. She looked out the window. The rain had stopped and the light was getting brighter.

Near the bottom of the box, she found the snapshot of Summer that always made Sofie's mom tear up. Her grandmother was thirty-four and her mom was seventeen in the photo. Their arms were around each other and their heads together. They looked like very beautiful sisters.

Sofie could hear her mom saying what she always said when she looked at the photograph: *It was the last time we had our picture taken together. Two weeks later, she got in a car with a friend. A beautiful, soft snow was falling.*

Sofie shivered. A person would know it was the last time only when it was too late. The fear of seeing her own mom for the last time nibbled around the edges of her thoughts. Once, after the worst boyfriend ever had broken Con's arm and gone to jail, she and Connie had been left alone in the trailer for a whole week, terrified their mom would never come back. Terrified they had seen her for the last time when she went off to a New Year's Eve party looking so beautiful and hopeful and smelling so nice.

Sofie dropped the photo back into the box like it was dangerous.

chapter 4

That night, her mom came home from the early shift bringing Lili and her sister and her sister's boyfriend. Everybody was already loud and happy.

Sofie saw the worried look on the old scarecrow's face. She could tell he didn't like her mom's friends, and they ignored him like an old mummy in the corner.

Lili called Sofie over, the way she'd done a hundred times before, and told her to shut her eyes and hold out her hand. Sofie knew Lili was going to put something special on Sofie's palm and close Sofie's fingers around it. Sometimes it was hair barrettes still on their card or a square of candy wrapped in foil or gum or a tiny plastic animal of some kind.

"You got the cutest kids on the planet, Ash," Lili said.

Lili's fingers brushed Sofie's palm as she laid something there. Lili smelled of beer and pot, and before long, Sofie knew, Lili would either be turning up the music and dancing like a wild woman or totally crashed in the corner. That was Lili. High or low.

"Open your eyes," Lili said.

Sofie looked at what she held in her hand. Lipstick? She looked at Lili.

"Well, you're growing up," Lili said, shrugging one shoulder.

No, she wasn't. She was going to be in fifth grade. That was nowhere near grown up. She didn't really want to be a grown-up. Not the way Lili was talking about.

"Won't be long until you have boyfriends."

She would never have a boyfriend. They were the worst.

Lili smiled at Sofie's mom. "Just like your pretty mama. She started young."

Con's face turned red and he seemed to grow another inch. "Come on, Sof. Let's go." He motioned toward the attic door.

The scarecrow watched, looking worried.

Sofie had been propped on her elbows trying to read for what felt like hours. She held a flashlight in a sweaty hand and pointed it at her book. The attic was so hot and sticky. The thudding music from downstairs made the floor of the attic quiver against her belly. She felt like she was inside a drum.

Where was the scarecrow? She'd hadn't heard him leave over the noise of the party, but she'd seen the look on his face—like he couldn't get away fast enough. Like something was chasing him and it was so close he could feel its breath.

Over the bass line that shook the house, she heard the sudden sharp *Rherr! Rherr!* of a police siren. She and Con scrambled to the window as red and blue lights swept the front yard.

The music stopped.

She told herself if they stood absolutely still, barely breathing, no matter how long it took, nothing bad would happen. Her heartbeat drummed in her ears. Bad boyfriends, social workers, and the police always meant trouble.

After a long time of hearing her mom's voice now and then and her laugh once, and the voices of the police, Sofie—finally—heard car doors shut. The spinning lights stopped. The police car pulled away. Her mom had worked her magic on the cops.

She flopped down on her pallet and heard Con settle on his. It didn't seem safe to speak even yet.

Finally, she picked up the flashlight. She was reading *The Paper Dragon* again for the third time. The words were easy enough, but really understanding how a poor artist could save his village from the biggest, fiercest fire-breathing dragon imaginable needed to be thought about. At the beginning of the book, the dragon was huge in the illustrations and the artist was very small and bowed. But at the end, the dragon had become a small paper dragon.

Sofie was deciding maybe the story wasn't about getting eaten by a dragon, but about people loving and taking care of each other, even when they were scared.

Her flashlight dimmed and went out.

She smacked it against her palm. Nothing. She'd been using it the last three nights, and the batteries were dead.

She couldn't just shut her eyes and go to sleep after the police had been there.

She lifted the sheet. "Connie."

"What?"

"My batteries died."

"I'll turn on the light."

The light was a bare bulb with a chain pull that hung from a rafter too high for her to reach.

"No. It hurts my eyes and I can't read by it."

She knew she sounded whiny, but if she couldn't escape into a story she didn't know what she'd do.

She scooted under the sheet to his side. Being very close in the darkness made her think of the bolt hole in the trailer.

That was where they lived with Jonah, the worst boyfriend. He beat their mom, and they weren't big enough to stop him. So when he came back to the trailer all jittery and loud and mad at everybody, their mom shot them that *Get out of here!* look. And they ran for the closet like a pair of meerkats and Connie blocked the sliding door with a screwdriver.

That was where she'd learned to read, pressed against Con's side, his breath on her cheek. In between boxes and the vacuum, using the flashlight that they kept hidden in the closet, whispering, Connie taught her to read his Magic Tree House books.

Jack and Annie were really Con and her. The kids on the cover even looked kind of like them. As they had wonderful adventures Sofie learned to recognize and sound out words. She hardly heard Jonah's angry bellowing or felt the trailer shaking when their mom got slammed into the wall.

"You want to watch a movie on my phone, Meerkat?" Con asked, as if he'd been remembering the same thing.

She couldn't think of anything in the world she'd rather do.

They bent over the phone together. She wasn't paying attention to the movie, and she didn't think Con was either. Gradually the house got quieter. Then quiet.

She was so tired. She scooted under the sheet and stretched out on her pallet and took a breath so deep it made her dizzy. Connie was rustling on his side of the sheet.

He touched her shoulder. "I'm going for a walk," he whispered.

"Now?"

"Yeah. I have to. Come with me."

She sat up. "It's the middle of the night."

"Come on, Sof. I'll keep you safe." He said it like a grown-up.

He was a blob against the pale light of the window. He was taking the screen out of the window. Wait. They were going *out the window?*

Maybe she was dreaming.

"Get your shoes, Sof."

"My shoes don't fit. I just have flip-flops."

That fact somehow told her this wasn't a dream.

"Then I'll put the flip-flops in my pocket until we get down. You might trip on the roof."

She couldn't believe she was doing this. But she found her flip-flops. Con put them in his pocket, then folded his long legs and went through the window. He reached for her.

She hunkered on the slope until Con helped her stand. The shingles were warm and gritty.

As she tipped her face to the sky, a breeze lifted her hair. She felt as if she'd hatched into the wide world. She'd shake out her feathers, run a few steps, and fly off. She'd catch a breeze and rise through the clouds the way she did in her dreams.

"How do we get down?" she whispered, suddenly not tired at all.

He spoke close to her ear. "I'll go first. Then I'll help you."

He led her to the edge. "Put your foot where my foot is," he said quietly.

As she did, something stubbed her toes. "Ow!"

"That's a grip I put there. When I tell you to come over the edge, hang on to that with both hands until I say turn loose, okay?"

"Okay."

If he had put the grip there, did that mean he'd done this before?

Lying on his stomach, Con scrambled over the edge of the roof. "Come on over," he said softly from the ground.

Was he kidding? He was ten feet tall. She was short. But she lay on her stomach the way Con had. Her T-shirt hiked up as she slid, and shingles scraped her belly.

Con touched her ankles. "Easy," he whispered. "Keep coming."

Her cheek pressed against the shingles as she clutched the handhold.

"Drop," Con said.

When he caught her, they tumbled backward and she bit her tongue and tasted blood. She rolled off him and got up, crunching a plastic cup under her foot and feeling whatever had been in it gush over her toes. Empty bottles in the grass caught the dim light.

"Yuk," she whispered. "Give me my flip-flops, Connie."

The backyard was trashed too, she saw, as Con led them between their house and the vacant house next door. They followed a trail of alleys where weeds in the gravel itched her ankles.

Martin Luther King Jr. Parkway was empty. A thing she'd never seen. The traffic light, two blocks away, changing from green to yellow, looked lonely. The night was so still.

Right in the middle of MLK, Con began to walk the center line like it was a tightrope. Was this a weird game of follow the leader, the way they'd used to do? Playing in a busy street even if it was empty felt dangerous.

When they heard the hiss of brakes, Con grabbed her hand and they dashed to the sidewalk. They hunkered in a bus shelter that smelled of pee. The lights of a big semi swept around the curve, then it passed and was gone.

"We're okay," Con said, taking her hand and standing up.

They were okay. But why were they doing this?

They followed the curving sidewalk down the hill to the park. The playground looked ghostly, and an eerie musical sound raised the hair on her arms.

"What's that?"

"Frogs. Calling their girlfriends."

"That's so dumb."

All that boyfriend girlfriend stuff was *so,* so dumb. She hated it.

Last week, Beth, the new girl in her swim class, had asked if Con had a girlfriend. Beth's cousin Jade wanted to know. Jade was the beautiful girl who came every week with Beth to swimming lessons. Sofie had discovered Jade was from Tennessee, which probably explained why she talked funny. And she was here to help with the twins who were going to be born soon.

Sofie said what she always said when girls asked about Con: *My brother doesn't have time for girls.* And she always looked very stern when she said it.

But she'd glanced at Con sitting in the bleachers. He was listening to music and seemed to be hanging out in his own cool world. But he was wearing a new T-shirt—the pink long-sleeved one with the fancy-schmancy logo he'd been so thrilled to find at the clothing pantry. And he'd gelled his hair. And the girl, Jade, was sitting one row behind him, a few feet away— but closer than she'd been the week before.

"You don't have time for a girlfriend, Connie," she said as he led her down the shadowy path to the duck pond.

"I don't have a girlfriend."

The closer they got to the pond, the louder the frog music became. As they walked out on a pier with a bench at the end, the pond seemed to thrum around them, to wrap them in magic. A big, bright moon made shadows.

Con sat down and she sat beside him, their arms touching. They could be the only two people on the planet.

"Do you like Jade?"

He snorted. "I've never even talked to her."

"But do you think she's pretty?"

If he said no, she'd know he was lying. Jade was beautiful, with her red hair and nice smile.

"I guess," he finally said.

"I think she's rich." The towels Beth brought to swimming lessons were thick and soft and snowy white. Jade's clothes looked like they'd never been worn before.

"So?" Con said.

Jade could break her brother's heart. Any girlfriend could—which was why he should never have one. Especially not a beautiful rich one.

She jumped at the *who-who-whowhowho* sound. She whispered, "Connie, is that a real owl? In person?"

Before he could answer, tree leaves rustled and a shadow swooped over them.

"Whoa," she said, her breath catching.

The owl called again, then she heard a second on the other side of the pond.

"It's just like on TV," she said. It was the coolest thing.

Con laughed.

The owls went back and forth for a while with their *whowhowho*-ing and flying from tree to tree, and finally she didn't hear them anymore.

Sleeping headless ducks drifted on the pond, twirling slowly. She knew they weren't really headless, they just looked that way with their heads tucked under their wings. It was so peaceful.

"How long have you been sneaking out and coming here?" she asked.

"A while."

"Why?"

When he didn't answer, she asked again.

"Why, Connie? It's dangerous."

Finally he said, "I can't explain." He sounded angry when he said, "I have to do it. Just in case."

"Just in case what?"

He rushed the words like he didn't want them to have time to be remembered. "I have to know I can face scary stuff and look after you too."

Oh.

She shivered even though the night was warm.

After a while, the moon began to sink behind the tall buildings downtown. The sleeping ducks kept drifting. The frogs kept singing, but more quietly. They didn't need to talk about what he'd said.

When they started home, she took his hand. Not in a babyish way.

At the house, Con climbed onto the roof and into the attic, then came to the door and let her in. She fell asleep the minute her eyes shut.

chapter 5

The next morning, passing sirens woke her. Heat and bright light poured through the window.

She got up and rummaged through her crate for underwear, a pair of pale blue denim shorts with fancy white ruffles around the back pockets that felt signature, and a red tank top.

In the kitchen, the clock on the stove said 12:05. Past noon. Normally she would have waked Connie and they'd have rushed to the Community Center before the lunch line closed, but yesterday their mom had taken them to the food pantry. Plus, the scarecrow had bought a big carton of blueberries yesterday. They were beautiful to look at, but they tasted kind of nasty.

Connie was going to be so mad about the stinky, gross kitchen. She shuddered when a big roach crawled out of an overturned can. It darted across the counter and disappeared behind the faucet. Butts floated in a glass of yellowish liquid. Wrappers from a fast-food place littered the table, and two french fries stuck up out of a container of ketchup like rabbit ears. But the Uno deck was where it should be.

Thank goodness the bathroom was empty, because she really needed to pee. She locked the door and turned on the shower for the water to get warm.

Under the spray, she squeezed watermelon-scented shampoo into her hair. Until this summer they had all used the same shampoo, but now Connie wanted his own, which was silly because watermelon smelled nice.

☆

When her mom tapped on the door and said, "About done in there?" Sofie was pulling on her tank top.

"Just a minute," she said in a muffled voice.

She opened the door and her mom wrapped her in a hug, so close she could feel her mom's heartbeat. Underneath the stink of cigarettes and partying, her mom smelled like a sunny day. It wasn't a smell like flowers or grass. It was a smell of belonging. Con had the same smell, though he sometimes shoved Sofie off when she tried to hug him.

Her mom gave her a long squeeze, kissed the top of her head, and disappeared into the bathroom.

Sofie went to the back door to see if the scarecrow's truck was there, which it wasn't. Which meant he wasn't in her room. Still, she tapped before she opened it. She tried not to see his stuff. She glanced to make sure her books were lined up along the baseboard and AnaMaria's drawings were taped to the walls. Then she stooped and picked up the pink lamp with both arms.

Her mom was coming out of the bathroom. Sofie couldn't see her mom's face over the lampshade, but she sounded disappointed when she said, "Oh, honey."

What? She didn't feel bad about leaving the old scarecrow in the dark. Somebody might have broken her beautiful lamp last night. She was taking it upstairs even if there was no place to plug it in. At least it would be safe.

The lamp was heavy. Only a rich lady like the one her mom cleaned for would have such a heavy lamp. Sofie clutched it against her stomach. The pink shade flared way out at the bottom and bumped her chin as she struggled up the stairs, and the cord hit her ankle with each step.

She was out of breath when she got to the attic, where Con was waiting to come down. She squeezed past him.

"There's no place to plug it in," he called over his shoulder as he went down the stairs.

Like she didn't know.

In her bedroom, the lamp had sat on an upside-down plastic crate beside her mattress on the floor. Here, she put it on the floor at the head of her pallet. The base was as glossy as glass and the color of strawberry ice cream. It looked like it had been swirled through the fingers of a giant's hand. It was a signature lamp, and her mom had gotten it for her when the rich lady was throwing it out. Her mom had wrestled it home on the bus. After her books, it was Sofie's most important possession.

She ran back downstairs and gathered an armful of random books. There wasn't room in the attic for many.

Then she went to help Con, who was slamming stuff around as he cleaned up the kitchen. Sofie fished the butts out of the yellowish liquid with a spoon and flung them in the trash, then rinsed the glasses. She got rid of the fast-food stuff, which smelled bad, then cleaned the table with a damp paper towel.

Finally, they each opened their own box of cereal from the food pantry. Her box made a snap as the seal broke, and the inner bag sighed a puff of freshness in her face. As she crunched, sugar sang through her body. Maybe a new box of cereal would make Con feel better too.

When her mom came into the kitchen dressed for work Sofie saw the headache in her eyes. Her mom filled a glass of water and drank it. She probably didn't feel very well.

But she looked beautiful in her shorts and silky shirt, and the platform sandals showed off her pedicure. The peony-pink glitter polish on her toes matched the polish on Sofie's own toes.

A few days ago, her mom had dumped a pile of treasures out of the pocket of her hoodie. The peony-pink nail polish. A little bottle of travel shampoo, though nobody was going anywhere. And for Sofie, a card of sparkly ear studs in rainbow colors.

When Con saw the treasures, he stomped off. And maybe Sofie should think her mom was bad, but she stole because she loved them and loved pretty things.

Peony pink was a beautiful color. Sofie hadn't known the word *peony* until she read it on the bottom of the bottle. Her mom told her how to say it. It made them giggle as they took turns saying *peony, peony, peony* while they polished each other's toes.

Her mom bent and kissed Sofie on the head, then twisted open a diet drink and lit a cigarette. Con's anger came off him like heat. Sofie wished her mom hadn't started smoking again, because it was bad for her and cost money, but her mom liked her comforts the way Sofie liked her sugary cereal. If they let her have her comforts, she wouldn't leave.

Her mom picked up the Uno deck and dealt.

Sofie arranged her cards. When Con didn't put down his phone, Sofie said, "Connie."

Finally her mom tugged the phone away. Con gave her a bad look, and Sofie thought for a second he was going to grab it back. But, looking bored, he gathered up his cards.

Sofie slid one foot into her mom's lap. She loved to have her mom pet her feet as they played.

When an alert sounded on her mom's phone, she gave Sofie's foot a squeeze and stood.

"See you after my shift." She tugged one of Con's ears. "Thank you for looking after Sofie."

Con ignored her.

Sofie stood to give her mom a long hug goodbye. Her mom brushed back Sofie's hair and smiled.

"Love you guys." She always said that.

"Love you too," they echoed.

Sofie was so relieved Con said it.

She was gathering up the Uno cards to put them away when Con said, "Look, Sof."

He held out his phone.

She didn't know what she was looking at.

"It's a light socket adapter," he said. "For plugging in your lamp in the attic."

That would be wonderful.

"There's an old extension cord in the shed that works. We could plug it into the adapter, then you could use your lamp."

But what about the cost?

Con earned money by doing jobs now and then for Mr. Bloom, and he was thirteen, which meant he could be a peer tutor when school started. And he was tutoring Tommy in algebra. Tommy, their mom's boss, was going to college again even though he was old.

But Con liked to save his money *just in case*.

And then she had a horrible thought. Did Con know something she didn't? Was she going to be in the attic forever? Was the old scarecrow *staying*?

As if he had read her mind, Con said, "Maybe it wouldn't be a bad idea to have Gunner stick around."

"Connie!" She glared at him. Didn't he know the old scarecrow was dangerous? The *three* of them had to stick together. In the circle.

The stupid boyfriends who moved in always left or her mom kicked them out. There had been a couple Sofie barely remembered because she was little. Then there was Jonah, whom she'd never forget. Then after Jonah was when their mom went off to Texas and left them for a week. She came home with a new boyfriend called Cowboy. Cowboy hadn't stayed long, and stole some of their stuff when he left.

That was when their mom kind of hit rock bottom. That was when she sobered up and started working at Tommy's Place. Somewhere their mom got the money to rent this house, and Con and Sofie had started at a new school. Connie had been in Mr. Bloom's room, and Sofie had met AnaMaria.

They were safe in a circle now, and the scarecrow needed to go.

"I don't want that old scarecrow here. And I want my room back." Though she did like being so close to Connie again, and if she had her lamp... "Why do you think he should stick around?"

"I think he's good for Mom."

"I thought you were mad at Mom."

He shrugged. "Yeah."

But Connie loved their mom as much as she did.

"We don't know anything about him."

"We know he's family. Blood family."

True. He and Con had the same thick, wiry hair with the little point on the forehead that their mom called a widow's peak. They were built alike. They had the same eyes.

Connie was getting attached to the old guy. She could tell by the way they messed around with the lawn mower and sat on the steps and talked.

"It's important to have real family around," Con said. "Just in case."

Just in case tied a knot in her middle.

"Let's go to Walmart and get the adapter," Con said.

The thought of being able to read by the light of her pink lamp was too tempting.

"Okay."

chapter 6

People were fishing on the bridge. Tackle boxes were open at their feet, and over the traffic noise, someone was playing music. Sofie fell into step with it. Gulls circled and cried.

Tommy's Place was on the other side of the street, up one block. She had always known Tommy, who was a friend—not one of their mom's stupid boyfriends, but a family friend. And ever since they moved to this neighborhood, their mom had worked for him.

Tommy didn't look at their mom the way boyfriends or wannabes looked at her. Sofie didn't know exactly what to make of Tommy, but somehow she just *knew* he was okay, kind of like she knew Mr. Bloom was okay. Some men were *not* okay, and she knew that too.

Once, a long time ago, when she and Con came home from school and Cowboy wouldn't let them in even though they could hear their mom yelling at him to do it, they went to Tommy's Place. They sat at a little table near the kitchen where Con did his homework and she read. Tommy kept bringing them treats.

Con hadn't wanted to tell Tommy why they were there. He thought Tommy would think he was a sissy because he couldn't make Cowboy open the door.

Finally, Tommy sat down with them. "You kids come here anytime. You class the place up."

No, they didn't. But the way Tommy said it made Sofie smile.

"I texted Ashley to see what was going on and she said that idiot boyfriend has left. Probably for good. You can go home now. Your mom's waiting for you."

Con put his stuff in his backpack and said, "Come on, Sof."

She saw Con stand as tall as he could when he offered Tommy his hand and said, "Thanks, man." Connie had learned to shake hands from Mr. Bloom, who shook hands with all his students.

"Anytime." Tommy smiled at Sofie. "Anytime at all, Princess. You're great kids, you know that?"

Why was Sofie remembering Cowboy and old stuff from years ago?

"Let's go say hello to Mom and Tommy," she said.

"Let's not," Con said.

But she ran across the street, dodging traffic.

"Sofie!" He caught up and grabbed her hand until they were on the other side. "That was dangerous!"

She saw fear in his eyes. "Sorry."

Their mom was clearing tables on the patio and Tommy was watering the hanging plants Tommy's Place was kind of famous for. This was a slow time.

"Mom!" Sofie called.

Her mom looked up and smiled. "Hi!"

"The princess and the professor," Tommy said. His muscles bulged as he lifted up a large planter to hang on a hook. "What are you guys up to?"

"Not much," Con said. "What's up with you?"

The way Con ignored their mom was mean.

"Guess what, Professor," Tommy said, grinning, brushing droplets of water off his black T-shirt.

Tommy had worn nice Levi's jeans and a black T-shirt at the restaurant every single day ever since Sofie had known him. It was his uniform.

"What?" Con said.

"I aced the algebra test."

"Cool."

The look of pride on Con's face made Sofie smile.

"Stop in sometime and I'll buy you a beer."

"I'll do that," Con said, grinning.

She knew Tommy was joking, the way he did. With his customers. With everybody. But even when he was joking, she also thought his eyes were a little sad.

"How about you, Princess? Still punching above your weight?"

He always asked that.

She nodded.

Con had explained that *punching above your weight* was a boxing metaphor, but since few or no princesses were boxers, Sofie didn't get it, but she knew he meant well by the way he said it.

"We just wanted to say hello to Mom."

"Not me," Con muttered under his breath. "Come on," he said more loudly, tugging on her hand.

"Where are you going, Connie?" their mom called.

When Con didn't respond, Sofie said, "Walmart."

Her mom waved, but Sofie saw the hurt look.

They walked a block in silence, heat bouncing off the sidewalk into their faces.

"That was really rude," Sofie finally said. "Why can't you be nice to Mom?"

"Because I don't like what she's doing."

Sofie sighed. Their mom was a beautiful glass with a crack in it, but the glass was full to the top with love for Con and her. Connie should think more about that.

"That's our bus," he said. "Hurry."

As they ran, the toe of her flip-flop caught on the sidewalk and pitched her forward. Con grabbed her arm so she didn't fall on her face, but her foot felt like it was split in half.

"Ow!" she howled, hopping. "Ow, Connie!" Her broken flip-flop lay on the sidewalk. And her foot hurt like anything.

"Just kick off the other one. Wait!" he yelled. The driver was shutting the door.

Great. Now she was barefooted.

But she ran with Con. They got on the bus and found seats.

A man across from her was staring at her feet. His eyes traveled up to her face, which suddenly felt like it was on fire. Then the man looked at Con, then at Sofie again.

"What are you staring at?" Con said.

The man turned away.

Sofie didn't look at Con, but she knew what he was feeling. She wanted to yell at the man *We're not homeless! We're not hungry! Our mom is at work right now and she loves us! Connie is going to be a doctor and I'm going to be a head librarian!*

As the bus gained speed and they went under the freeway, Sofie realized Dylan was sitting just a few seats in front of them. Had Con noticed?

He and Dylan had been like two pages in an open book when they lived in the trailer and Dylan lived a block away. Sofie felt like she had two big brothers. But now, if they were in the same place, they stared right through each other.

Sofie hated what had happened. She was glad Dylan got off the bus at the next stop.

Finally the bus stopped at Walmart, and they got off, along with a lot of other people.

There was a sign by the door: SHOES AND SHIRTS REQUIRED.

"Smile and keep walking," Con said quietly, steering her by the shoulder. "Nobody will notice."

He said, "How are you?" to the greeter so she looked up at him instead of down at Sofie's feet.

"We're going straight to the shoe department," he said, his arm brushing hers.

Sofie, who was almost trotting to keep up, stopped.

Were they going to steal a pair of shoes? Just put them on and walk out? Her mom might be brave enough to do that, but she wasn't.

"Connie," she said in a low voice, "I don't want to steal shoes."

His eyes were fierce. "I'm not going to steal them, Sof."

"You're going to *buy me new shoes?*" she asked in a squeak.

She had had brand-new, in-a-box, straight-from-the-store shoes just once in her whole life. Jonah had bought them for her to start kindergarten. Those shoes had been shiny, the color of grapes, with a little strap across the top. Sofie had loved the way they smelled. She loved the sharp, crisp corners on the box. She especially loved knowing no feet but hers had ever been in them. She had begged her feet to stop growing so she could wear the shoes forever.

She couldn't believe Connie, who was all about *just in case* with his money, wouldn't take her to the Salvation Army store across the street.

"*Why?*"

"Sof, you ask why too much."

"No, I don't."

"Because I want to," he finally said. "Okay?"

"Okay, I guess."

They found the aisle with her size. Her hands were shaking as she picked up a pair of gray sneakers with pink laces. They were pretty. And then she saw the shoes of her heart. They were red canvas with white soles, with a thick black line between the red and the white.

She pointed. "Those."

Con found a box of her size and she tried them on, silently saying *Sorry, sorry* for dirty feet and promising to always love and cherish them. She felt them come alive, the canvas hugging her feet, the soles making her bouncy.

They were absolutely signature shoes. Then she saw the price and nearly passed out, but she wanted the shoes and they wanted her.

"Come on," Con said. "Let's go pay for them."

He carried the box and she walked beside him. He was the best brother on the planet.

When they went through checkout, the lady noticed the box was empty and looked at them.

"My sister's flip-flop broke," Con said. "It was an emergency. She's already wearing the shoes."

The way her tall, good-looking brother with cash explained it all so naturally erased the humiliation of having been stared at on the bus.

"Thanks, Connie."

"You're welcome."

She wanted to give him the biggest hug, but while he went back to get the socket thingy she went in the restroom and washed and dried her feet and again slid them into her amazing new shoes. She looked in the mirror. She could see herself only from the middle up, but the shoes had made her beautiful.

chapter 7

Because it was The First Night of the New Shoes and because it was the first night she could read in the attic by the light of her lamp, Sofie was taking her slow, sweet time choosing her book from the pile by her pillow.

Her eyes went to *The Higher Power of Lucky* because it was brighter than all the others. The gold sticker shone in the lamplight. But Sofie couldn't read about a dead mom. It was just too horrible.

There was a Baby-Sitters Club book in the pile. Reading those was like eating popcorn, they went down so easy. She and AnaMaria loved them.

But there was also a thick, interesting-looking book called *The Underneath*, and it had drawings—which most thick books didn't have. Plus, it had two silver stickers, which was almost as good as a gold.

None of the books felt quite as interesting as her new shoes. She had washed them, even the soles, and put them back in the box, but without the lid. They were two comfy miracles staring at her—miracles because Con had spent so much money on new shoes for her.

Her heart was suddenly so full she didn't know what to do. She had to tell Con how happy he'd made her or she would burst. She lifted the sheet. He was propped on a pillow listening to music with his eyes closed.

"Connie," she said, loud enough that he would hear.

He opened his eyes. Eyes she had always looked to, no matter what.

She'd meant to say what a great brother he was and thank him again. But everything welled up in a huge wave. Her amazing, wonderful red shoes. The terrifying red and blue lights of the cops last night. The unreal trip to the duck pond that brought her so close to her brother.

Con put down his phone. "What's wrong?"

"Nothing," she said, trying to stop bewildering tears.

She saw Dylan's stone face.

Con sat up, cross-legged on his pallet, looking scared. "Come on, Sof. Spill it."

Why was she bawling? Why was she thinking about Dylan all of a sudden? Though in her bones she knew.

Con pulled her against his side.

"Did you doze off reading and have a bad dream?"

She shook her head no.

"Then what?'

"I had a feeling."

A big scary skulking feeling trying to creep inside the circle.

"I just wanted to say thank you again." She struggled to keep her voice from breaking, and wiped the tears away with her fingers. "For my shoes." She swallowed, her mouth dry. "Did you see Dylan?"

She felt him catch his breath.

"Yeah," he finally said.

They sat in silence.

"It just reminded me is all."

She had dragged the fearful thing into the light. Now they had to look at it.

"Are you afraid Mom is going to ditch us again?" Con asked.

"No." But the parties were getting wilder. Even the scarecrow, who acted like their mom was the moon and stars, looked worried. Sofie had overheard him talking to Con. The scarecrow always left when the parties started. Sofie kind of wished he didn't.

"She probably won't do it again, Sof. But I'm older now. I can take care of us. I won't be afraid this time."

Last time they had been *so* terrified. The first three days, they'd stayed inside the trailer. There'd been one pizza in the freezer, a little milk, a little bread, a jar of peanut butter, two cans of tomato soup—which Sofie didn't like—a half carton of juice, and a puckered apple. On the fourth day they'd gone back to school, and Sofie had been so thankful for the free breakfasts and lunches because Connie didn't have to worry.

They'd walked to school with Dylan and his mom, pretending everything was normal. But they were terrified that their mom didn't want to be their mom anymore. How could she now not love them? But if she loved them, why didn't she come home?

They had slept on the couch so they wouldn't miss her call if it came on the landline. Sofie remembered lying awake watching Jack Frost paint patterns on the window, feeling Con warm and strong, asleep beside her.

After six days, which felt like six months, Con finally broke down and told Dylan. And even though Dylan swore never to tell anybody, he told his mom. And his mom called Social Services.

When the social worker got there, their mom, Con, and Sofie had been playing in the snow, giddy. Their cheeks were still red and tear-streaked from *sorry, sorry, sorry* and the hugs of forgiveness they'd showered on her.

They'd been playing the circle game where they all fell down at the end. They'd fallen into a happy tangle and their mom had said softly, "I will never, ever go off and leave you again. I promise."

And that was when the social worker pulled up, got out of her car, and came toward them, past the front door of the trailer and their swing set, asking their mom if she was Ashley Jones.

Their mom swore she'd *never* leave her kids alone. Dylan's mom was a nut job. A troublemaker. A liar. Someone who called Social Services to make trouble. Someone who used drugs and neglected her own kid. Dylan was a liar too.

What could Con and Sofie do but back up their mom? They were terrified they might be separated and sent to foster care if they told the truth.

When they saw Dylan at school the next day, he had looked so confused and crushed. Like he didn't recognize them. And the shame of the lie turned Con hard and cold, and that turned Dylan hard and cold.

Her brother had never had a real friend since. He had gym buddies and nerd buddies. And he was always reminding Sofie of the danger of letting people get too close. And she didn't. Not even AnaMaria. Sofie shared everything else—her books, her clothes, her dreams. Her secret terror of the night crawlers washed up on the sidewalk after a hard rain. But she acted like her mom was the most normal mom in the world.

So why couldn't Connie see the danger of letting the old scarecrow get close?

"I don't think we should get close to him," she said.

"Who?"

"*Him.*"

Earlier the scarecrow had bolted from the table the way he did and gotten in his truck and left—which was fine with her. He made her think of a zombie—a scarecrow zombie—with his wrinkly skin that sagged under his eyes and dark spaces where teeth should be.

But that afternoon he'd mowed the yard, which was Con's job, and Con had said *Thanks, man!* like Con was a grown-up and they were friends. And now he was back, in her room with the door closed.

"Come on, Sof. It won't kill you to say his name. And I'm not going to get close. But we might need him if..."

"Okay." They didn't need to talk about it.

Footsteps sounded on the porch and she heard her mom's voice through the window. Was there going to be another wild party? She strained to listen. Her mom was talking on the phone. She was by herself. She had walked home.

There would be no party tonight. When there was a party, their mom came home with a few of her wild friends, and others on the way. The handful of friends her mom had known a long time, like Lili and her sister, were nice to Sofie and Con if they were sober enough to notice them. But others could be really rude. And scary.

But no worries tonight.

Sofie felt suddenly lighthearted. Why had she been crying and talking about Dylan and worrying about the old scarecrow? Everything was fine. Her mom was home.

"I'm going to go down and say hello to Mom," she said.

Con grunted something and went back to his side of the attic.

"You come too. We can show her my shoes."

"No."

If she tried to talk him into it he'd just get more annoyed, so she felt her way down the dark stairs alone.

Her mom was at the sink shaking ibuprofen into her palm. She tossed the pills back and washed them down with water. The light over the sink showed frown lines between her brows.

"Are you okay?" Sofie asked.

"Hey," she said, drawing Sofie into a hug. "Con upstairs?"

Sofie nodded. Her mom smelled like barbecue and cigarettes.

"I slipped on the wet patio this afternoon and fell on my butt. I didn't think I hurt myself, but I'm stiffening up. I'm going to take a shower."

The clock on the stove said almost midnight. Sofie shook a little of her cereal into her hand and ate it. It had lost some crunch, but it was still good.

Then she noticed her mom had brought home a sack of food from work, which she did when there were leftovers. The smell made her mouth water. There were four barbecue sandwiches.

She took two up to Connie, and she settled onto the couch with her own, leaving the last one for her mom.

She watched *Moulin Rouge* with the sound off so she didn't wake the scarecrow. Her mom loved that movie. But tonight, the actress who played Satine was annoying with all that red hair. Sofie hoped Beth had told that red-haired girl, Jade—and what kind of name was Jade, anyway?—that Con was too busy for girls.

Her mom came out of the bathroom in pajama pants and T-shirt. She settled on the couch beside Sofie, leaning forward, her head between her knees.

"What are you doing?" Sofie asked.

"Stretching my back," her mom said in a muffled voice.

"Want me to rub it?"

"That would be nice." Her mom took Sofie's hand and placed it.

Sofie circled her hand gently, feeling her mom's warmth through the thin T-shirt.

"You need to rub hard. It hurts down deep."

She got on her knees and put her weight into the massage. After a while, a trickle of sweat ran down her cheek from her hairline. She stopped rubbing to wipe away the sweat.

Her mom sat up, her face flushed. She let out a deep breath. "Thanks, my sweet Sofie." Her mom kissed Sofie's hand and stood slowly. "'Night. Love you."

"Love you too. Don't forget you promised to come to my swimming lesson in the morning."

"I remember."

Her mom's hand, when she touched Sofie's cheek, didn't smell like cigarettes or barbecue. It smelled like watermelon. Sofie smiled.

"What?" her mom said.

"Nothing."

"Something."

Sofie shrugged. "You smell good is all."

Upstairs, Sofie lifted the sheet between their beds.

Con looked at her.

"Mom fell and hurt her back at work."

He went back to his screen.

She dropped the sheet with a sigh.

It was barely daylight. A car door slammed and there were footsteps on the porch. The murmur of her mom's voice. Footsteps. A car door. Then nothing.

She lay there for a few seconds before she let her heavy eyelids drop. She'd dreamed it. Her mom was still asleep. At home with them. Where she belonged.

chapter 8

Her mom was dressed in shorts and a tank top. She had put on lipstick and twisted her hair on top of her head with a pretty scarf. But she was pale and shaky-looking, even though there hadn't been a party last night.

Her mom's eyes widened as she stared at Sofie's shoes. "Where did those come from?"

Sofie felt her face break into a huge smile. "Connie bought them for me. At Walmart yesterday."

Her mom's eyes flew to Con, who was pouring cereal out of his box.

"What?" he said, but Sofie saw a smile trying to escape.

"Did you really, Connie? With your own money?"

His face was red now. He nodded.

Tears shone in her mom's eyes. "You are such a good kid." She put her cigarette down and crossed the kitchen, walking stiffly, to put her arms around him.

He didn't push away. He did love her. Earlier when Sofie was brushing her teeth, she'd heard them talking. Con was telling their mom if she was hurting, maybe she should take the day off, and their mom said she couldn't pass up Friday tips.

"If you don't feel like coming to see me swim today, Mama, it's okay," Sofie said. "You can come next time."

Her mom shook a couple of pills out of the bottle and swallowed them with her diet drink. "I'll be okay."

Con watched and frowned. He glanced at Sofie, but she didn't understand the look that flashed in his eyes for a second.

On the crowded bus, Sofie squeezed in beside her mom, and Con held on to a pole. Sofie tucked her feet under the bench as far as she could so nobody stepped on her shoes.

Her swimming instructor told her she was a good swimmer, and she had heard the head instructor telling Con that too. That instructor had suggested that their mom come to one of the lessons.

Sofie hadn't learned to swim until this summer, and now the water magically held her up. When she stretched out on her back or stomach and moved her arms, she thought maybe it was a little like flying. Being a fish was next best to being a bird.

She was going to tell her mom this, but she saw her mom's eyes were closed and her head drooped. Maybe her back had hurt so much last night she hadn't been able to sleep.

As they neared the bus stop closest to the Y, Sofie touched her mom's arm. "Time to get off, Mama."

Her mom startled and looked at Sofie. Then she blinked. "Oh."

When she stood, she took Con's arm.

Sofie swam the breaststroke the length of the pool and back, raising her face to breathe when her arms lifted her out of the water, relaxing her face back into the water when her feet and legs were doing the work and her arms were resting. Over and over she stroked, listening to the splashes of the other swimmers, voices that echoed a little, an instructor's whistle.

She thought about the silver sailfish charm AnaMaria's mom always wore on a chain around her neck, often touching it. Sofie imagined she was her mom's beautiful sailfish charm that her mom was proud of and would always cherish.

Con had told the instructor their mom didn't have money for extras, and the instructor said there were scholarships. Sofie wasn't sure what a swim team was or if she wanted to be on one. But when she and Con did well in stuff it made their mom look more like other moms—moms whose kids had dads. Everybody knew her mom had boyfriends who sometimes lasted only a day or two, and mean kids teased Sofie with awful words.

That was why she was going to win the Student Explorer Award. That would show the mean kids. And so would being on a real swim team. And just wait until Con was a doctor and she was a head librarian. Then they would all see how excellent her mom was.

As Sofie paused for a few seconds at the end of the lane, she glanced into the bleachers. Her mom's eyes were on her. Sofie smiled and waved. Her mom smiled and waved back. Sometimes she wished their mom was like regular moms, because then they wouldn't have to protect her. Sometimes that got kind of exhausting.

She saw Con stand up and walk toward the door. Where was he going?

Jade and Beth were coming in. Beth headed for the open lane beside Sofie, and Jade walked on, her hair catching the light. When Jade and Con met, Jade smiled and said something. Con blushed and shook his head, smiling.

"Connie, aren't you going to watch me swim?" she shouted.

He turned and glared at her. Then she remembered. She wasn't supposed to call him Connie in public. He had made her promise. He said it sounded babyish. But to her it didn't.

He walked toward her. "I'm going to get Mom water, okay?" he said quietly, his eyes full of annoyance.

"Okay. Sorry."

Then the instructor blew her whistle and Sofie had to pay attention.

During the lesson, she looked into the bleachers now and then. Con sat with Jade instead of their mom. And he wasn't watching Sofie. The main instructor was sitting by her mom. At least they were watching her. Well, her mom was kind of flirting with her hands and her hair the way she did.

When the lesson finished, she pulled off her goggles and swim cap, which felt really good, and wrapped her towel around her waist. She stumbled when she started toward her mom because it was hard to walk after being a fish.

The instructor stood. He smiled at Sofie and gave her two thumbs up before he turned away.

Her mom looked a little confused. She reached for Sofie's hand to stand.

"Are you okay, Mama?"

Her mom shook her head. "I called Gunner and asked if he could pick me up. He's on the way."

Only for a second, Sofie liked the old scarecrow.

"I'll take more ibuprofen and rest a little. Then I'll feel like going to work."

Jade was talking to Con, which annoyed Sofie especially because their mom wasn't feeling well.

She heard Jade say "I'm taking Beth to the Botanical Center for lunch."

To Sofie, it sounded like she was *tacking* Beth there. Jade's slow, warm way of talking cast a spell on Con.

"Do y'all ever go there? You and Sofie?" Except in Jade's mouth, it was *Sofay*.

The Botanical Center was across the river, and she and Con sometimes walked around and looked at plants and trees. They didn't have money for the fancy restaurant.

Unless Con suddenly decided they did. Like he'd decided to buy her shoes.

Her mom was sort of gazing into space and Connie looked like he'd fallen under an enchantment that stole his voice.

"We can't," she told Jade. "Connie has a class at East High and I'm doing crafts at the Community Center. Mama is going home to rest her back before she goes to work."

After a *free* lunch at the Community Center, Connie would take the pedestrian bridge across the freeway to East High, where gifted middle-school kids had summer classes. She wished she was old enough for those. But she would hang out in the Craft Room at the Community Center until Connie picked her up and they walked home.

On the way, they might pet the chickens if the lady was outside again. They had discovered the chickens last week when they cut through the alley. Sofie loved the burbling sounds they made as they pecked in the grass, and the way they turned their heads to look at things. The lady had seen Con and Sofie watching and she picked up a butterscotch-colored chicken and brought it to the fence for them to pet. Sofie would like to do that again.

That was their summer Friday routine—what they did while their mom worked for Friday tips. Jade had no business butting in. But Con was glaring at Sofie. Was it because she'd called him Connie again?

"Oh." Jade looked disappointed. "Y'all are so busy." But her smile said being *so busy* was just the best, most amazing thing ever.

Con looked like his brains had been scrambled.

"Maybe next week," Jade said.

For a scary minute Sofie thought Con was going to say he'd skip class today. She wanted to poke him to make him right.

He nodded. "Sure. Next week." He kept nodding.

Jade put her hand on Beth's shoulder and started toward the door. She looked back. "See y'all then."

No. Sofie would not let this happen. Connie was hers.

chapter 9

When Con came to get Sofie at the Community Center, Mr. Bloom asked him if he had time to clean and organize the sports equipment storage area. While she waited for him, to keep her mind off her mom and how she was, Sofie went to the library and made sure the books were alphabetized.

As she worked, she checked to see if there were any Baby-Sitters Club books she and AnaMaria hadn't read. They'd read so many, but there were over a hundred books in the series according to the media lady at school. So now and then Sofie found a treasure. But today she didn't.

She also watched for picture books that weren't too babyish and had beautiful illustrations. And books with stickers on their covers. Today she took *Tuck Everlasting* because the lady she was helping said her daughter really liked it.

Sofie sat cross-legged on the library floor to read. Connie would know where to find her.

She wasn't sure about the idea of never getting older like the Tuck family. Of course, she would like for their mom never to get any older, because she would always be beautiful. But Sofie personally needed to get older so she could become a head librarian. And being older than her mom would be extremely weird.

She was reading near an open doorway to an alley where books and clothing and stuff came through in bags and boxes. A robin hopped past, then turned and seemed to be looking into the library, right at Sofie.

The lady who worked there said quietly, "Maybe he's a book bird."

The robin hopped three times in a circle and flew away. Sofie smiled. That was a good sign.

When Con came to get her, he looked like he had money in his pocket.

"Ready?" he asked, reaching a hand to help her up.

"How much?"

He just smiled.

On the way home, they cut through the alley and the chickens were pecking in the grass, but the lady wasn't out. Sofie asked the butterscotch chicken to come over and be petted, but the chicken didn't.

At home, the house was empty—which meant their mom was at work and the scarecrow was wherever he went. Sofie put the giant card she'd made for her mom on the kitchen table and propped it against the wall with the Uno deck. It said *I hope your back stops hurting soon, Mama,* and she'd added lots of glittery hearts. All the glue made it sag in the middle, but her mom would love it.

Con sprawled on the couch. Sofie put *Coco* in the DVD player and claimed one end of the couch, pushing Con's big feet away.

She put her feet on the coffee table. She had pale feet and short toes, like her mom. Her pinky toe was just a bead, actually. Con's toes were long, like they could wave at you if they wanted.

He was texting.

"Who are you texting?" Jade?

"Mom. To see how she's doing."

So she didn't miss the ping of a text back from their mom when it came, she muted the sound on *Coco*. She knew the words by heart anyway.

What would they do if their mom's back didn't get better? Maybe Con could mow yards, but the mower didn't work very well. And she was too young to work in a real library. Maybe she could help the lady with her chickens. But the lady probably didn't have money to pay her.

Ping.

She smiled. Con was sending a text back.

"What did she say?" she asked when he was finally done.

"Who?"

"Mom."

"It wasn't mom."

His face was so happy she knew. She looked away.

She always, always, always cried at the end of *Coco*—wet-faced crying that stuffed up her nose. She was wiping her face on her T-shirt when the truck rattled to a stop in the alley. She could tell Con was asleep from the way he breathed.

When she touched his foot, he startled. "What?"

"He's back."

Con stretched and sat up as the scarecrow poked his head into the living room.

"You heard from Ashley?"

"No," Con said.

"I guess that means she's doing okay. She's going to call me when her shift ends, and I'll pick her up." He turned and went to the kitchen.

Sofie heard the refrigerator open and close, then she heard him go out on the back porch. He sat there a lot when her mom wasn't around. Maybe because he knew Sofie didn't want him here. Maybe he felt bad about taking her room.

Con's phone pinged again.

Sofie picked at dried glue and glitter on her fingertips as Con bent over the phone like it was a tiny living thing he was keeping alive with his thumbs.

She couldn't bear it.

In the attic, she felt for her lamp in the darkness. The warm light made her feel better, but the room was so hot her scalp prickled with sweat. She found the chess set on Connie's side and took it downstairs. Con was still curled over his phone in the dark living room.

She went to the back door. "Hey."

It took the scarecrow a while to turn and say "Are you talking to me?"

"Do you know how to play chess?"

When he stood, the kitchen light showed the surprise on his face. "Do you?"

She nodded.

"Maybe you could teach me."

She sighed. He was probably too old. But Con had forgotten she even existed, and worry about her mom was nibbling around the edges of her thoughts.

"First we have to set up the board." She opened the box where the glossy black and white pieces nestled. "The black pieces are yours. Put them on the squares the same way I put my pieces on, with your queen on a black square."

She could feel his concentration as his eyes moved between her pieces and his own.

"Like this?" he said, looking at her.

When she nodded, he smiled.

She told him about pawns and bishops and knights and rooks. How each piece could move. That the knights could leap over other pieces. She told him about the king and queen. How the queen was powerful, but the king was precious. When the king was captured the game was lost.

"Whoever wins says *checkmate*." She was longing, after months, to say it.

"Are you pretty good at this game?"

"I don't know. Connie is teaching me." She had never played anyone but him, and she had never won, but it was taking longer for him to get to checkmate.

"This won't be a real game," she said. "You'll be learning."

He nodded, looking pleased.

She'd teach him the way Con had taught her. She'd explain her moves, and when he made a move, she'd explain why it was good or bad and let him take it back if it was bad. Not because she liked him, but because she wanted to be a good teacher.

Later, when they were taking a break, he said, "There are grapes in the refrigerator."

He was making a cup of tea.

When she stood, her sweaty legs stung as they pulled away from the chair. She stood in front of the open refrigerator door, her eyes closed, loving the cold on her front. Finally, she opened her eyes and tore off a stem of grapes.

"Who taught Con to play chess?" he asked

"He taught himself mostly. From books and online."

She looked at the clock on the stove. Could it really be ten? She'd forgotten to worry.

Con came into the kitchen, his hair wild, squinting in the light, gripping his phone like it was growing out of his palm.

"Mom will be calling anytime," he said.

Sofie thought her mom would be happy she was teaching the scarecrow to play chess. And she would love Sofie's card.

Bugs tapped the screen and the smell of tea drifted across the table when the scarecrow sat down.

"What are you up to?" he asked Con.

"Nothing," Con said, blushing.

"There are grapes in the refrigerator," the scarecrow said.

"I'm not hungry." But he took one of Sofie's.

His phone had stopped dinging. Maybe that annoying girl had gone to bed.

Sofie saw Con checking his phone even when it hadn't dinged. The clock said 10:20. He got grapes out of the refrigerator and stood eating them, looking at the chessboard, but Sofie could tell he wasn't really paying attention. She felt the scarecrow wasn't paying much attention either.

10:40.

"Why don't you text her?" Sofie said.

Con fiddled with the chess pieces Sofie had captured from the scarecrow. "I already did."

At eleven fifteen, the scarecrow stood. "I'm going to get her."

"Sometimes when they're really busy, Mom works later," Con said.

She heard the hope in his voice.

The scarecrow had the look he always got when he was about to jump up and get in the truck and go wherever he went.

As the screen door closed behind him, Con stood at the sink, staring out the window into the darkness. A bug thumping against the screen made her jump.

chapter 10

By twelve thirty the scarecrow still wasn't back with their mom, and Sofie felt awful dread, sickening and itchy, curling around her throat. "We have to do something."

Con was still as a stone, staring out the screen door. He nodded.

The night wasn't empty like it had been when Con took her out walking with him. Cars rumbled their pipes and blasted music. Somebody who smelled bad lay on the bridge and cursed them as they hurried past. Con grabbed her hand and they ran the rest of the way to Tommy's Place.

The front lights were off and the patio was dark. Sofie was counting on the truck being in the parking lot and her mom and the scarecrow sitting inside with the windows down, talking, her mom smoking. When her mom saw them, she would tease them for being worry warts.

But the parking lot was empty. Bugs swarmed the tall lights. Sofie leaned against Con, still holding his hand.

Maybe they had just missed their mom. Maybe the truck had pulled out of the parking lot a minute before they got here and her mom and the scarecrow were almost home.

A door slammed and footsteps crunched in the gravel. Her mom was coming around the corner of the building.

But a man stepped into the light.

"Tommy," Con called. "It's me, Con. And Sofie."

Tommy came closer, peering at them. "What are you guys doing here? Is everything okay?"

"We don't know where our mom is," Sofie said. She hated herself for sounding like a little lost baby.

"She said her back was bothering her and she left about ten thirty," Tommy said. "She didn't come home?"

"No," Connie said. "We're worried."

"Did an old man come looking for her?" Sofie asked.

"Yeah. Her grandfather. Summer's dad. Gunner, right? I told him he'd just missed her. Like by two minutes."

She caught Con's glance. Did the scarecrow and Tommy know each other?

"Ashley probably went to a friend's house and lost track of time," Tommy said.

"Yeah," Con said. Sofie felt how hard it was for him to sound calm.

"Why don't I take you kids home?"

She didn't really want to go home to an empty house. She wanted her mom.

"Thanks," Con said.

She and Con got in the backseat. Tommy's car smelled like new shoes, and it was so quiet Tommy would probably hear her swallow. He might hear her thoughts.

"Can one of you give me directions to your place?" he asked.

Sofie wasn't sure she wanted Tommy to see where they lived.

"I will," Con said, telling him to cross the river going south and keep going until the light, then two blocks further on turn right. They lived three blocks down on the left.

"So Princess," Tommy said, pulling out of the parking lot, "how are the swimming lessons? Ashley says you're going to the Y for them."

"Okay." Right now, swimming seemed too hugely silly to talk about.

"What do you like about it?" Tommy asked, his eyes searching for hers in the mirror when they stopped at a light.

"Everything." She was barely able to get the word out.

Tommy held her eyes, waiting for more, but she couldn't. Then the light changed and he drove on.

"You know, your mom talks about you kids all the time. Everybody at the restaurant knows you're stars in school. Ashley couldn't be any prouder. Con, she's told anybody who will listen that you're tutoring me in college algebra. You should hear her."

She wished Con would say something, but he didn't. He sat so still, staring out the window.

Was Tommy figuring out that things weren't right? Could he feel how scared they were?

"If Ashley did go to a friend's house," he said after a while, "do you have any idea whose? Maybe we could go by and make sure everything's okay. She might need a ride home if her back is bothering her."

"No idea," Con said in a voice that sounded far away.

She might have gone to Lili's, but Lili and her sister moved a lot. Sofie wasn't sure where she lived anymore. And even if Sofie and Con did know, they shouldn't be taking Tommy there.

Tommy said, "It's late for you two to be on your own."

"We're not on our own," Con said, his voice suddenly deep. "Our granddad is staying with us. He's probably there now. He's got a truck. He can go get Mom if she needs a lift home."

With all her heart, Sofie hoped the scarecrow really was there. She would make him feel so welcome.

Tommy stopped in front of the house and turned to look at them. "Go in and make sure your granddad is here, okay? I'll wait. If he's not, I can text Ashley and let her know you're with me. You can stay at my place until she turns up."

"Okay," Con said.

She followed Con up the sidewalk and stood close as he tried to unlock the door. She wanted to lean into him. He fumbled, tapping the key against the lock.

Inside, the emptiness of the house felt huge, and it seemed to take a long, sickening time to walk to the back door and see no truck in the alley.

"I'll go tell Tommy Gunner is here," Con said.

Sofie stared at the empty spot where she'd hoped the truck would be. She should have been nicer.

When Con came back, he said, "Mom could be at a party. And Gunner could just be wherever he goes all the time."

She looked up at him. He was pale. No, he was white. He was terrified. It was happening again.

She barely made it to the bathroom before she threw up the grapes. Con knelt beside her, holding her hair.

"Sofie." She heard the tears in his voice. "Don't be scared."

But the fear was in her bones. "I'll try."

At the top of the stairs, where it felt hot enough to melt butter, she turned on the lamp and Con locked them in.

He pushed away the sheet that separated them. She didn't ever want him out of her sight again.

He said, "I've got an idea. It will be cooler on the roof. Maybe the moon is still up."

She turned off the lamp and he helped her through the window.

They sat on the slope, their knees pulled up, bare arms touching. A breeze made leaf shadows move in the streetlights.

After a while he said, "It will be easier this time, Sof. We're older."

She nodded to make him feel better.

"And it's kind of like the worst thing that could happen has happened. And now we don't have to worry about it happening," he said.

A surge of fear and anger filled her. It was not the worst thing that could happen. The worst thing was that their mom wouldn't come back.

"Or maybe Mom is just at a party," she made herself say.

He was silent. She could hear him breathing. She matched her breath to his.

After a while, the moon slid out from behind a cloud and seemed to watch over them. That made things a little better.

She opened her eyes. She didn't even realize they'd been closed, but the attic was getting light. Her swollen eyes ached.

She turned her head to look at Connie, sprawled on his pallet, one knee bent, his eyes open. Had he slept?

Her book lay splayed where she'd dropped it. When they came in from the roof, she'd tried to read *Tuck Everlasting*. Her eyes moved along the lines, but her own family filled her mind. She'd told herself they were characters in a story. Something bad had happened, the way it always did. But they were brave and strong and smart. And everything would be okay in the end, because it always was.

"Did Mama come home?" she asked, her voice raspy.

Con shook his head.

She stared up at the rafters. They were like ribs, like she and Connie were inside some creature that had swallowed them.

"Were you awake all night? You might have fallen asleep and not heard Mom come in. She might have snuck in so she didn't bother us."

"I was awake all night," he said, his voice dull.

"Could we look?" she said.

His face, with its wide mouth, looked very still in the dim light.

"Connie?"

"We can look."

When they came out of the dim stairwell into the kitchen where the glittery giant card and the chessboard were still on the table, she felt the emptiness. Neither their mom nor the scarecrow had come home. They were on their own.

chapter 11

For the last week, whenever they were home, they had stayed in the hot attic. The downstairs, without their mom and the scarecrow, felt as scary as an unknown planet.

Sofie caught her hair up on top of her head and fastened it with a scrunchie. The sweat drying on her neck felt good. Her tank top and shorts were damp with sweat.

Con, inches away, was stretched out on his back with his eyes closed, listening to music.

They decided their mom and the scarecrow had gone off somewhere in the truck. It killed her to know their mom had picked that awful old scarecrow, whom Sofie had been starting to like, over them.

At night, they turned the lights on everywhere in the house so it looked normal. They ate at the Community Center, and when seconds were offered, they always said yes even if they weren't hungry. Sofie was never actually hungry, but Connie coaxed her to eat. He bought peanut butter and bread. They had an almost full jar of jelly and a little bit of cereal from the food pantry, plus two oranges and grapes the scarecrow had left.

Sofie drank water instead of juice. They ate what they had, even if they didn't like it much. Like canned corn, which was kind of nasty. But potato chips, which Con also bought, made it better.

One night somebody had knocked on the door. When they didn't answer, the person pounded and yelled, "Ashley, come out, come out! I know you're in there, girl."

It was Lili. Con had opened the door and said their mom was at a friend's house, but he didn't know the friend's name. Lili was so stoned she didn't seem to recognize them and turned away mumbling.

Was that someone knocking now? Or was it just an old-house sound? Con's eyes were still closed. He didn't hear. Her heart raced. Might it be Social Services or the police?

They tried to be so careful to do all the usual things. But today she hadn't gone to swimming lessons, because going felt impossibly sad. Could that have given them away?

The knocking was louder.

"Con," she said quietly, shaking him. "Somebody's knocking."

He sat up, alarm in his eyes.

"Turn off the light," he said. "Keep still."

She did, though her heart was trying to get out of her body.

Con was taking out the screen and stepping through the window. She scrambled to her feet. She was going with him.

But he waved her back. "I'm looking to see if there's a car in the street."

Like a police car. It might be a police car. Sofie's head nearly burst with the buzzing in her ears.

Con moved away, then back inside quickly. "It's Tommy," he said, unlocking the attic door and rushing down the stairs.

Sofie followed, her legs wobbling with relief.

"Remember the plan," Con said over his shoulder before he opened the door.

She nodded.

Tommy held boxes, and she smelled barbecue.

"Sorry if I scared you," he said. "We just closed and I thought maybe you'd like some leftovers."

Memories of her mom coming home from work with warm, tasty-smelling containers of food from the restaurant washed over Sofie, leaving her breathless.

Con opened the screen. "Come in."

In the kitchen, Tommy put the boxes on the table. His muscles showed through his T-shirt and the curly, golden hair on his arms caught the light. Of her mom's friends, he was Sofie's favorite. He didn't party and he didn't do wild stuff. And he felt solid and cozy.

"So is your mom around? I haven't seen her all week, and she's not answering my texts." He looked at them, a question on his face. "Did she get a new job and not tell me?"

He asked the question kind of like he was joking, but Sofie saw the seriousness in his eyes.

"She didn't tell you?" Con said.

Tommy blinked. "What?" He looked at Con, then at her.

"Mama needed a break," Sofie said. "She went on vacation with friends."

This was the plan they'd made. She tried to mirror Con's look of *No big deal.*

"She went off and left you kids alone?"

"No, Gunner's here," Con said.

Tommy's eyes were angry. "So that night you came looking for her, scared out of your socks, Ashley had gone on vacation without telling you?"

Sofie didn't want Tommy to think their mom was bad. "She called right after you left. She was sorry she'd worried us."

"It's just how she lets off steam," Con said.

Tommy shook his head like he was trying to clear it of something. "Are you saying Ashley has done this before?" he asked, his voice louder at the end of the question.

"Yeah," Con said. "She makes sure we're okay, then she takes a little vacation."

"To where?" Tommy asked, shock in his voice.

Con gave the answer they'd agreed on. "Texas. With friends."

Tommy was shaking his head again.

"She just walks out on her job? Doesn't answer my texts? I've been scrambling to cover her shifts all week."

He couldn't fire their mom. Working at the restaurant was the best, longest place their mom had ever worked.

"Mom will be back soon," she told Tommy. "I know she's sorry she didn't tell you."

"It's kind of our fault," Con said. "We were supposed to tell you."

"We forgot," Sofie said.

They were making this part up as they went. Why hadn't they thought about their mom getting in trouble with Tommy? That was dumb.

"Where's your great-granddad?" Tommy asked.

The suddenness of the question made Sofie blink. What was the story they'd made up about the scarecrow?

Con was opening a box of barbecued wings, trying to act casual. "He's at work. He got a job as a night watchman."

He picked up a wing and looked like he was enjoying it.

All week, food hadn't tasted very good to Sofie. But to show Tommy there were no worries about anything, she pulled a french fry out of a bag and nibbled on it. It was warm and salty. Saliva filled her mouth. She ate a few more, then dipped one into barbecue sauce and felt heat burst on her tongue.

Tommy was leaning against the counter with his arms crossed. Having a living, breathing grown-up in the house made Sofie feel better. She felt her appetite waking up. She sat down at the table and ate a few more fries dipped in sauce.

Tommy stood watching them eat. Sofie felt his eyes. She hoped they looked like two regular kids whose mom was on vacation and whose great-granddad was at work.

"So where does your granddad work?" Tommy asked. His voice sounded different. He was watching her with a look she didn't understand.

Did he suspect?

"Some warehouse downtown. I don't remember."

Tommy nodded, but his expression made her uneasy. Like he'd just figured out something that was hard to believe. Had she given them away?

She tried to keep her hands steady as she dipped a french fry and put it in her mouth. Con had food on his face.

"Well," Tommy said. "Anything I can do for you kids?"

"We're good," Con said. "But thanks for coming by with food."

"Now that your granddad has a job, you've got a little money coming in?"

Con nodded, chewing on a wing.

She willed herself not to look at Tommy. The rent was due soon. And they had opened the mail. Their mom hadn't been paying the water bill.

She thought Tommy was getting ready to leave. But instead, he pulled out a chair and sat at the table with them.

"I've known your mom a long time," he said.

Since he was looking at her, she nodded.

"Yeah, we know," Con said.

"You were just a baby when I met her," he said to Con.

She thought Tommy looked kind of embarrassed when he said, "We were all kind of wild in those days. And Summer didn't seem like Ashley's mom. More like her sister. And after Tish and Summer died together in the accident . . ." He shook his head. "I lost it."

"Who's Tish?" Sofie asked.

"Tish was my wife," Tommy said quietly. "Tish and I were a few years older than Ashley. And Summer was like a big sister to all of us. I was a bartender then at this place called The Fishing Pole. I changed it to Tommy's Place when I bought it."

Sofie thought he still looked embarrassed for some reason. He sat there, seeming not to know what to say next.

She wondered why he was telling them this.

"I'm sorry your wife died," she said. That must have been very sad.

"Yeah," Con said.

Tommy nodded.

"Ashley has always been so proud of you two. You're what keeps her going."

"Yeah," Con said.

Tommy stood up. "You let me know if you hear from her. Yeah?" he said, looking at Con.

"Yeah."

"And tell your great-granddad I said hi. We know each other from the last time he visited Ashley. He stuck around quite a while that time.

"And you keep punching above your weight, Princess." He smiled at her.

She nodded. "Thanks for the food."

"Why don't you give me Gunner's number?" Tommy said to Con. "Maybe he'd like to catch up sometime. It's been a lot of years."

Sofie saw Con's dark eyes go darker for a second. They hadn't thought of this. They were caught.

She felt dizzy with the possibility of just blurting out the truth to this nice person who cared about them. To shake off the pretending and the terror.

But she knew Tommy would call Social Services, because that's what grown-ups did. That's what Dylan's mom had done.

"Sure," he said, giving Gunner's phone number to Tommy.

"Thanks," Tommy said. "I'll give him a call."

Her heart was pounding when Con got up to follow Tommy to the door. She heard him lock it after Tommy was gone.

Con came back, his face pale and his hands shaking as he wiped barbecue sauce off his face with a paper towel.

"I know," he said, looking at her. "Maybe I shouldn't have given him Gunner's number. But I'm not sure Tommy really believed us, and I didn't want to make him more suspicious."

He sat down and began to eat again.

How could he do that? The food suddenly smelled nasty. But Con was always hungry.

The house felt so empty. She wanted to go back to the attic where they were safe, but she couldn't leave Con down here alone.

"What will we do if Tommy calls him?" she asked.

He looked up from his food. "It depends on what happens. Gunner probably isn't paying any attention to his phone."

Sofie picked up the Uno deck from its special place on the table. She stared at the cards, ran her fingers over them. Saw her mom's hands as they played. They were not safe inside the circle anymore, because her mom had broken the triangle.

She got up and threw the deck in the trash as hard as she could. And she threw away the stupid giant card.

chapter 12

Sofie jerked awake when Con kicked her. He was thrashing on his pallet, having the nightmare. She scooted out of the way.

"Connie, it's alright."

She didn't know he still had the awful dream.

"Connie, Connie. It's just the dream. It's not real."

He suddenly gasped and sat up, his eyes wide, staring at her without seeing.

"Hey, it's Sofie," she said. "We're in the attic. At home." She kept her voice low and soothing.

Sun was coming through the window.

"It's me," she said. "Everything's okay."

He stared at her through the fog of the nightmare. He tugged at his hair like he wanted to pull it out, and talked so fast she could hardly understand. "Sof, we should have gone to the police. Mom didn't leave us. Something happened to her. I think she fell in the river and is drowning. She grabbed my hand and I tried to pull her free but something held her. We have to help, or the police have to help. Somebody . . ."

His words stopped and he stared at her, the fear in his eyes changing. He covered his face with his hands.

She wrapped her arms around him. His heart was pounding. He was crying. She slid her hands along the bumps of his spine, the blades of his shoulders.

The sun threw their shadow on the wall. When she was little, she would climb into the top bunk and he would make hand shadows. Lop-eared bunnies, elephants, reindeer. She hadn't understood then that he couldn't make the shadows without the sun. She had thought he could do anything, all by himself.

"It's just the same old dream, Connie. None of it's real." She stood and took his hand. "Come on now. Get in the shower."

He shook his head.

"Yes." She tugged. They had to be strong.

Like they'd been doing all week, she kept guard outside the barely open bathroom door while Con took a quick shower. She'd grabbed a pair of baggy shorts and a tank top from her crate without looking. She didn't care anymore about a signature look.

She sat on the floor and read. A few days ago, at the Community Center, she'd found a treasure trove of seven Baby-Sitters Club books she hadn't read. And probably AnaMaria hadn't either, since they shared everything.

When she finished her shower and dressed, she found Con outside the bathroom door texting. She hadn't seen him text anyone all week. All the dings from that rich girl had finally stopped when he didn't text back.

"Who are you texting?"

"Gunner."

"*Why?*" Who cared about that old scarecrow anymore? She couldn't believe she'd tried to teach him to play chess.

"I guess I'd just like to know they're alive, okay? And I wouldn't text Mom for a million dollars. I'm done with her."

"Connie, we can't really be done with her."

He stood and put his phone in his pocket. "I can," he said, his face hard.

No. They would be mad at her like they were the last time. But she would say *Sorry* and they would forgive her because they couldn't live without their mom, and she couldn't live without them. Connie knew that.

They cleared away the cartons from Tommy's visit last night and ate the last of the cereal from the food pantry. In another week they'd be eligible to go to the food pantry again, but they couldn't get food without a grown-up. Her cereal was soft and stale, so she poured a little milk over it. All the fruit was gone. They would have to spend Con's money to buy food soon if their mom and the scarecrow didn't show up.

The time before, their mom had been gone a week. Sofie was pretty sure this was day nine. Con's dream couldn't be true, could it? *Had* something terrible happened?

That thought suddenly loomed so big Sofie couldn't breathe. She had to have a mom because she didn't have a dad. *Nope,* her mom said when Con brought it up. *No dads.* She said whoever their dads were, they'd fathered great kids and that was all that mattered.

And that had felt fine when her mom was standing right in front of her, but now it felt really scary.

Con's phone dinged.

She watched his face as he read the text. Please, please let it be their mom.

He texted something very short back. "Tommy. He wants to drop food off again tonight after work."

The little gust of hope died. But she also sighed with relief. Connie wouldn't have to worry about buying food today.

"Does he say anything about talking to the scarecrow?"

"No."

Thanks goodness.

"Connie, what if mom never comes back?" Her lips felt numb as she asked the impossible question.

"I'll take care of you, Sof."

He said it with such courage, but he was thirteen. Being on their own would be terribly hard. She swallowed.

"I'll take care of you too, Connie. I'll be really strong, you'll see. But it will have to be just the two of us. There won't be room for anybody else." She couldn't have that girl in their life. "Pinky swear it will be that way."

He stood looking at the floor for what felt like a long time. Then he linked his pinky finger with hers and nodded. She loved him so much.

She went in the bathroom and shut the door. Her mom's towel hung where her mom had left it. Sofie buried her face in it.

chapter 13

That night, June bugs banged against the screen. A car went by with loud pipes and the music cranked up. The night was hot and jumpy.

Across from her, Con was finishing his book. It was the one Mr. Bloom gave him—*Holes*. Connie liked it so well he was reading it again.

She stretched her leg out to the side and touched him with her foot. He startled, but didn't tell her to move it.

Sofie had whizzed through three Baby-Sitters Club books and was ready for something else. She eyed *The Underneath*. It looked interesting, but it was big and some of the paragraphs were long and it had words like *Liberia, centenarians,* and *pirogue*. But it also had words like *corn snakes, rat snakes, gumbo,* and *bayou*. Those words pulled her in.

She studied the illustration of the ginormous alligator circling a man standing in a little boat. A *pirogue*, she decided. The illustration put the reader up in a tall, tall tree looking down on the man and the alligator. It made her a little dizzy, but also curious.

The illustration of the redbone hound and the calico cat sitting side by side said they loved each other. And in another illustration Sofie was being glared at by the biggest snake imaginable. She felt like she was hunkered down low, face to face with the snake, who might bite her on the chin. She didn't like that snake. Probably somebody would kill it so the story could have a happy ending.

They heard the knocking at the same time and locked eyes. It was too early for Tommy.

Con went to the window and stepped out on the roof to look.

"I don't see Tommy's car," he said.

She thought about the people her mom hung out with. Or...could it be their mom at the door? She might have lost her key.

The knocking started again. It sounded like it was at the back.

"Turn off the lamp," Con said.

With the room lit by streetlights, he handed her the big yellow umbrella they'd put by the attic door. He took the mop.

"We don't know for sure who it is," he said.

Did he think it was their mom? Was that why he said *don't know for sure*? Her hand holding the umbrella shook as she followed him.

Light from the kitchen glowed at the bottom of the stairwell, and with each step down, cooler air rose to meet her. At the bottom, she felt lightheaded.

Con put his mouth near her ear. "Don't say anything. And stay behind me."

She crowded close against his sweaty T-shirt.

"Who is it?" Con called in a rough voice.

"Gunner."

The mop banged against the floor and hit her bare toes when Con dropped it to unlock the door and throw it open.

There stood the scarecrow.

She didn't want him.

"Where's Mom?" Con said.

The old guy looked bewildered, as if he didn't understand the question.

"Where's our mom?" she said, suddenly icy with fear.

He frowned and shook his head. "I'm sorry. I don't know where Ashley is. I've been gone," he said, as if they might not have noticed.

He had a black eye and a cut across his nose. In the bright light, he looked older and more chewed up than ever.

"Mom disappeared the same night you did," Con said. "We thought you were together."

He shook his head. She saw understanding slowly creep over his face. "You kids have been on your own? All this time? Over a week?"

The words filled the kitchen. Sofie could almost see them. Yes. They had been on their own. *All* on their own. All this time.

She nodded, fighting back tears.

"Something must have happened to Ashley," he said, grabbing his hair the same way Con did, his eyes searching their faces.

"She's probably okay," Con said. "It's not like she hasn't done this before."

"Gone off and left you alone before?"

Con nodded.

"That's not right." His voice rose. "That shouldn't happen. Have you heard from her?"

"No," Con said.

"Have you tried to get hold of her?"

"No."

"Why not?"

"I tried to get hold of *you* several times. You didn't answer my texts."

"What texts?"

"On your phone?"

The scarecrow looked clueless for a minute. Then he said, "It's probably in the truck. Or somewhere."

This meant Tommy couldn't have talked to the scarecrow.

Con's phone pinged.

"Tommy is almost here," he said, looking at it. His eyes went to the scarecrow. "We told Tommy Mom had gone away with friends for a while because you were here looking after us. Nobody can know we've been by ourselves."

She watched the scarecrow's face as he thought about this.

"And we told him you had a night watchman job at a warehouse down-town," she said.

He frowned, but then he nodded.

"And Tommy thinks she's staying in touch with us," Con said.

"And he thinks she's with friends in Texas," she said. "That's where she was last time."

He turned even more pale. The cut on his nose stood out and his black eye seemed to glare. He looked fearsome.

"Where have you been?" Con asked.

He looked at the floor. "On a bender. I spent the last two days getting cleaned up. And I just came from a meeting. That helped me find the back-bone to show up here. And I find out you two were alone...." He shook his head. "I'm sober now. And sorry."

Maybe that was where he'd been going all those times. To meetings for people who didn't want to drink or do drugs anymore. Sometimes her mom went to those.

Tommy knocked at the front door, and Sofie let him in.

"Hey, Princess. You guys hungry?" He looked as happy as Santa delivering Christmas packages.

"Yes," she said, though her stomach was in a million knots.

In the kitchen, he put the boxes on the table. His eyes widened when he saw how beat up the scarecrow was. But he smiled and shook hands. "How are you, Gunner?"

"Doing okay. How about you?"

"Fine. I'm sorry we didn't have time to visit when you were in the restaurant last week looking for Ashley. I guess you don't have to work tonight?"

Sofie watched the scarecrow struggling not to get tangled in the trails of the story she and Con had just told him. If only they'd had a little more time.

"Uh, no," the scarecrow finally said. "Not tonight."

Tommy gestured to Sofie and Con. "Have these two been staying in line for you since Ashley's been away?"

The scarecrow was taking too long to answer. His eyes moved over Con with something like amazement and to her with that strange expression he often got. His whiskery knot of an Adam's apple moved when he swallowed. He finally said, "They're good kids. Real good kids. They take care of each other."

The warmth in his voice made her eyes prickle with tears. She felt a little proud of how she and Con and managed on their own.

"That they do," Tommy said.

The words seemed to roll around the room. *That they do.* And Tommy's expression seemed to say *And they shouldn't have to.*

Was Tommy suspecting the truth? Sofie fought the need to look at Con. Instead, she looked at Tommy and told herself he was a strong, friendly, nice bear who would never hurt them and would try to protect them. A good friend to their family. And with all her strength, she fought the scary thought: good friends sometimes call Social Services.

His eyes were kind when he said, "What did you hear from your mom today, Sofie?"

Like every day, nothing. Nothing, nothing, nothing. She wanted to scream it and then turn into a puddle of tears. But Con was looking at her. *Say something.*

"Mama went out on a shrimp boat."

It was so hard to make stuff up fast.

"Ashley?" Tommy asked, sounding surprised.

She shrugged. Why not? She'd seen an interesting-looking book in the Community Center library about a girl whose dad owned a shrimp boat in Texas. Sofie had paged through it, thinking she would like to go out on a shrimp boat with its great long wings. They weren't called wings, but that's what they made her think of.

She hadn't taken the book because the last few pages weren't there, so she'd never know how it ended.

"That really doesn't sound like Ashley," Tommy said. "Gunner, remember back in the day when we took that pontoon boat out on Saylorville Lake?"

The scarecrow nodded. "Poor Ashley."

For a while nobody said anything.

Her mom must have gotten sick—so sick Tommy and the scarecrow still remembered it. Maybe it was wrong to make things up. Maybe she and Con were going to be punished for lying.

"Does she say when she's coming back?" Tommy asked.

"Soon," Con said. "Not for sure when, but soon."

"It doesn't seem like her to be so irresponsible about you kids. Ashley's always been a wild thing, but she's never let you kids down."

Sofie tried to keep her face perfectly still.

"You're not going to fire her, are you?" Con asked.

"That's the part of being a boss I don't like," Tommy said. "So probably not. But tell her to get in touch with me."

Tommy bopped Con on the shoulder. "Don't worry about your mom getting fired."

To the scarecrow, he said, "Since you've got a night watchman job, is it okay if I look in on these two every night after work?" He smiled. "Just to make sure they're not out terrorizing the town when they should be home reading."

He laughed at the looks on their faces. "Yes, Ashley is always talking about all the books you kids read. She says you get it from her."

Even the scarecrow laughed. And Sofie stopped holding her breath.

"And speaking of smart kids," Tommy said, "I could use another tutoring session. There's a test coming up."

"Sure," Con said.

It would mean money. Tutoring grown-ups paid really well.

Tommy looked at his calendar. "How about tomorrow at three o'clock? The place should be pretty dead then. We can sit on the patio. You come too, Sofie. Tell me about what you're reading. And Gunner, you come too. We'll have a late lunch."

Food.

Sofie was so grateful for Tommy. As long as he didn't do the terrible, terrible thing he might do.

Tommy didn't stay much longer. After he was gone, the scarecrow—who looked like he was about to topple over—said, "If I'd known...I would never have..." His voice trailed off as he shook his head. "I'm sorry."

And Con, who looked like lightning had struck close enough to lift the hair on their arms, said, "You're back now. We can make this work. No matter what happens, we have real, blood family with us now. And that changes everything."

Sofie thought for a minute Connie might reach out and hug the banged-up old man, but he just took a long breath and said, "Let's eat."

Sofie sat down and took a sandwich out of the bag. It was warm and a little steamy through the paper. A tangy, appetizing smell floated up as she unwrapped it, making her feel Tommy's kindness. He liked to feed people.

"Are you sure Ashley just went off?" the scarecrow asked after a while.

"Pretty sure," Con said.

The scarecrow shook his head. He looked beat up, worn out, about done with everything.

"You should eat," she said. She tilted the bag of sandwiches. "There's plenty, see?"

He wasn't who she'd been hoping for when they opened the back door, but here he was.

chapter 14

Sofie stretched and yawned. She'd fallen asleep full of sandwiches. And the last thing the scarecrow had said last night was that as long as he was welcome, he wasn't going anyplace.

"Hey, sleepyhead," Con said. "About time."

She curled onto her side and looked at him sprawled on his side of the attic, hair falling in his face.

"Maybe Mom will come home today," she said.

He grunted something.

"How long have you been awake?"

"A long time."

He had waited for her.

Her red shoes, scrubbed last night and put to bed in their box beside her pallet, glowed in the light coming through the window.

"Is he still here?" she asked.

"Aren't you ever going to use his name?"

"No."

"*He*," Con said, emphasizing the word, "left for a while and is back."

In the kitchen, Sofie saw bananas on the table beside the pretty eggs from the chicken lady. Last week, the lady had called out to them in her language—which sounded kind of angry, even though she was smiling—and hurried to the fence with two eggs, one blue and one green. The green egg she placed in Sofie's hand. *And* the egg was warm, which had been more startling than the color. The lady had explained all about them, pointing to the chickens, but of course they didn't understand. They'd said thank you, and the eggs were still on the table where the Uno deck used to be. Maybe the scarecrow would know if it was okay to eat colored eggs.

The bananas looked so cheerful, like they were smiling. She peeled one and ate it, the fresh flavor making her mouth tingle.

"You want one?" she asked Con.

"Sure."

The scarecrow was sitting on the back step with his tea. Was it because he wanted to be there, or because he thought he wasn't welcome in the house?

She stepped outside. "Hey," she said.

He looked up. His face, with the dark circle around one eye, was even more terrible in the daylight.

"Why are you sitting out here?"

"I like being outside," he said. "Don't you?"

"Kind of. I guess." She thought about adding *If you want to be inside, it's okay.* But that didn't feel like the right thing to say.

He smelled like tea and toothpaste when she sat beside him.

"I ate a banana," she said. "Thank you."

His smile showed those awful holes. "You're welcome."

Con came out with toast on a plate and set it on the step. Her toast had peanut butter on it. Con's had peanut butter and strawberry jelly.

"Help yourself," he told the scarecrow, who took a piece with jelly.

"I've been trying to call Ashley all morning," he said. "But nothing happens. She just starts talking on her answering machine. Why doesn't her phone ever ring?"

"Because she's blocked your calls," Con said.

As the scarecrow figured out what that meant, he looked so hurt.

"Why would she do that?"

Con faked a *Who cares* shrug.

They ate in silence. A pair of cardinals flew in and out of a bush between their house and the vacant house. The toast tasted good.

After a while, the scarecrow took a photo out of his billfold to show them. Sofie stared. It was her in someone else's clothes. And there were palm trees, but she had never been to a palm-tree place. And who was the man with his arm around her?

Con took the photo and stared at it. "What the heck is this?"

"Be careful with the picture," the scarecrow said. "It's precious."

"Let me look again," she said.

"I don't get it," Con said, handing over the picture.

It was her, but it wasn't. The eyes weren't hers. They were the eyes that looked at her from the framed photo on the table in her mom's room.

"It's not me, Connie," she said. "It's Summer, right?"

She looked at the scarecrow, who nodded.

"Your grandmother. When she was your age, Sofie." His voice was raspy.

So the tall man with thick black hair and dark eyes was him, looking down at his daughter. No wonder he sometimes stared at Sofie.

"I didn't do right by my California family, but I especially let down Summer because she was so young when I left. I went to prison shortly after that picture was taken."

Was that where he'd been all this time?

"I have a lot to make up for, and I'd like to try. If Ashley's not around, or not reliable, I'd like to help." He cleared his throat. "It would be a pure gift to me to look out for you kids."

This beat-up old guy made her sad. But also glad. She gave the picture back to him.

"Why didn't we know about you before?" Con asked.

"Ashley was probably ashamed to tell you I was in the joint. But she stayed in touch. She wrote to me and sent me money sometimes."

"Why were you in prison?" Con asked.

"Drug-related stuff. Parole violations."

She didn't know what those were, but she didn't want to ask.

"The good thing about being locked up for somebody like me is getting clean. Twelve years last time."

He drained the last of the tea from his mug, his hand trembling a little.

"Sobriety is a great feeling, once you get past withdrawal. You tell yourself it feels so good to be sober, you'll never be any other way. When I came here, I was going to three or four meetings a day, determined to not to screw up again." He shook his head, not looking at them. "And then I went to get Ashley after work that night. Tommy said she'd just headed home, so I started back here, but seeing the people having fun in the bar had tickled my addiction. I stopped at a place, telling myself I'd have one beer." He made a sound of disgust. "I was stupid. Twelve years of sobriety down the tube."

He could have been here with them the whole time. They wouldn't have been so scared. How did they know he wouldn't keep disappearing? She didn't want another person in her life who did that.

Con said, "You're sober now."

The scarecrow nodded. "Yes. And I mean to stay that way."

"How'd you get the black eye and cut nose?" she asked. Her hand went to her own face as she thought about how painful the blows must have been.

"I remember a dark parking lot and a couple of guys." He sighed. "Two days ago, I woke up in front of a convenience store in this little town north of here where I grew up. I thought of you kids and Ashley, and felt lower than dirt for letting you down. And, of course, I had no idea you two were on your own."

"I thought you grew up in California," Con said.

The scarecrow shook his head. "I grew up in Tyler, about fifty miles northwest of here. You don't remember, but you visited there when you were little. You, your mom, and I went to visit my brother. He's no longer living, but we had a good time that day."

A breeze stirred, ruffling the leaves of the oak tree. She looked at Con. They knew more about him now.

chapter 15

Sofie followed Con, who followed the scarecrow, who was pushing a wheelbarrow loaded with tools and seed packets and long sticks. The low morning sun gave them huge shadows, making them look like a parade of freakishly tall people led by a strange giant insect. The wheelbarrow squeaked and rattled on the grass path, stirring up some smell that tickled her nose.

This early, there was nobody else at the Community Gardens except the person at the entrance who asked them to sign in. Sofie had looked at the sign-in sheet, curious to see what the scarecrow wrote. *Delbert Jones*. She couldn't call him Delbert. She couldn't call him Gunner like her Mom and Con did. So she called him *Hey*.

He had been back for almost two weeks. With his first Social Security check, he'd taken them to thrift shops looking for boots for her and Con. Hers had come from the boys' bin, actually. They were a little big, but she loved them. She had never even imagined having such things on her feet. She liked the clomping sound they made. They were brown like the soil in the garden, and the leather laces smelled very serious when she pulled them tight.

The scarecrow went to meetings every day, and he offered Sofie her room back, saying he could sleep on the couch. Of course, nobody could bear the thought of sleeping in her mom's room, surrounded by the forget-me-not-blue walls.

Sofie said no to the scarecrow's offer because she wanted to stay with Connie. She'd gotten used to him being right there where she could see him and touch him with her foot. She'd carried up more books and a few of AnaMaria's drawings. The drawings, taped around the window, made a pretty frame.

AnaMaria had sent a postcard showing three ginormous *cacti*—the plural of *cactus*, according to Con—against a fiery sunset. No one had ever sent Sofie a postcard. She hadn't even known postcards were a thing. The scarecrow said people once used them like cell phones. A smile had been hiding in his eyes when he said that. She propped the postcard against the box where the red shoes rested when she wasn't wearing them.

"These are our plots," the scarecrow said. He put the wheelbarrow down and pointed to two patches of big, fat, fuzzy-headed dandelions.

In the plot across the path from theirs, vines with pretty leaves and blossoms sprawled everywhere. A pretty sign said MILLIE'S WATERMELON PATCH.

"Hey!"

He looked at her, the brim of his cap pulled low against the sun.

"Let's plant watermelons."

"We're almost into July," he said. "Too late in the season."

"I'll bet it's not." He surely didn't know everything.

"Seeds need their own temperature range to germinate. To wake up. And they need their own number of days to be ready for harvest. And that needs to happen before it gets too cold." He pointed to the watermelon bed. "The melons in that bed will be ripe in late August."

She stared at the pretty vines and imagined plump, green watermelons appearing. She loved the way a cold mouthful of melon burst into juice in her mouth on a hot summer day.

Last week, the scarecrow had talked the Parks and Rec lady into letting them have two abandoned plots. The lady argued it was too late to plant anything, but he told her they could plant carrots, snap beans, chard, and peas now. And in August they could plant lettuce, radishes, and spinach. The lady had looked at him for a long minute and then said, "Oh." Then she smiled and gave him a registration sheet. While he filled it out, the woman kept looking at Sofie like she must be very proud. Sofie was deciding the scarecrow wasn't so scarecrow-ish, really. He was more just very old.

When he jammed the shovel into the ground with his boot, it made a long, interesting, gritty *shush*. He lifted up the dirt, then turned it over so the dandelions were on the bottom and dark, shiny dirt was on the top. She saw part of an earthworm sticking out. Probably it was surprised to be upside down in the sun.

After a few more shovels of dirt, the scarecrow said, "Con, you could take the wheelbarrow and get us a load of compost." He pointed to a sign that said COMPOST PILE with an arrow.

Sofie helped Con unload all the things from the wheelbarrow onto a bench. The long sticks, the strips of cloth, the tools you could cut or hack or dig with, the packets of seeds...they all seemed mysterious.

"What is compost anyway?" she asked Con.

"Dead and decayed stuff."

"Eww." She shuddered. "What kind of dead and decayed stuff?"

"Plants. Animals."

"Animals?" That was disgusting.

"People."

"Connie, not!"

She saw the tease on his face. "The compost here is from plants. But people *can* be composted. I learned it last year."

The horror made her a little dizzy, but gardening was turning out to be an adventure.

She rattled the packet of chard seeds. Just the word *chard* sounded nasty. Like something you might pull out of your nose. She didn't plan to eat chard, though the picture on the packet was pretty.

"Don't fill the wheelbarrow so full you can't push it," the scarecrow called to Con. "Keep checking for how heavy it's getting."

"Don't worry, I know what I'm doing," Con said, standing very straight and tall as he walked down the path.

Sometimes Connie seemed to like having the scarecrow take charge of things, and other times he didn't. He was the same way with Tommy, who stopped by the house most days and texted Con a lot. *Just to stay in touch,* Tommy said, *until your mom gets back.* But he'd gradually stopped asking about their mom. A couple of days ago, he'd taken the scarecrow to get a new battery for his truck, then sat on the back step and talked for a long time and never mentioned their mom once. Probably he'd figured out she'd gone off and left them like a pair of old shoes she was tired of.

Was she? Just tired of them?

Sofie ignored the huge, tangled question that always hung around. Instead, she watched the scarecrow turn over scoops of dirt. Some of it stayed stuck together, and some of it crumbled into pieces. There were lots of worms. Huge ones, tiny ones. The biggest black beetle she'd ever seen scurried over the clods and disappeared.

She wanted a job too.

"Hey, what can I do?"

He stopped digging, He had a bandana tied around his forehead, making him look like an old pirate. She couldn't help but smile.

"How about building teepees for the snap beans?"

"What are snap beans?"

"Beans that say *snap* when you break them in two."

Was he kidding? She searched his eyes for the hidden smile. "Are they going to live in the teepees?"

"They'll vine up the poles as they grow. Just lay out three bamboo poles and tie them together about eight inches from the top with one of those strips of cloth. Don't tie the poles too tight, because we're going to spread them out at the bottom."

He kept working while he explained. He was strong for an old guy, and he didn't look so ancient in the garden.

He'd told her and Con about working in the prison garden for eight years and learning about growing food. He was good at it and he liked it. The day he got out, he stopped at the farmers' market outside the prison and bought a crate of strawberries he'd grown inside the fence. Those were the ones he'd given her mom that first day.

She wrestled with the long bamboo poles, beginning to sweat as the sun got higher. She could hear a little traffic—but mainly she heard birds. The garden was by the woods and a bend in the river, like a place in a book she had read.

As she swiped sweat off her face, she understood why the scarecrow wore his bandana. Next time, maybe he would have an extra one for her.

After she tied the first three bamboo poles together, she dragged them to their plot to see how they would work when she spread the legs out.

"Hey!"

When he looked at her, she said, "Is it okay to step in the dirt?"

"That's not dirt."

It looked like dirt to her.

"Dirt is something you want to wash off. Something bad. Nobody wants dirty stuff, right?"

"I guess."

"That's soil. Soil is where things grow. And it's okay to step in it."

She stood up the poles, which wanted to go all wobbly. And the tie kept slipping. When she finally got it arranged in a neat triangle, the ends of the tie fluttering in the breeze, she thought of her mom and Con and her, three in one inside a safe circle. Three weeks. That was how long her mom had been gone. Much longer than last time.

"Look at that," the scarecrow said. He was smiling at what she'd done. "That's a fine teepee for snap beans."

"Thanks." He was kind of a nice old scarecrow.

chapter 16

She had never seen Con so sweaty and dirty. She was too, and she hadn't worn socks so her boots were making a blister, but they also made interesting prints in the soil. She turned in a tight circle, creating a flower-petal print like something AnaMaria might draw.

"Connie, come and see," she called, when he returned with his third or fourth load of compost.

Compost had turned out to be just dark brown stuff, kind of like soil. It didn't stink. She'd touched it and it hadn't felt nasty until she thought about it, then she'd scrubbed her hand on her shorts.

Con tipped up the water jug that was in the shade of the bench. It made a *glug, glug, glug* sound as he drank.

Then he came to see what she was pointing at.

"Cool," he said.

"You make one. We'll see what your boots look like on the bottom."

Con turned in a tight circle, making a larger flower-petal print beside hers. Then he picked up the handles of the wheelbarrow and started down the path for another load.

Sofie heard his phone ding as he walked away, and she ran to catch up. It might be their mom. But the way he was grinning froze her.

"Hey," he said.

Sofie could barely hear Jade's voice.

"Yeah, I'll show you," he said, as if he wasn't supposed to be shoveling compost but could just stand around talking. As if he wasn't breaking his pinky promise.

Jade said something Sofie couldn't make out. Why couldn't she talk like ordinary girls Con had never cared about? Why did she have to sound so different and ... and *nice*?

Sofie's anger grew as Con turned in a slow circle, his phone held out. "These are some of the garden plots. And see the woods behind the gardens?" Then he swung the phone back the other way. "And over there is the Des Moines river. You can't see it. But that opening where there are no trees is a bluff. You can look down and see where the river bends."

He kept turning in his circle.

She heard Jade say, "There's Sofie. Hi, Sofie!"

She really *really* wanted to make a horrible face. Connie had *promised* her it would always be just the two of them. She glared.

"Hey," Connie said, suddenly bringing the phone to his face, "text me in ten, okay?"

When the phone was back in his pocket, he looked at Sofie, his face reddening. He glanced at the scarecrow and lowered his voice.

"I know, Sof."

There was shame in his eyes.

"I know I promised, but you've been taking up with Gunner..."

"No, I haven't!" She'd never do such a thing.

"You eat the doughnuts he brings you. You teach him chess. You—"

She kept her voice down, but she felt like yelling. "I ate doughnuts one time! And I teach him chess because I like to teach stuff. I'm not *taking up with him.*" She put the last in air quotes to show how stupid the idea was.

"That's not how it looks to me," Con said. "You broke our promise first."

Was Connie jealous of the scarecrow? That was ridiculous. Connie would always be the most precious person in the world to her. Always.

"If he's going someplace, you tag along like a puppy. You've been doing it all week."

She didn't want that to be true. "If I have, I'll stop."

"It's too late now. I'm not going to mess with Jade's feelings again. It really hurt her when I ghosted her."

He picked up the wheelbarrow and pushed it down the path, his back very straight, his shoulders saying *Leave me alone.*

She swiped away the tears that stung her eyes, but they came again. Was what Connie said true?

She didn't think it was, but she ran through the last week. When the scarecrow went someplace that wasn't to a meeting, he usually asked Con and Sofie if they wanted to go along. She had gone to the grocery store with him so she could show him what she liked best. She'd gone to the Social Security office with him because it was across the street from the library with the stained-glass windows where she was going to work someday, and they'd visited there after his appointment.

She'd gone to the farmers' market with him because of the music and balloon animals. And it had been a pretty day with a breeze and the smells of strange food being cooked. The nice old scarecrow had bought them crispy fried things with interesting stuff inside called samosas. And they took two home to Con.

All those times she'd gone somewhere with the scarecrow, Connie could have come too. But the only time Con went was when they were looking for boots. Those other times . . . had he stayed home on purpose to talk to Jade? And now he was trying to blame everything on Sofie?

She ran down the path after him and caught his arm. "Have you been talking to Jade all week? Is that why you stayed home when he asked us if we wanted to go with him?"

When she looked up, his face was as miserable as she felt inside. He shook his head no.

"Oh, Connie." She wrapped her arms around him. "Let's not fight."

He didn't hug her back, but he didn't push her away.

"I didn't mean to break our promise," he said. "It just kind of happened. One day Jade texted me for the first time in a long time, and I answered. It was when you said you wanted to go to the farmers' market with Gunner and he looked so happy about it."

She nodded. In her heart, she knew the scarecrow loved Con. But she was the one who made his eyes sparkle.

She sighed. "So, is Jade really nice?"

Con nodded so hard she thought his head would come off.

"I really like her, Sof. I can't lose her now."

Those words hurt her heart.

chapter 17

Sofie was hot and windblown and sun-toasted when they got home, and all she wanted was a cool shower. She'd poked and patted seeds into soil with her bare hands, so now her fingernails and palms were lined with dirt, and her knees were caked because she'd knelt to do the planting.

The scarecrow was storing stuff in the shed. But after he got cleaned up, she hoped he'd make a big pan of scrambled eggs. He bought pretty eggs from the chicken lady, and he knew just how to cook them with cheese and butter. And they'd have toast and fresh strawberries and bananas.

Connie unlocked the back door and let her go in first. When she stepped through the door, her mom was standing in the middle of the kitchen.

Her heart almost leapt out of her body. "Mom!"

"Where have you been? I've been waiting to see you, but look at you! What have you been doing to get so dirty and where's Gunner?"

Her mom was wearing clothes Sofie had never seen and putting off a weird energy. And talking so fast.

The last time she went off and left them, she had come home and scooped them into hugs and kisses. There had been tears and *sorrys* and more hugs. And promises. That's how it was supposed to be. That's how they found their way back inside the circle.

Her mom glanced around as if tracking an invisible fly. "I met some-body in Vegas. You'll like him. He's nice. He's gone to take care of some stuff now, but he'll be back soon to stay."

Sofie felt Con's grip on her arm. They knew stupid boyfriends. He would not be nice. And they would not like him.

The scarecrow came through the door carrying the carton of strawberries they'd bought at the fruit stand. The sweet smell floating off them made Sofie a little sick.

"Ashley." His voice was hard, and her mom blinked with surprise. "You should never have gone off and left these kids on their own."

Her mom went white, then pink. She shrugged and shook her head, making her dangle earring flash. It was so sparkly it hurt Sofie's eyes.

"They weren't on their own. I knew they'd be fine with you, Gunner." Their mom tried to smile. "I needed a change of scenery. Like really, really *needed* it, that's all. Just a little time on my own."

She turned her smile on Con and Sofie. "But I'm back now."

Sofie wanted that to be wonderful, but her stomach was churning.

"Thanks for taking care of everything," her mom said to the scarecrow, as if he'd babysat them for a few hours and could leave now.

If a stupid boyfriend moved in, would the scarecrow have to move out?

She felt the scarecrow growing taller and larger. Her mom must have felt it too, because she shut her eyes for a few seconds and, when she opened them, Sofie got a tiny flash of their real mom.

She opened her arms to them. "Could I please have a hug? I need one."

Con's grip tightened on her arm, but Sofie crossed the room, taking him with her.

She felt him stiff as a bamboo pole as their mom pulled them to her. But Sofie hugged their mom deeply, burying her face, searching for the sunny-day smell of belonging. When she found it, tears flooded her eyes.

Con broke the hug.

Her mom said, "Wow, you've really grown, Connie. You're a lot taller than when I left."

"I doubt it," he said, his voice cold. "You were gone three weeks. Nobody grows that much in three weeks."

Their mom was so restless, the way her hands went to her hair and then to her pockets. She looked confused.

"Con," the scarecrow said.

He had put the strawberries on the table. Weirdly, Sofie noticed that the berries matched the sweat-soaked red bandana he still wore.

His voice was firm. "Take Sofie to the Community Center for the afternoon. It's not too late for lunch."

But they were so dirty. And their mom needed them.

"Come on, Sof," Con said.

The new clothes and super-sparkly earring unsettled her.

"Come on," Con said again, tugging her arm.

The scarecrow's face was a mix of feelings.

"I don't want lunch," she said, following Con down the back steps.

She was really just tired. If she could lie down on her pallet and nap. She didn't need a shower. She didn't need food. Her mom's return was a new, exhausting kind of not-right.

In the alley, Con kicked a broken brick into a trash can, then he kicked it again, sending a squirrel up a tree. When the squirrel thrashed its tail and jabbered at them, Con picked up the brick and threw it.

"Connie!"

The brick hit the tree trunk and bounced back into the alley.

"It's not the squirrel's fault," she said, her heart pounding.

"I know." His voice was sullen, but he called, "Sorry, squirrel."

"Shouldn't we stay at the house?" she asked. "Something's wrong with Mama."

"She's higher than the space shuttle. And things are going to get worse when the stupid boyfriend shows up. Gunner wants us gone."

"But will he be okay? The stupid boyfriend may be big."

"Gunner's big."

"But he's old."

"He's tough."

This didn't feel right, but she walked beside Con. The sidewalk, the passing cars, the houses looked sort of speckled. And she couldn't quite breathe. Seeing her mom in the kitchen like that was just so shocking. It was what she'd longed for, so it should feel wonderful.

As they crossed the bridge, their boots rang out on the metal walkway. The sounds of their walking together cheered Sofie a little, though she didn't understand why.

"Maybe we should stop at Tommy's," Con said.

"Why? We're stinky dirty."

"Maybe he'd want to know Mom's back."

"But she's not back in a good way, Connie."

"I know."

As they walked past Tommy's Place on the other side of the street, Sofie understood why Con wanted to see Tommy. Tommy was steady and warm and made people feel good. Now that their mom was back, would he disappear from their lives? Just be their mom's old friend again, who sometimes asked Con to tutor him and called Sofie Princess?

Sofie looked at the pretty flowers on the patio and the people eating. She caught a whiff of food and heard the music and voices.

"I don't think we should go there right now," she said, fighting tears.

They didn't belong.

At the Community Center, Mr. Bloom was at the front desk. He smiled, but Sofie felt him take in how they looked.

"We've been working in the garden," she said.

"And we wanted to get here before the lunch line closed," Con added. "Come on, Sofie, let's go wash our hands."

In the restroom, she used soap and warm water and paper towels to clean her hands and knees. She wiped a smudge off her forehead. Because of the wind and humidity, her hair made her look like a large dusting tool.

Because they came here all the time, the people serving the food knew what they liked and didn't like. And Sofie knew that the lady who gave them their drinks had no teeth at all, a beagle who was going blind, and a new great-grandbaby. For some reason, the lady always called Sofie *Sofia mia*.

Con's phone dinged while they were in line and she watched the smile that crept across his face in spite of everything. He read the text, but he didn't text anything back.

"Aren't you going to answer?"

"Later."

"What does she know about . . . ?" She spread her hands to take in the free lunch, their mom, the scarecrow, everything.

He shook his head. "Nothing." The way he said it meant *And she never will.* "Her aunt and uncle have tickets to a baseball game Sunday. They're inviting both of us."

Slowly, like the sun coming up, his neck and face and even his ears turned bright red.

She sighed. She didn't want to ever be a teenager.

The young mom with the sweet baby waved at Sofie. Sofie waved. But today there was a guy at her table. Sofie hoped with all her heart he wasn't a stupid boyfriend.

They carried their trays to where they sat unless someone—someone new who didn't know better—was already there. It was right by a large humming window fan that made the air feel fresh.

Sofie stared at the food on her tray. She really liked garlic mashed potatoes, but today she could no more eat than she could fly. Con was eating. Was there anything that could make him not want to?

"What's going to happen, Connie?"

He put down his fork and looked around the room that was so familiar, where they'd come for meals since Sofie was in second grade.

He looked at her. "I don't know, Sof."

chapter 18

Sofie sat at a picnic table behind the Community Center and watched Con kick a soccer ball around with some older kids. The wonderful morning with the scarecrow in the garden felt so long ago she could hardly remember.

After lunch she'd alphabetized books, but that hadn't taken her mind away from worry about her mom and the scarecrow. Was the bad boyfriend there? Sofie knew he was bad, not just stupid, because something had happened to her mom while she was away. Was her mama going to be like Lili now? Not able to keep a job? Not have money to rent a house?

A kitten crept out of the weeds at the edge of the alley and found a piece of food on the ground by the dumpster. The kitten was so scruffy it made Sofie's heart ache, but the delicate way it sat and ate, as if it were having tea with the queen, made Sofie smile. A dragonfly touched down and sent the kitten into a fit of leaps and pounces. Then something spooked it and it vanished into the weeds.

Sofie clung to that as a sign. The ratty little cat had found a meal, and dragonflies were lucky according to AnaMaria. This meant her mom was not going to end up like Lili. They would be okay.

When the Community Center closed at eight, the soccer field felt creepy with nobody around, so they went to the park. But the playground was empty and they were the only people at the duck pond. In the long thick shadows, the ducks were starting to go to sleep, and their floating headless shapes were scary.

Con texted the scarecrow they were coming home. They had a hard time figuring out what his text back meant because he couldn't text very well, but the bad boyfriend hadn't shown up, and their mom was locked in her room.

It was dark when they went down the alley behind their house.

The scarecrow was in the kitchen, clutching a cup of tea like somebody was trying to pry it out of his hand. A shoe, which must be her mom's, though Sofie had never seen it before, was under the table. It was a silver ballerina flat, like something a princess might have lost when she fled. The carton of strawberries they'd bought that morning was still on the table.

Sofie could hear her mom's voice, loud and angry, through the wall.

The scarecrow set down his tea and stood, putting one hand on Sofie's shoulder and one on Con's, as if they were his crutches.

"You need a meeting, man," Con said, his eyes worried. "Go. We're okay here."

No, they weren't. What was Connie saying? Sofie heard something hit the wall and her mom's furious voice.

The scarecrow shook his head. "I'm holding on okay. But it's good to see you kids."

Sofie thought she heard her mom crying. Sofie had always been able to comfort her mom, and her mom could always comfort her.

She slipped away from the scarecrow's hand on her shoulder and went to her mom's door. "Mama?" She called more loudly. "Mama, it's Sofie. It's okay. I'm here."

There was quiet on the other side of the door, and speaking loudly had calmed Sofie's pounding heart. In the crack of light under the door, she saw the shadow of her mom's feet appear. Her mom was just inches away.

"Sofie?" Her mom's voice didn't sound angry anymore. It sounded hoarse and curious. And tender.

"Let me help you, Mama. Can I come in?"

"Sofie, is that really you?" There was hope in the question.

She sensed Con and the scarecrow coming close and motioned them away.

"Yes, Mama, it's me. What do you need?"

She turned and made a fierce gesture to Con and the scarecrow to go back to the kitchen. She thought of her mom brushing peony-pink polish on her toes and of them laughing until their ribs hurt over the funny word *peony*. She thought of her mom kissing them goodbye every morning and saying she loved them.

She heard the lock slide away and her mom opened the door, the light behind her making her a tall silhouette. She touched Sofie's hair and drew her into the room.

"Oh Sofie," her mom said, dropping to her knees and cupping Sofie's face. "My sweet Sofie, where have you been? You've been gone so long."

Her mom's eyes were tender and so full of love. She touched the back of her hand to her nose and blotted it. "I have a cold."

Like Lili always had a cold. Only her mom's cold would go away. Sofie would help. Con would help. The scarecrow would help.

"Now you're here," her mom said, "will you help me look for it?"

"What are we looking for?"

"The diamond ring. I'm afraid somebody took it. It's worth a lot of money, you know. And I do mean *a lot*."

She glanced at Sofie as if Sofie were a grown-up. But her mom was mixed up, like Lili got mixed up. Sofie took her mom's hands.

Loud pipes came down the street and slowed in front of the house. Sofie saw distraction in her mom's eyes.

"Look at me, Mama."

Her mom pulled her eyes away. She frowned.

"Mama—"

The sound of the pipes stopped. The car had parked in front of their house.

Her mom's gaze turned on Sofie, suddenly full of the most terrible suspicion. Almost of...hatred.

"You little shit," her mom screamed, yanking her hands away and jumping to her feet. "You had me fooled for a second. But you're with him! You took it!" Her eyes said she had no idea Sofie was her daughter who loved her so much. She grabbed Sofie's shoulders and shook. Sofie's head snapped back before her mom flung her into the table with the pretty green candle. "You little shit!" she screamed again, raising her fists high and striking herself in the thighs. She cried out a terrible cry.

The scarecrow and Con were in the room now and trying to hold her mom, who was fighting like she had no idea who they were.

Sofie lay on the floor with the little table overturned beside her. There was a wad of dried gum stuck to the underside. The green candle rolled slowly under the bed. It was probably making a sound as it went, but her ears were ringing and she couldn't hear. The photo of the famous Summer Jones was face down. Sofie's elbow hurt.

A short guy Sofie had never seen before stood in the doorway, seeming to bounce a little on his feet. He was putting his hand in his pocket and pulling out something—maybe the missing diamond ring, which would make her mom calm down. Then slowly, Sofie's confused brain let the thing take its true shape. A gun.

The scarecrow saw what the man was holding and jumped away from her mom, then swooped in and scooped Sofie up and over his shoulder and charged past the bad boyfriend, nearly knocking him over.

"Come on, Con," the scarecrow yelled. "Now! Out!"

Con seemed frozen. His hand on their mom's arm.

"Connie," Sofie called, "come on!"

And finally, after what felt like forever, he followed them at a run across the backyard and into the truck. The old truck lurched down the alley, making gravel fly.

chapter 19

Wisps of hair stuck to Sofie's sweaty face. The scarecrow had found a fan at a place that gave away things that didn't work but maybe could be fixed, and he had fixed it. It hummed on the counter, blowing across the kitchen one way, then back the other way. It brushed over Sofie, stirring her hair, and then on to the scarecrow, ruffling papers on the table. She longed for it to brush over her again.

She kept seeing the gun take shape from the bad boyfriend's pocket last night.

Today, they were pretending everything was okay. The scarecrow, acting as if last night had been a bad dream they'd all three happened to have, was going over a short list of places that hired felons.

"I'll bet Tommy would hire you." She kept her voice light as she got bread and peanut butter out of the cupboard.

The heartbreaking suspicion on her mom's face kept flashing through her mind.

This morning, the scarecrow looked a thousand years old, with bags under his eyes. And Sofie felt like she was walking on glass that was cracking under her feet. But they were pretending it was a normal Sunday and she and Con were going to have fun at the ballpark with Jade's family.

Con had been in the bathroom forever. She went to the door and knocked.

"What?"

"Do you want a peanut butter sandwich?"

"Yeah."

"Are you about done?"

She remembered the way her teeth had chattered in the truck as they drove around not knowing where to go. The scarecrow had driven without his lights until they figured out why people were honking at them.

At Tommy's Place, they had sat in the parking lot for a while unable to speak.

"We should call the cops," the scarecrow finally said.

"No," Con said, his voice hard.

He clutched her wrist like she was being carried away by a river.

She heard them both breathing.

Finally the scarecrow said, "You kids go in and tell Tommy you need to stay here for a while. I'm going back to the house."

"No." She and Con both said it at the same time.

"Listen," he said. "Ashley needs help. You kids don't know anything about this kind of thing. I do. And I know what she would want most if she was herself is for you to be safe."

She had touched his hand on the steering wheel. "It's too dangerous."

Guns killed people. Connie might have died. Her mom might have died. The scarecrow might have died.

Who could have imagined her mom would ever *shove* her? And call her that?

"Sof, are you absolutely sure you're not hurt?"

Connie kept asking as if he'd forgotten he'd just asked.

"I'm sure, Connie."

At the scarecrow's insistence, they had finally gotten out of the truck and gone into the busy restaurant.

Tommy had spotted them and come over. Like the scarecrow, he put a hand on each of their shoulders.

"Spill," he said, his face worried. "What's happened?"

"Mom's back," Con said.

Sofie waited for him to go on, but he didn't. She looked up at him. Tears were filling his eyes. His mouth twisted.

"Come on," Tommy said, rushing them through the crowded, loud restaurant, into the kitchen, then to a tiny room that looked like a closet and an office.

Sofie couldn't bear Con's face. Her big brother didn't cry. She put her arm around him and leaned against his side as he shook with sobs.

"It's okay, Connie," she said very quietly.

Tommy looked like he was imagining the worst possible things.

"It was Mom's stupid boyfriend," Sofie said, still hugging Con. "He had a gun and Con was very brave." He'd wanted to stay with their mom.

But the scarecrow was really brave too. He was going back.

As Con's sobs settled, she kept patting and tried to tell Tommy what had happened. She skipped the part about her mom being mean to her.

"We need to call the police," Tommy said.

"No!" Con yelled, his face twisted and wet.

"We'd end up in foster care," she told Tommy. "Maybe not together. That's why we can't ever *ever* call the police." Panic tightened her throat. Had they made a terrible mistake coming here and telling the truth? "Promise, Tommy! No police, no matter what. Promise!"

"You kids." He took a deep breath, then squeezed Con's shoulders. "Look at me, Con."

When Connie raised his eyes, Tommy said, "I'll do everything I can to help. And I won't call the police."

Then he cupped Sofie's chin, lifting her face. It was a strange feeling. His hand was warm and steady even after what they'd just told him about the gun. His eyes asked for her trust. "I promise, Sofie. I won't call the police."

She nodded, then sighed. They were safe.

"So did anybody get physically hurt? Or was it just dangerous as all get out?"

She sensed Con was about to tell Tommy what their mom had done, and she gave him a tiny shake of her head.

Her elbow hurt from hitting the little table. Her heart hurt from being called a little shit. And she felt betrayed by her mom, who was supposed to take care of her kids.

"We're okay," she said.

He looked from one to the other. "You're sure."

They both nodded.

"Let me make you some food," Tommy said. "Are you okay to hang out here until closing?"

They nodded.

"You want to come out and sit at a table?"

This little room with no windows felt safe. Like a tornado shelter.

"We're okay here," Con said.

Quickly, Tommy brought plates of hot food and a pitcher of water and put everything on the little desk. Con was leaning against the wall and Sofie was sitting in the chair behind the desk and the smell of the food made her stomach swirl. She shook her head no.

"Ice cream?" Tommy asked.

Something cold. And sweet. That didn't smell. She nodded.

"Caramel sauce? Chocolate sauce? Both?" He smiled.

She nodded.

After a hundred thousand years of staring at the file cabinet, the wastebasket, and the vacuum in the corner—but seeing mainly the gun taking its cruel shape and her mom's beautiful face on an ugly stranger—Con's phone rang. She heard the scarecrow's deep voice. The stupid boyfriend was gone and their mom was okay. But the scarecrow had talked to Tommy, and Con and Sofie would spend the night at his place.

Sofie looked at the clock on the wall. Almost another hour until closing. How had the scarecrow got rid of the bad boyfriend? Was the scarecrow safe?

Con sat on the floor and leaned against the file cabinet. He held his phone with his hand resting on his leg. His head was bent. After a while, Sofie thought maybe he was asleep. She hoped so.

She was so tired. She'd give anything for a book.

Finally, she put her arm on Tommy's desk and laid her head down. She shut her eyes and pretended she was reading the story she was making up as she went.

When she woke she was in a big bedroom, in the glow of a nightlight, with a cover over her. The room was cool.

She found Connie on a couch in a very large room listening to music. She curled up beside him and went back to sleep.

When she woke again, it was morning and Tommy was making coffee in a kitchen that was all metal and shiny. Con was sitting in an orange leather chair texting with Jade.

Would Jade still like her brother if she knew about last night?

"Hey, Princess," Tommy said. "Still punching above your weight?"

His kind face said the question was serious today.

"I'm okay."

He made a cup of coffee with the same care the scarecrow used when he made his tea. Sofie wanted to see the scarecrow. She thought of the way he held his tea mug. It was more than something to drink. It helped him. Kind of like her books helped her.

Sofie sat on a tall stool at the bar and watched Tommy make breakfast. He was barefooted, in shorts and a T-shirt. She had never seen his bare legs and feet. Like his arms and neck and probably his face if he didn't shave, they were covered with reddish-brown frizz that looked soft. She tried not to stare. But as he flipped the pancakes and turned the bacon and put carrots and celery and oranges in a weird-looking machine he called a *juicer*, he made her think of a nice bear who knew how to cook fancy.

"So Professor," Tommy said, "there's a test next Friday. Got time for an hour or two of review this week?"

Con nodded without looking up from his phone.

Jade was the most annoying person on the planet, but Sofie was glad somebody made her brother feel good. And Tommy made Con feel good too. For no really good reason, she gave Tommy her best smile. He looked very pleased.

As he was driving them home he caught their eyes in the mirror. "Gunner is a good guy, but he's got a lot on his plate. If he gets in trouble—which we all hope he won't—but if he does..." He paused. "You call me, okay?"

They nodded.

"For sure, man," Con said.

When they were parked in front of the house, he'd turned to look at them, his eyes very serious. "I know you're terrified about ending up in separate foster homes," he said. "But listen. Stop worrying about it, okay? It won't happen."

Sofie felt Con bristle. Tommy didn't know that. Not for sure. It felt like bad luck to say it.

"Maybe not," she said. "But remember you promised. No police."

After a second, Tommy nodded. "You have my word."

And here they were back home. And the scarecrow was not in trouble, or at least he was pretending not to be. He was looking for a job, Con was primping in the bathroom, and Sofie was washing grapes to go with the peanut butter sandwiches for a snack with the scarecrow and Con before she and Con went to the ballpark. A nice normal family like Jade's or Tommy's, doing what normal families did.

Would the gun coming out of the bad boyfriend's pocket in slow motion ever quit circling through her head? Would the shock of crashing into the table?

The scarecrow told them their mom was okay and needed to sleep, but Sofie went to the room where the most terrible thing in her life had happened and cracked the door. Drawers hung open and stuff was dumped everywhere. She opened the door wider. The little table lay on its side. She picked it up and put it back where it belonged, telling herself her mom had been on drugs and hadn't meant to be so mean. Still.

The glass on Summer Jones's photo was not broken, thank goodness. Sofie returned it to the table. How would her mom feel if she'd broken the picture? Would her mom remember what she'd done to Sofie?

She felt under the bed for the green candle. Her mom didn't stir. Sofie found the candle and put it beside the photograph. Then she went to the other side of the bed so she could see her mom's face, but it was hidden by her hair, and Sofie was afraid to brush it away.

The scarecrow said he'd make their mom eat fruit and go to meetings with him. He said she'd be okay. He'd see to it. But she wouldn't be working for a while, and she probably shouldn't go back to Tommy's Place because of the booze. He would have to get a job. Soon.

The scarecrow was too old for a job. And Con was too young for a real one. The worry that their mom might become like Lili gnawed at Sofie.

Con finally came out of the bathroom. He had dark circles under his eyes and he was pale. But he looked nice. Like a boyfriend any girl would be proud to have.

As they walked to the ballpark, Con took her wrist again. Gently this time, not hanging on like last night. "Are you okay, Sof?"

She felt tears spring up, but she blinked them back and nodded. When she could find her voice, she said, "How about you?"

"Sure, I'm fine."

chapter 20

Sitting on the couch, Sofie's mom looked like she could be blown over by the fan, or might crumble if a car backfired. But she motioned Sofie to sit on the floor between her knees. She had a brush in her hand.

Con was still asleep. He and Jade had texted all night. Once he snorted with laughter and woke Sofie. He and Jade had met at Tommy's Place for dinner yesterday. Jade's uncle had dropped her off and picked her up. Connie had come home at 9:30 with what was probably a smear of lip gloss on his face.

It was very annoying.

As her mom began to braid Sofie's hair, Sofie looked at her mom's feet on either side of her, at the glossy toenails. The peony-pink polish was gone. The new polish was perfect, with tiny blue forget-me-nots. She ran her fingers lightly across the polish. It felt like warm glass.

"That tickles," her mom said, wiggling her foot.

Sofie did it again, making her mom laugh at little. Laughter was probably a good thing.

Yesterday, her mom had slept almost all day except for when the scarecrow woke her up to go to a meeting.

When they got home, Sofie had seen shame in her mom's eyes. She'd touched Sofie's cheek and said she was sorry. Truly. Then she'd gone into her bedroom and shut the door. Sorry for what? Did she even remember?

This morning, the scarecrow was off buying groceries and Connie was asleep. It was just her and her mom.

Her mom brushed her finger along Sofie's skin to the place where her neck became her shoulder. "Your beauty mark," she said, tracing around the tiny dark speck on Sofie's skin.

Her mom always told Sofie an angel had put that little dot there to mark her as special. When she was little, Con had tried to wash it off.

It wasn't really a beauty mark from an angel, it was just a mole. The doctor said. But she didn't correct her mom.

She hoped the scarecrow hurried with the grocery buying. The stupid boyfriend with the gun had been gone for a few days, and her mom was better. But things weren't the same. Sofie had to think about everything. Before, she could trust the love in their bones.

"The polish on your toes is lasting a long time," she said.

"Because it was done by a professional."

Sofie didn't want to hear or think about anything her mom had done while she was gone.

Her mom kept braiding, catching small strands of Sofie's hair first on one side of her head and then the other. Normally, Sofie would have loved it, but now she wished the scarecrow would come back.

"Can you hurry and finish the braid? I need to wake Connie so we can get to the Community Center for lunch."

"About done," her mom said.

Sofie heard the scarecrow's truck in the alley. Her mom finished off the braid with a twisty, and Sofie ran up to the stairs to the attic.

She found Con awake. Texting.

He glanced up. "I know," he said, dismissing her.

She turned and went downstairs. It wasn't fair.

Downstairs, her mom's door was closed again and the scarecrow was in the kitchen.

"Look what I've got. I bought it at the produce stand down by the river."

He held the watermelon out to her, a smile cracking his face so wide open she saw two dark holes.

When she reached for the melon, he said, "Careful. It's heavier than it looks."

She cradled it, cold against her arms.

"I paid extra for a cold one," he said.

She understood it was for everybody, but he'd bought it for her. "Thank you."

She was hoisting the melon onto the counter just as Con came into the kitchen dressed in shorts and a T-shirt, and wearing the leather boots he wore everywhere now.

"Look," she said.

"Cool."

"We should eat it now," the scarecrow said. "Go get your mom."

She found her mom in the bedroom standing by the table with the candle in its green glass holder and the picture of Summer Jones. Her mom was staring into space. Did her mom have even a whisper of memory?

"He bought a watermelon," Sofie said. "Do you want some? It's nice and cold."

Her mom looked at her, a long look, her eyes coming alive. Sofie shivered. Her real mom was coming back like a flower opening or the sun rising.

Sofie stepped into her hug and let herself be rocked from side to side. As her mom sobbed, she buried her face in Sofie's hair. Sofie patted her mom's back.

"Oh baby, I love you so much. I'll make it up to you, you'll see. I'll never do it again."

Sofie kept patting, murmuring, "I know, Mama. I know."

She had her mom back. Her heart nearly burst with joy.

In the kitchen, the scarecrow was using their biggest knife to cut the melon in two. The halves cracked as they came apart and juice puddled on the counter. Then he divided the halves in half for the four of them.

"When I was a kid," the scarecrow said, "we ate watermelon outside, standing in the shade, so we didn't make the kitchen sticky. My mother hated a sticky kitchen."

She and Con glanced at each other. The idea of such an old man having a mother was strange.

"Come on," he said, opening the door.

She caught the slightest eye roll from Con. But carrying their pieces of watermelon and spoons, they went out.

They stood in the shade of the oak tree. Con leaned against the trunk. Their mom looked almost like herself as she scooped out a big bite.

The scarecrow dug his spoon in too.

A breeze stirred and Sofie got ready for her first bite of watermelon this summer. But she heard crunching gravel in the alley.

A police car with two cops in it was driving by slowly, the driver staring at them. The car stopped.

Had the scarecrow stolen the melon? Instead of paying extra for a cold one, had he just taken it? Her eyes flashed to him. He looked scared, but not guilty.

Con's face had turned the greenish white of the watermelon rind. Had *he* done something bad? Surely not.

Her heart stopped as the cops got out of the car. They had so much stuff around their waists she expected them to clang as they walked. Tools for stopping people. For catching them and taking them away and locking them up. And side by side, the two were coming into the yard to get somebody. She saw it in the way they moved.

She looked at the scarecrow again, who was looking at her mom. Her mom was standing very still, her eyes wide.

And then, coming around the side of the house, was another cop and a man not in uniform. That man was short and wore almost rimless glasses that sparkled in the sunlight. Sofie thought he looked merry, like a mall Santa who turned up in the wrong time and place. And Tommy, of all people, a few yards behind them, almost running, who stopped when he saw everybody and looked from person to person, his eyes landing on Sofie.

One of the cops said, "Ashley Jones?"

Sofie's mom nodded.

"I have a warrant for your arrest," his partner said, pulling cuffs off his belt and moving close to Sofie's mom. "Put your hands behind your back."

Sofie watched the watermelon and spoon gradually, gently leave her mom's hand. The spoon tumbled and spun slowly, catching the light, diving into the grass handle-first and sliding a little before it stopped. The watermelon sounded like a living thing falling from up high, landing with a damp thud and exploding, bits of pink stuff flying. Sofie looked at her spattered leg. A drop of watermelon clung there for what seemed like a long time, then began a slow, cool roll down her calf, ankle, and into the grass.

When she looked up, her mom was being folded into the backseat of the police car. She stared at them, mouthing *I'm sorry, I'm sorry.* For a long time the car stayed, as if waiting for something—the motor running, the windows up, their mom's lips moving.

Maybe the police were finding out they had arrested the wrong person. Their mom's name had accidentally got put on an arrest warrant and any minute the car door would open and their mom would get out, her hands free. The cops would apologize and leave. Maybe her mom would sweet-talk the cops the way she did when they came to break up parties. Was her mom doing that now? Sofie's heart was pounding so hard as she waited for this she thought she might die.

Then slowly the car moved down the alley and out of sight.

Sofie's hands fell to her side and her watermelon and spoon dropped to the ground.

The short man with the sparkly glasses was standing close to her and Con now, saying he was an advocate for children with parents in the criminal justice system. Sofie didn't understand any of that except the word *criminal.*

"Our mom isn't a criminal," she said, struggling to find the breath to explain it calmly. "She's..." Her brain had turned off. "She's..." Even her voice didn't want to work. "...our mom," she whispered, hoping that if the man couldn't hear her, Tommy, who'd also come to stand beside her, would explain.

She looked up at Tommy. His eyes were sad and kind, but he didn't try to explain, he just squeezed her shoulder.

chapter 21

"Come on, Sof," Con said, his voice sounding far away.

He led Sofie to the porch and sat beside her, his arm tight around her shoulders.

She stared at the place where her mom had stood eating watermelon. Sofie saw it again, over and over. Her mom being handcuffed. Her mom being handcuffed. Her mom being handcuffed. Like an ugly flashing sign that never quit, that she couldn't look away from.

Her mom wouldn't be able to wipe her face or blow her nose with her hands locked behind her back. Who would help their mom? Would somebody take off the handcuffs so she could eat and go to the bathroom?

"Maybe she won't have to stay in jail," Con was saying. His voice was coming from a long way off even though his lips were close to her ear. "Maybe we can post bail like in the movies and she can come home today."

Where would they get money for that?

The streak of watermelon splatter on her leg was drying. She touched the French braid in her hair, remembering the feel of her mom's fingers, the smoothness of the skin on her mom's legs, the tiny forget-me-not toes.

The twinkly guy crossed the yard from where he'd been talking to Tommy and the scarecrow. He sat on the porch steps with Con and her, talking to them, telling them why their mom had been arrested. She didn't listen.

The scarecrow and Tommy were still by the fence, talking to each other now. She didn't listen to them either.

She could hear the traffic on MLK. It was a nice steady hum with other sounds dotted through it. Horns and loud mufflers and trucks changing gears.

The twinkly guy kept talking, and Con, still far away, was talking too.

"Will they leave the handcuffs on long?" she asked.

The twinkly guy looked surprised. Then he said, "I don't think so."

"Sofie, you need to pay attention," Con said, squeezing her shoulder. "They don't know what to do with us."

She looked up at him. There was terror in his eyes. But she was so tired. She wanted to crawl inside a book and fall asleep. A breeze stirred, making her more tired. The twinkly guy was mostly bald, with hair only around the edges. It ruffled in the breeze in a peaceful way.

By the fence, Tommy put his hand on the scarecrow's shoulder and the scarecrow nodded. They both came toward her and Con.

The twinkly guy stood. "I'd like to walk through the house now, Mr. Jones, if you'd give me a quick tour."

The poor scarecrow looked like all his blood had been drained out. "Okay."

As they went inside, Tommy sat on the step by Sofie.

"How are you holding up, Princess?"

"She's okay," Con said, keeping his grip on her shoulders. "Did you call the cops? *Why?* You promised!"

"I didn't call them," Tommy said. "They showed up at the restaurant, hoping Ashley would be at work. They didn't want to arrest her in front of you kids. I followed them here. I hoped I could help."

How could Tommy help? And then she saw a way.

"You could give them money so Mom can come home." Get her out of those terrible handcuffs. "Post bail like in the movies."

She felt Tommy take a deep breath. She stared at him, trying to beam all her love, hope, and fear into his mind so he would do what she wanted.

Finally, he nodded. "I'll try."

"Today?" she asked. "Right now?"

His face was sad. "It doesn't work that way, Princess."

chapter 22

They lay in the attic sleepless. The scarecrow was pacing downstairs. Sofie heard the microwave door open and close. He was making tea. Then back to pacing. He'd been doing it for hours.

Her mind was loud and jumbled and jerky. She kept trying to shape the day into something she could hold, like a ball or a globe. Something that would stay still so she could look at it and understand.

She counted the scarecrow's steps from the front door to the back door. Seventeen. Turn. Seventeen. Turn.

Connie had pushed back the sheet between them again. He lay on his back, his head and shoulders propped on a pillow. His eyes were open but he wasn't looking at anything. He still held his phone in his hand like it had grown there, but the phone had been quiet for a very long time. Sleeping. Maybe dead.

Much earlier, he had read aloud a message from Jade saying the twins had been born. He'd texted something back, then said he was turning off his notifications. The way he said it was like *The End*.

To her surprise, that felt terribly sad.

He bounced the side of his fist against the floor and muttered, "Why won't Gunner stop pacing?"

The pacing stopped.

Their eyes met as they waited for it to start again, but it didn't.

"He's worrying too," she said.

The advocate—whom the scarecrow called the twinkly guy—had stayed a long time, looking at the house and talking to the three of them together, then just to the scarecrow, then to her and Con together. Watching them from behind his shiny glasses, asking so many questions—mostly about ordinary things like where they went to school and where all they'd lived. Why Sofie had so many books lined up around the edge of her room.

But he also asked about things they didn't like to talk about, like stupid boyfriends and drugs and alcohol and guns and being left alone.

Finally, he'd asked them if it was okay with them if the scarecrow became their legal guardian for a little while, until they discovered what was going to happen with their mom in the justice system. And until Social Services could make more permanent plans for them.

Since the scarecrow had been looking after them for weeks already, it was fine with them. And their mom would be home soon, thanks to Tommy, so they wouldn't need permanent plans.

"I can't just lie here," Con said so quietly she thought he was talking to himself. "I've got to do something."

"What time is it?"

She felt like a week had passed since the cops came down the alley. And she felt like it was still happening.

He looked at the phone in his hand. "Almost four."

"Let's go to the duck pond," she said.

He sat up and began to put on his boots. "We should go out the window. Gunner is probably still awake and he wouldn't think it's a good idea."

She took her red shoes out of the box.

Con helped her through the window. Tonight the air was sticky, and there was no moon or breeze.

Carrying his boots, Con led her to the edge. He dropped his boots, then swung himself down.

"Come on over," he said quietly.

This time he didn't fall down when he caught her.

"What are you kids doing?" the scarecrow asked.

Sofie let out a squeak of surprise and Con jumped a foot. The scarecrow was sitting on the front steps, in the shadows.

"It's dangerous to be out this time of night."

His voice sounded weird. Was he drinking?

"Dangerous to jump off the roof."

"I do it all the time," Con said.

Sofie felt him trying to act all macho. Should she say it was her idea because no matter what she did, she couldn't sleep?

Con sat down in the grass and began to put on his boots. "What are you doing out here?"

The scarecrow sighed. "Fighting the urge to go find a bottle." He sounded so tired. "I know where there's a meeting at six. I'm trying to hang on."

Sofie sat beside him. She was so glad he hadn't been drinking she felt dizzy.

"I'd like to give Ashley a piece of my mind. How could she have been so stupid, letting that guy suck her into all that? Now. With you kids half grown." He smacked his hand against his knee. "It about kills me."

His words hung in the air, which was still and thick.

"I don't know if I can handle this," the scarecrow said.

Sofie's hand went to her heart. He had to.

"And I see myself in Ashley," the scarecrow said. "I did stupid stuff that took me away from my kids."

"You won't do stupid stuff again," Sofie said. "I know you won't." She didn't know any such thing, but if she believed it, maybe it would be true.

She wished Connie would say something. But at least he got up and came to sit on the steps with them.

The scarecrow slapped at a mosquito. "The dregs of the night," he muttered.

"Morning will be here soon," Con said.

"Have you been to the duck pond at the park?" Sofie asked the scarecrow. She felt him shake his head in the darkness.

"Well, when the ducks sleep, they put their heads under their wings." She saw it in her mind, and it made her smile a little. "They look headless."

Nobody said anything. A cricket chirred in the grass.

"Don't you think that's kind of funny?" she asked.

The scarecrow's voice sounded lighter when he said, "If you think it's funny, Sofie, it's probably funny."

"After your meeting, come home and we'll go to the duck pond," she said. "We'll show you."

Of course, the ducks would be awake then. But sometimes they took naps.

Somebody's stomach growled loudly. Sofie couldn't remember when they'd eaten. If they'd eaten. She'd been ready to take her first bite of cold watermelon when the world turned upside down.

"We should make breakfast before you go to your meeting," she told the scarecrow.

"Eggs," Con said.

Later, when it was beginning to get light and the rattle of the truck down the alley had faded, Sofie stretched out on the couch and put her feet in Con's lap. He didn't seem to mind. She closed her eyes and told herself she was a duck, drifting on the pond, with her head under her wing. She was safe. The water would hold her up.

chapter 23

Sofie sat in the front seat of the social worker's car parked in the shade. The air conditioner ruffled the papers in the open file between them.

It was cool in the car, but she still felt drippy with sweat, as if she were being twisted up and wrung out. Con and the scarecrow sat on the front steps where she could see them. She tried not to fidget, but her feet and hands wouldn't be still. In the well around the seatbelt fastener, her fingers found part of a broken purple crayon. She smelled it. Which was dumb because it just smelled like crayon. She put it back, guiltily.

The social worker—who said to call her Elizabeth—looked like a mom. Maybe the crayon belonged to her child. Surely a mom would understand how much Sofie needed to see her mom.

The social worker took a folded piece of paper out of the file and handed it to Sofie with a smile.

"Your mom tells me you're a great reader. Can you tell me what this says?"

Sofie looked at the paper.

"It says it's okay for you to interview me alone and record our conversation." There was her mom's pretty signature at the bottom. *Ashley Ann Jones.* "Have you seen her?"

"I saw her yesterday."

"Isn't she pretty?"

"Yes, she is. You must miss her."

"Did you know she's the daughter of a movie star?" The social worker needed to know her mom was a lot more than just somebody in jail.

The social worker stopped going through the file and looked at Sofie. Probably she didn't believe her.

"So you're the granddaughter of a movie star," she finally said, smiling again.

She smiled a lot. But what she said made Sofie feel good.

She laid the paper with her mom's signature on her bare leg and smoothed the fold. "Can I keep this?"

The social worker looked surprised. "No. Sorry. I need it for the file."

Sofie handed it back, then shut her eyes. She tried to concentrate on nothing except the backs of her eyelids. She heard the scratch of the social worker's pen against paper. Then the sound quit.

"So Sofie, to start, do you have any questions?"

She opened her eyes and everything jumped with brightness. "When will my mom get to come home?"

"Well." The social worker took a breath. "It depends on several things. But I understand the charges are serious. So we should plan on it being a while."

"Like a month?"

"Almost certainly longer than that." She cleared her throat. "Much longer, Sofie."

Sofie stared at the social worker. She felt as if the whole world had begun tilting from side to side and she was about to be pitched off. That could not possibly be true.

The social worker had her mom mixed up with somebody else. That was all.

It was ridiculous to think that she could be without her mom for *much longer* than a month. The social worker was probably new or a substitute.

"What grade will you be in, Sofie?" the social worker asked in a kind voice.

She really didn't want to talk to this person who was confused about her mom. But the advocate said she had to.

"Fifth," she said.

"Where do you go to school?"

Sofie told her, and the questions went on.

They were easy at first. She talked about school and her teachers. About Mr. Bloom who would be her teacher next year. About AnaMaria and how they ate lunch together and played at recess.

And then she had an awful thought.

Would AnaMaria want to be Sofie's friend if Sofie's mom was in jail?

But thanks to Tommy her mom would be home soon and AnaMaria would never know.

As the social worker's questions got harder, Sofie wished she and Con could answer them together. She glanced at her brother sitting on the steps. He was lining up his feet even with each other and looking at his boots.

"Do you feel safe at home, Sofie?"

"You mean now?"

"Now and in the past."

Bad memories flashed through her mind, but she said, "I feel safe because I'm with Connie." She found herself adding, "And our great-granddad."

The scarecrow was old, but he was strong. And he'd do anything for her and Con. He'd somehow gotten rid of the stupid boyfriend. He'd tried to take care of her mom. And he was fighting to stay sober.

Did she need to tell the social worker about the trailer a long time ago and hiding in the closet? Even then she'd felt kind of safe because Connie was right beside her. Her mom hadn't meant for him to get hurt. The social worker probably already thought their mom was a terrible person.

"Has anybody ever hurt you or your brother or your mom?"

She was thirsty, as if the questions were sucking her dry. If the social worker asked Con, what would he say? If she said no, and Con told the truth, would she get in trouble?

She stared at him through the window, trying to send him a message and get one back.

Finally, she spoke very quickly and softly, as if her answer wasn't important. "A long time ago, Mom had a bad boyfriend. He hit her and stuff. When Connie tried to help, he got hurt and the boyfriend went to jail. But our mom didn't do anything wrong."

She promised herself that as soon as the social worker was done with her she could run inside and gulp down a glass of delicious, cool water.

Did anybody ever live in their home except her mom and granddad and brother, the social worker asked. Stupid boyfriends sometimes, Sofie explained.

"Do you get along okay with your great-granddad?"

She nodded. "He cares about us." As she said the words, she felt the truth of them grow into a little block of warmth deep inside.

"How about your brother?"

"He's the best brother in the world."

That made the social worker laugh. "You sound very definite about that."

She raised her foot to show the social worker her red shoes. "Connie bought these for me. New. At Walmart. With money he earned."

Finally, the social worker said she didn't have any more questions. Was there anything Sofie needed from her?

"Let me see my mom. Please. I need to know if she's okay."

"We'll talk about that when we're all together with your brother and granddad. She needs to see you too. And make sure you're okay."

Those words warmed Sofie so much she forgave the social worker for being mixed up.

"Why don't you ask your brother to come and talk to me now?"

She scrambled out of the car.

"She wants to talk to you next," she told Con, rushing past him, up the steps and inside, into the kitchen where she ran a glass of water. The glass clicked against her teeth and water dripped down her chin because she was shaking. The social worker's words—*much longer*—were shoving to break free of the box with a tight lid where she'd put them.

The scarecrow came into the kitchen. "You don't look so good, Sofie," he said, his face worried. "Eat some grapes. The sugar will help."

If an army of hungry zombies were marching down the street, he would tell her and Con to have some grapes. Or a pear. Or a banana. But she nodded.

"I will. But go sit on the steps so Connie can see you."

After he left, she tried again to drink water. This time, her hand was steadier. She had a second glass and felt kind of dizzy. The little jars of strawberry preserves she and the scarecrow had made a few days ago were lined up on the window ledge. They caught the sun like ruby jewels. They were a good-luck sign. The social worker didn't know what she was talking about.

Before she left the kitchen, she wiped away the water spatters in the sink and rinsed and dried her glass and set it on the shelf. She and Con and the scarecrow had spent all day yesterday cleaning. They wanted to make things look as nice as possible. Con and Sofie had taken the bus across town many times to help their mom clean rich people's houses. In the beginning, they'd gone because there was nobody to look after them. Now, they were good helpers.

Even though Sofie's stomach was swirly, she put a bunch of grapes on a paper towel and went to sit beside the scarecrow on the steps. She saw Connie look their way and she sat up straight and sent him a message. *Be strong.*

When she bit into the grapes, they were crisp and sweet.

She put them between her and the scarecrow. "You have some too," she said.

Now and then Con looked their way.

"How long did I talk to her?" she asked.

"About fifteen minutes."

"It felt like hours." She crossed her arms on her knees and laid her head against them, shutting her eyes. Then she remembered Con, and sat up straight.

Their mom had been in jail for a week, which felt like a year. She and Con had stopped going to the Community Center for lunch. But yesterday, Mr. Bloom had knocked on their door with containers of food. He'd met their granddad and told him what fine kids Con and Sofie were. She had felt herself blossom at the kind words, but Con had slumped, his hair falling into his eyes.

He wasn't texting with Jade anymore, which made Sofie feel guilty because she had wanted Jade to go away. But now she thought he needed Jade to cheer him up. When she told Con that, he'd look surprised, then shaken his head no. He said he didn't want to talk about it.

"Did everything go okay with the social worker?" the scarecrow asked. "You look kind of..." He stopped talking and waited.

She wouldn't say the horrible words *much longer* out loud. She wouldn't lift the lid and let them out or they might destroy their hope.

"I'm okay."

After a while the scarecrow said, "Your mom got her problems from me. Like poor Summer. They both got bad stuff from me."

"You're not bad," Sofie said, which was what she always said when he said that.

Someone who was bad wouldn't hang around trying to help her and Con.

"But people pass things on to their kids. And grandkids. They don't mean to. But they do."

He leaned forward and clasped her foot, shaking it. It was kind of like a hug.

"When you're as old as me you'll have a lot of memories. Sometimes I even forget what my memories are until something happens to make me remember. Con makes me remember being a kid."

She looked at the scarecrow, trying to find a kid in that big bony body.

"I was tall for my age too. All I cared about was playing basketball and baseball with my buddies. Then in high school, I mainly played basketball and chased girls.

"We lived in this little town where my dad had an insurance agency. My brother Jack had already gone off to college with big ideas. I didn't have big ideas. I took things as they came and had fun."

Like her mom.

"And then I got drafted and sent to Vietnam. That doesn't mean anything to you, Sofie. But it was an awful war. I used drugs and booze to escape."

She didn't know what her mom was trying to escape. Maybe sadness.

"When I was discharged from the service in California," the scarecrow said, "I found a pretty girl and married her and had a son right away. Donna and I had a lot of fun at first. California was the place back then."

The scarecrow looked softer and very sad.

"But Donna was smart and was done with being wild, and then we had another son. I knew I wasn't living up to my obligations, and rather than doing something about it I stayed high most of the time. And then I got in with bad people and things from the war started to haunt me and I did really stupid stuff. By that time, Summer was your age. I got myself sent away for a good long time."

"That's not going to happen with mom," Sofie told him.

Not going to happen, not going to happen, not going to happen. She would fight the social worker's words with her own words.

"I've been in and out of prison ever since," the scarecrow said. "The California family moved on without me. My two sons don't want any more to do with me, which is what I deserve. And Summer..." He shook his head.

"I'm old, Sofie. *Old* old. But if I could do good things for you and Con in these last years, I'd die happy."

He raked his fingers through his hair the same way Con did, making it stick up.

"Looking after you two may be the one thing I want enough to stay clean. We've got to convince this social worker I'm up to being your permanent guardian."

"You mean permanent until Mama comes home soon."

He nodded.

They would help each other. She and Con would help him stay sober. He would help them stay together. They all had to be together when her mom got back.

Finally, Con got out of the car and came up the walk.

"You're next," he told the scarecrow.

He flopped down beside Sofie.

"How did it go?" she asked.

He shrugged.

"Did she ask you if anybody had ever hurt us?" she asked.

"Yeah."

"Did you tell her?" She was holding her breath, hoping she hadn't given away something she shouldn't.

He nodded. "I figured they'd find out if they didn't already know, since Mom pressed charges. I reminded the social worker that Mom had called the cops."

She let out her breath.

"I hope Gunner can hold up his end," Con said. "He's our only hope."

chapter 24

When it was time for the social worker to come in, Sofie led the tour the way they'd planned. She was a little excited. They'd worked so hard to make the house nice.

"This is the living room," she said.

The social worker nodded and smiled.

Nothing matched, and up close the couch smelled like all the people who'd ever had it. But the air smelled like fresh linen today because the scarecrow borrowed a can of freshener from the car wash where he'd been working for the last few days.

"This is his bedroom," she said, looking at the scarecrow. She stopped thinking of it as hers when she carried all her books up to the attic and piled them as high as she could on either side of the window.

The sheets on the scarecrow's mattress were smoothed and the pillow fluffed. His things were put away in the tiny closet and the door was closed. A wooden chair he'd bought at Goodwill sat by the closet door. The windowsills were clean and he had gone around the house this morning for any mouse poop that had been dropped overnight.

"This is the bathroom," Sofie said, stepping across the hall.

The scarecrow also borrowed special cleaner from the car wash to take off rust stains in the sink and toilet. The smell made her sneeze.

"Bless you," the social worker said.

"Thank you."

In her head, she had practiced saying the next five words. "This is my mom's room." She said it without her voice breaking.

Everything was put away. She and Con had done it yesterday while the scarecrow worked on the bathroom. It felt kind of like their mom had died and was never coming back. But Sofie didn't want the social worker to think her mom was a slob.

The social worker looked at the table with the candle and the picture of Summer, but she didn't ask. She seemed to understand how hard this was for Sofie. She smiled and turned away. "Next is the kitchen?"

Their granddad had polished apples and put them in a bowl and set the bowl on the table like something on TV. Sofie thought that was a nice touch. She watched the social worker's face to see what she thought about it. The social worker smiled. Sofie saw her look at the strawberry preserves with the light shining through them.

They'd decided Con should take the social worker to the attic. And they decided to call it the *upstairs*.

"I'll show you the upstairs," Con said.

Sofie listened to the two sets of footsteps on the stairs. She could see it in her mind. Her books on both sides of the window, the sheet drawn closed down the middle, their bedding spread out neatly on the floor. Their tidy clothing crates. They had made it look as good as they could. But she was afraid it would look poor and shabby to the social worker.

She heard the social worker and Con talking, but she couldn't make out the words. They were talking a lot. Until now, the social worker had mainly nodded and smiled. The scarecrow looked worried. What could be so interesting about an attic?

Sofie wished she had been the one to take the social worker up. She could have done a better job of letting the social worker know how safe and cozy it felt, especially with her lamp. And now her books. It was a wonderful place with her brother right there. And they went out on the roof at night to cool off—though they definitely weren't going to talk about that to the social worker.

When Con and the social worker came downstairs, neither looked happy. But the social worker was friendly when she told them she appreciated spending time with them individually and getting a tour of the house, which was very orderly and clean.

"But Sofie needs her own room," she said.

Sofie blinked. She didn't want her own room. Not anymore. She opened her mouth, but Con's warning look made her close it.

The social worker looked at their granddad. "I understand the room you're in used to be Sofie's."

He nodded. He was pale under his garden tan and she saw a sheen of sweat on his forehead.

Despite Con's warning, she spoke up. "He offered it back to me a long time ago, but I don't want it. I like being in the attic with Con."

Con caught her eye and she realized she'd said *attic* instead of *upstairs*.

"That space is substandard. There's no real floor. No real walls or ceiling. You can stand up only in the center." The social worker was not smiling now. "It's hot and dim and poorly ventilated."

But going out on the roof was nice. She bet the social worker couldn't do that at her house.

"That's a change that must be made," the social worker said. "I could be okay with one person in the attic, I guess. Under the circumstances. But everybody needs their own bed—or at least a mattress—and Sofie needs her own room."

She turned to their granddad. "As the temporary guardian, Mr. Jones, can you make those changes happen?"

He looked ashamed and responsible. "Yes," he said.

"When I get back to the office, I'll text you the number of an agency that can provide free mattresses," she said. "You text, right?"

He nodded.

Not really. But she and Con could help him.

The social worker said it was nice meeting them and she'd be back in a week or two to see how things were going. And she'd make her report to the advocate, who would be in touch with them. Did they have any questions?

"When can we see our mom?" Sofie asked.

"The visiting hours are posted online. The dos and don'ts. Check those out and go when you feel ready."

It was as easy as that?

This news made her floaty with relief as they stood in the door watching the social worker drive away. Then Sofie turned to Con and her granddad, all their faces asking each other how the visit had gone.

"I wonder if she thought the bowl of apples was corny?" the scarecrow asked.

"No," Sofie said. "She liked it. I could tell."

His face turned pink and he smiled.

"Man, she did not like the attic!" Con said.

"I'm not moving downstairs," Sofie said. "No way."

Her granddad looked at her, his face kind but determined. "We'll have to do what she says, Sofie. She has a lot of power. What if she tells the court I'm not a fit guardian?"

That thought was terrifying, but Sofie was sure she would lie awake all night, afraid and worrying, if she moved downstairs.

"You used to be mad because Gunner was in your room," Con said. "This is your chance to take it back."

What a terrible thing to say. The scarecrow was standing right there and she saw the hurt look on his face.

She glared at Con. "He offered my room back a long time ago. And remember I said no? I don't want it back."

"Then take Mom's room."

What was wrong with her clueless brother? He sounded like the social worker.

"That's the stupidest thing I ever heard. She'll be coming home. Soon."

Maybe not *soon*, soon. But before too long.

Con's expression hardened. "Sof, you'll be a head librarian before she gets out. By then, this house and the dump next door and this whole neighborhood will be torn down."

She gasped and the scarecrow looked like he'd been punched.

"You don't know that." She glared at Con. If he was right, the scarecrow would probably be dead by then. "You don't know everything," she cried as her face started to break. "You don't know *anything*!" Her throat burned as the words were torn out of her. "You're trying to get rid of me."

She saw the guilt on his face and a piece of her heart tore off. Her brother really didn't. Want. Her. In the attic with him.

She caught her breath and ran past them and out the front door. She would live someplace else. If her mother was never coming back and her granddad was going to die and Con didn't want her...

She was across the porch and down the steps before she heard the screen door slam shut behind her. She heard Con and the scarecrow call her name, but she ran as fast as she could. The world blurred with tears. Surely, they wouldn't keep her mom in prison as long as Connie said.

Con caught up with her, his hand brushing her shoulder. He sounded out of breath when he said her name. He clasped her arm.

She slowed to a stop, but she kept her face turned away and yanked her arm free. Her nose was stuffy from crying and she was out of breath from running. It was hard to talk, but Con needed to understand her mom couldn't be gone for a long, long time because Sofie couldn't live without hearing her mom say *I love you* every day. She couldn't live without her mom's laughter. Without her mom, the word *peony* was heartbreaking.

She glared at him through her tears. "Why did you say that about me being all grown up before mom gets out of prison? You don't know that."

"I don't know that for sure," Con admitted.

Of course he didn't.

She couldn't possibly grow up without her mom.

Who would Sofie hug every morning? And their mom needed to be home to play Uno.

A thought stabbed her. "Is all this because I threw the Uno deck in the trash?"

Con looked so sad her fury died.

"No, Sof."

"Then why?" Tears were streaming down her face again. "Why?"

He put his arm around her shoulders. "Because Mom is Mom."

A kid went by on a bike and looked at them like they were acting very weird in the middle of the sidewalk.

But Sofie didn't want to go back to the house and face the scarecrow. He was so kind to her. She couldn't believe he was going to make her move downstairs where she'd never sleep. For that, she kind of hated him. But the thought of him dying before her mom came home was horrible.

"We're going to have to make changes, Sof," Con said. "We can't stop time until Mom gets home." His face was pale. "And Gunner's right. We've got to do what the social worker says or else . . ." He shook his head. But the fear in his eyes said *or else we might be separated.*

"So will you take Mom's room?" he asked.

"No!" She would die of heartbreak in there.

"Then you need to go back to your old room and we'll let Gunner have Mom's room."

That felt so wrong. Even if the scarecrow was nice, the room would begin to smell like him instead of her mom. She saw her mom, so beautiful, stretched out in her bed, her feet poking out from under her silky sheets.

Finally she said, "He mustn't move her things." But then she took a deep breath and swallowed hard. The room would make the scarecrow sad too. "Unless he really, really needs to."

chapter 25

The day was hot and steamy. Sofie sat between her granddad and Con in the truck, her heart jumping around like a frog.

"Are you kids ready for this?" her granddad asked.

"Ready to get it over with," Connie muttered.

For the past two weeks he had disappeared into the attic. Sofie saw fury and misery in his eyes. And she felt the scarecrow hanging on from one meeting to the next.

Connie was sitting pulled away from her so their arms didn't touch. She ached to lean against him, but not if he didn't want her to.

She wished he'd come to the garden with her and the scarecrow. The snap beans starting to grab hold of the teepees with their wavy little arms felt hopeful. And when she came home from the garden, tired and dirty, she could sleep. Con looked like he never slept.

The social worker's visit had been two whole weeks ago, and until yesterday Con had refused to visit their mom, and Sofie wouldn't go either because she knew it would break her mom's heart if Connie wasn't with them. And the scarecrow didn't want to go without them because he thought they should all go together.

But Tommy had come over yesterday on his day off and talked Con out of the attic to go have a couple of beers—which Sofie knew was silly guy talk. But Con had gone.

When he came back three hours later he said he'd had a good time. They'd gone to an arcade and Tommy had taught him to shoot pool. And he'd go see their mom but he didn't want to talk about it.

Sofie had been so grateful for Tommy she didn't know what to say, so she had smiled her very, very best smile. And he had nodded as if to say *You're welcome, Princess.*

When the scarecrow got on the interstate, Sofie clenched her fists. She was afraid the rickety truck might die or fall apart right in the middle of whizzing traffic. Also, she thought the scarecrow was too old to be going fast. And deep down, she dreaded getting to the jail any sooner than they had to.

"Being in jail is rough," the scarecrow said. "Your mom will be in a bad way. We need to do all we can to lift her spirits."

Sofie fought tears at the thought of her mom being in a bad way, but last week the advocate had explained things and now Sofie felt all mixed up about her mom.

The advocate told them she was pleading guilty for a lighter sentence. After a sentencing hearing, she'd go to prison—almost certainly for many years, the advocate said—because she and the stupid boyfriend had bought and sold drugs in more than one state, burglarized rooms in a Las Vegas hotel, and robbed a convenience store in Nebraska. A person who worked there had been shot and seriously hurt by the stupid boyfriend with their mom standing right there.

Those details made Sofie so angry she never wanted to see her mom again. Her mom had gone off and left her and Connie all alone, and then done those mean, awful things. And because she'd done them, now they'd be without her for a long, long time.

But maybe their mom had done those things because the stupid boyfriend made her. Maybe he'd threatened her with the gun. If she didn't do them . . . he might have killed her. Sofie shoved that thought away.

She looked at Con, his face set. Maybe the boyfriend had lied about her mom so *he* got a lighter sentence. She and Con had lied once. They said Dylan's mom was lying when she was telling the truth.

All this went around and around in Sofie's head, but her real mom—the one who was funny and kind and beautiful—kept sneaking back into Sofie's heart. That mom would come home soon. Somehow. Because Sofie needed her.

Could they be at the jail already?

Her mom had seemed so far away the last three weeks, on another planet. She felt Con's surprise too. He grabbed the door as if he wanted to hold it closed as they turned into a big parking area.

There were no other buildings close to the jail, which was huge. It looked kind of like an office building except there weren't many windows, and those were all up high. They parked near a sign saying COUNTY JAIL VISITOR ENTRY. Someone had sprayed graffiti on it.

They walked up a long, wide sidewalk. Outside the entrance, a woman in a red shirt, her hair tied in a bandana, sat on a bench talking on her phone.

Con held the door open for Sofie and the scarecrow. He looked so miserable and scared Sofie feared he might let the door close behind them, then run back to the hot truck and lock himself in.

She was shaking inside. Con let his hand brush hers and she looked up at him. For a second, she saw her real brother. The red-shoe brother.

There were other people coming and going, but she didn't look at them and hoped they didn't look at her. When the scarecrow said they were here to visit Ashley Jones, Sofie wished he hadn't said it so loud.

At the security gate, the scarecrow took off his belt and boots and put them in a plastic tub. Then he emptied his pockets and pushed the tub onto the conveyor belt. The guard motioned the scarecrow through the security arch. On the other side of the arch, the scarecrow took his things out of the tub, then turned and motioned her to be next.

She didn't have anything in her pockets and she hadn't even worn her sparkly studs because she knew she couldn't have any metal on her body. She slipped off her red shoes and put them in a bin. She hoped the guard would smile and maybe say something about them, but he just waved her through the arch.

When the alarm went off with a huge staccato blare, she leapt off the floor and then froze, her heart pounding. What had she done?

The guard motioned impatiently for her to come through and the awful blaring quit. He smelled like garlic as he passed a short, fat wand all around her, her shorts, her top. He told her to lift her arms.

She looked at the scarecrow. What was going to happen to her?

When the wand passed over her head, it beeped.

Her hands flew up and touched the barrettes that held her frizzy hair in place. She felt her face flame. "Sorry," she whispered. Then more loudly, "I'm sorry."

"Take those out and put them in the tub," the guard said. "Then go around and come through again."

Her legs were shaking so much she was afraid she'd fall, and she didn't know if she should go through the arch again or around it. What if she did the wrong thing?

"Come on, Sof," Con said in his deep voice. "It's okay."

When Sofie came around, Con squeezed her shoulder. Tears filled her eyes, but she went through a second time and didn't set off the alarm.

She sat beside the scarecrow, who was lacing his boots. Con was coming through the arch. She slipped on her shoes and tried to put the barrettes back in her hair but her hands were shaking and slick with sweat. She tried not to cry, but tears rolled down her hot cheeks and a little sob exploded.

"Hush now," the scarecrow said. "You don't want your mama to know you've been crying."

Con stepped up to the scarecrow, his face white.

"You don't get to tell my sister not to cry. It not her fault we're here. Sofie's not doing anything wrong." He spaced the words so they felt like blows. "Old man."

"Connie!" He shouldn't talk to the scarecrow that way.

The scarecrow didn't say anything. He laced his other boot and stood.

"Here," Con said to Sofie. He took the barrettes from her hands and fixed her hair so at least it didn't fall in her face. She blotted her cheeks with her palms and wiped her hands on her shorts.

They stood in silence for a minute.

"Ready?" the scarecrow said.

She nodded.

There were several people in the visiting area, and Sofie's eyes darted around. Her gaze slid right past the pale person in the bright green scrubs until the woman called, "Sofie!"

Sofie threw her arms around her mom, who looked so different and smelled so different, but the familiar softness was home. Sofie hung on.

"We're not supposed to do that," her mom said, loosening Sofie's arms.

Sofie had read it in the dos and don'ts online, but forgot. Guards standing around the room watched them. One was staring at Sofie. She'd done another wrong thing.

"We're supposed to sit down," her mom said, pointing to metal tables with benches on either side, all bolted to the floor.

When Sofie tried to sit beside her, her mom said, "You guys are supposed to sit across from me. Rules."

The rules said they could have twenty minutes. Now that she was across from her mom, Sofie didn't know what to say. Her tongue felt like wood.

"How are you?" her mom asked, looking at them like they were food she was starving for.

"Fine," she and Con said at the same time.

Their mom looked at the scarecrow. "How's your new job, Gunner?"

"Fine."

"How's jail?" Con said in a voice so snarky Sofie winced.

His mom's head moved as if he'd slapped her.

Sofie jabbed Con's leg with her finger.

"What?" he said, pretending he didn't know.

Why was he being so horrible? But she saw the pain in his eyes.

Her mom was staring at the light from one of the small, high windows that ran around the room. Sofie couldn't bear it if the only part of outside she saw was a small square of sky.

"There's nothing to do here," her mom said. "Nothing, nothing, nothing."

"You were doing a lot when you were on the road with that nut with the gun for three weeks," Con said.

Her mom flinched but kept staring at the light.

"Did you think about how Sofie could have got killed when he started waving the gun around?"

His voice was quiet so others didn't overhear, but Sofie felt the rage coming off him. She leaned against his arm.

Their mom kept staring at the windows, but Sofie saw her swallow hard and her mouth quiver.

The scarecrow looked sad. He probably knew how their mom felt.

"We were so scared, Mama," Sofie said. "When you didn't come home, we thought something awful might have happened to you. We thought you might never come back. We were terrified of foster care, of being apart. I'd have died if I'd been separated from Connie." The huge knot in her throat ached when she said, "That would have been your fault."

Her mom closed her eyes and sat very still.

The scarecrow cleared his throat and leaned across the table a little. "Prison will be better, Ashley. You'll see," he said.

Sofie stared at him. Wasn't prison worse than jail?

"There's nothing worse than county lockup," he said. "That's where you wait until you find out if you're going to get to go home. If you're not going home, you stay locked up in jail until you can be sent to prison. Hopefully it won't be much longer."

Her mom got even more pale. "My lawyer says I'll probably be sent to a federal prison first. In another state."

It took a while for the words to have meaning to Sofie. Another state. Far away. The scarecrow's truck couldn't make it far away. They didn't have money to go far away.

She caught her breath. "*Why?* Why can't you stay here?"

Although she was angry at her mom, Sofie still needed her close. "How will we visit you in another state?"

She was being too loud. She saw a guard watching. She put her hand over her mouth, her heart pounding.

Even Con looked truly crushed at this news, but the scarecrow nodded like he'd been expecting it.

Her mom shook her head, her limp hair falling around her face.

Sofie's beautiful mom with the movie-star hair and the single dangly earring who claimed all their energy was dead. She'd been killed by this drab, sad mom who did truly bad things. So how could Sofie still love her? How could her being far away until she was old—maybe as old as the scarecrow—break Sofie's heart?

"When you get to prison, you'll have things to do," the scarecrow finally said, his voice scratchy. "After a while, you'll get a job. You'll make friends. You'll probably be able to take classes if you want to. I know."

Anger flashed on her mom's face and she snapped at the scarecrow. "You're telling me prison is something to look forward to?"

Again, the guard was watching.

The scarecrow's voice was tired. "No. But it's a lot more permanent and settled than this. You'll make peace with it, Ashley."

His words cut Sofie's heart. She felt the stretch of time. The way her world was being changed forever.

Sofie reached across the table, her hands open.

After a few seconds, her mom took them.

"We love you, Mama." Sofie fought to keep her voice steady as she was being crushed inside. "Don't we, Connie?"

When he didn't say anything, she looked up at him. He nodded. His face was red, like he might explode.

"It's okay," she said, holding her mom's hands. She didn't care what the guard thought. And she knew why Connie couldn't touch her mom right now.

Finally, her mom turned loose of Sofie's hands and brushed tears off her cheeks. She took a deep breath and said to Sofie, "Tommy came to see me a couple of days ago."

Her mom shook her head as if it was weird that Tommy had visited her in jail. Then she opened her mouth as if she were going to say more. Then her face turned pink and she didn't say anything.

"Tommy has been a godsend to me and the kids," Gunner said.

Her mom nodded.

"He brought us leftovers while you were gone," Con said.

"I know."

While her mom was on the run with her awful boyfriend had she ever wondered how they were getting food? Had she thought about the water getting shut off? Of the landlord evicting them because they didn't have money for rent? Of what could happen to them?

She saw embarrassment and shame in her mom's eyes.

"I love you kids," she said. "Believe it or not."

Sofie nodded.

As they stepped back into the heat, Sofie stared at her red shoes taking one step after another, seeming to move on their own, having nothing to do with her. The lady in the red shirt was still on the bench.

That night after her shower, Sofie went into the kitchen to get a banana. The kitchen light was off because it was so hot and the brightness made it hotter. Her pajamas stuck to her.

Con and the scarecrow were sitting on the back step talking. As she slowly peeled the banana, she couldn't help but hear.

Con was kind of apologizing for yelling at the scarecrow and the scarecrow was saying it was okay. But Con said it seemed like the scarecrow cared more about their mom than about Sofie. And the scarecrow said that wasn't true. He wished with all his heart that he could go back and be a better man—especially for little Summer—but he'd take care of Con and Sofie as long as the court would let him. Con said he would take care of Sofie. He always had and that was his job.

Sofie ate her banana, licking her fingers at the end, then she folded the peel and put it quietly in the trash. Every time the scarecrow was two minutes late for anything she worried. Was he off somewhere drinking? What if he left them again? Would somebody beat him up again—maybe kill him this time? And Connie was so, so angry.

They needed to make a triangle. And they needed a circle.

chapter 26

The shouts of little kids at afternoon recess came through the open windows. Sofie's sweaty arms stuck to her desk. It was the first week of school and Mr. Bloom had the windows cranked open. A fat black fly droned past, landing on the head of the kid in front of her.

The kid craned his neck, knowing the fly was somewhere. She watched for a while as the fly explored the boy's hair.

He was new this year, and she'd seen him looking at the Student Explorer Award and asking questions about it. She'd pointed out Con's picture on the wall and said that was her brother.

How long was the fly going to stay in the boy's hair?

She caught AnaMaria's eye. AnaMaria was trying not to laugh. Should they tell him?

Sofie decided it was mean not to. She wouldn't want a fly lost in her hair. So she leaned forward and poked him. When he turned, she pointed to her own head. His eyes widened and he swung his hands around his head and the fly droned off and out the window.

"Thanks," he whispered.

She shrugged.

She looked at her red shoes and the shoes of other girls. Hers were definitely the best. She would outgrow them before long, but she had her boots.

Con had his boots too. This morning, he'd gone stomping off down the street refusing to get in the truck for a ride to school. Stomping was how he walked all the time, like he was about to kick something. He was rude to the scarecrow. He wouldn't really talk to her. He didn't fix his hair, which was so black and thick and wild it made him almost scary looking.

Her attention went back to what Mr. Bloom was saying. Sometimes she daydreamed Mr. Bloom was her dad. But Mr. Bloom looked nothing like Sofie. He had jet black hair and brown skin.

At the end of the school day, she and AnaMaria joined the stream of kids twisting down the dark, narrow stairwell and popping out into the sunlight-filled entry in front of the office. AnaMaria's mom was talking to the office lady. When she saw AnaMaria and Sofie she smiled and waved.

"My mother is going on the trip to the Science Center with us next week," AnaMaria said. "She got off work especially."

Sofie saw the pride in AnaMaria's eyes. AnaMaria had beautiful dark eyes like her mom.

"I have the best idea," AnaMaria said, suddenly facing Sofie and gripping both her shoulders the way she did when she had a best idea. "Have your mother come too! We'll be like twin sets."

Sofie didn't know what to say, but she was *so* glad AnaMaria didn't know her mom was in jail. Sofie was always searching faces, trying to tell if the person knew or not.

But what should she say to AnaMaria, whose hands were still on her shoulders?

"Do, Sofie. Ask her to come. Our moms can sit together on the bus, and we can sit together. Of course," she added, as if anything else would be too weird to even think of.

"I already asked her," Sofie said. "She has to work." The lie tasted nasty.

AnaMaria sighed and dropped her arms to her sides and shrugged. "Okay. You can sit with my mom and me. There will be room in the seat."

Sofie nodded, the knot in her throat aching.

Outside, she waited for the scarecrow's truck to cough to the front of the pickup line. The truck was kind of embarrassing, but she was so relieved to see it in the line she felt like dancing.

The scarecrow was like an ancient twisted tree. Not going anywhere. Her mom had swooped around like a beautiful butterfly until finally she flew off and left them. Sofie knew her granddad would never leave her and Con unless the monster that had always chased him caught him.

"Hi," she said, fastening her seat belt before he let out the clutch and they lurched forward.

"How are you?" he said.

"Hot." She leaned her head back and let the air from the open windows tickle her sweaty scalp and try to blow away the stink of the lie to Ana-Maria. "How are you?"

He smiled. "Getting by."

His uniform carried the sharp, soapy smell of the car wash. His hands on the steering wheel looked chapped.

At the house, she dropped her backpack and washed her hands and got out two bowls for the ice cream. Con wouldn't be home for a long time because he was tutoring at the Community Center after school. That was the only thing that cheered him up.

While the scarecrow changed out of his stinky car-wash clothes, Sofie scooped ice cream into bowls. The night Tommy brought her ice cream in the little windowless room, the spoon had been icy cold in her hands, and she had felt something besides terror for a few minutes.

Before school started, Tommy had stopped by to ask if they needed help getting school supplies or anything. Con told him no, they could take care of themselves. They knew a neighborhood church where there were free backpacks and markers and all kinds of school stuff. And about the time school started, the clothing pantry at the Community Center got in a lot of kids' clothes that seemed practically new. And sometimes Lili brought them back-to-school treats that she'd shoplifted.

"We can look out for ourselves," Con told Tommy. "But thanks, man."

"How about you, Princess?" Tommy had asked hopefully. "You need anything?"

When she'd smiled and shaken her head no, he looked so disappointed it made her sad.

Their spoons clicked against their bowls as she and the scarecrow ate in silence. Some things, like ice cream, were so good you shouldn't talk. But right in the middle, he said, "You need to stay in your own bed at night. I'm afraid of getting in trouble with that social worker."

She let her spoon clatter into the bowl and stared at the ceiling. She didn't think the scarecrow knew. She had been sneaking to the attic and sleeping beside Con.

"I can't sleep downstairs." Why couldn't anybody understand that? "And the social worker won't know if we don't tell her. She said I needed my own room, and I have my own room."

The social worker didn't say she had to sleep every single minute in it. What if Connie left in the night? As she tried to fall sleep downstairs, she imagined she heard him climbing down the roof and going away. And the fear he'd never come back kept her awake.

She explained this to the scarecrow.

"And when I find him up there, I need to sleep by him to make sure he doesn't leave."

Her granddad's jaw hardened. "You need to stay in your own bed, Sofie. I could tell that social worker meant business. If she finds out you're sleeping in the attic again, you'll be in foster care before you can blink."

He was quiet while she thought about that.

"If Con swore he wouldn't go out at night, could you sleep downstairs?" he asked her.

"I don't know."

If the worry got too bad, she'd have to go up and check.

That night, after they got back from the garden and Sofie was toweling off from the shower—who knew picking green beans was such itchy business?—she heard the scarecrow almost yelling at Con.

"How would you feel if the police picked you up, and the social worker found out, and the court decided your wandering around at night was a sign I wasn't up to being your guardian? They're already worried I'm too old. And not always reliable."

She listened, her hair dripping down her back.

"You've got to use your head, Con. Believe it or not, I remember how it feels to be young. And the stuff boys do." The scarecrow calmed his voice. "Can you swear to your sister you won't sneak out at night?"

She didn't hear anything except moving-around sounds.

Finally, Con said, "How about I promise not to climb down and go walking? But I can still go out on the roof."

"Going out on the roof is dangerous," the scarecrow said. "What if you fell off and broke your neck? Don't you think that would reflect on me? Don't you think they'd take Sofie?"

"I'm not going to fall," Con said. "I've been going out there the whole time we've lived in this house. I know what I'm doing."

Then they must have gone out on the back porch, because she couldn't make out their words, though she could hear the rise and fall of their voices.

She put on her pajamas and untangled her damp hair. She felt in her bones that her brother would always look out for her when she needed it, but she also felt a change coming and knew it couldn't be stopped.

And she knew she had to do anything she could to make her brother happier.

chapter 27

After school the next day, Sofie ran the short distance to the scarecrow's truck, feeling fat raindrops smack her shoulders. Her granddad pushed open the door for her and she jumped in, dropping her backpack on the floor. His hair was wet, and the shoulders of his car-wash uniform were soaked. Everything smelled wet.

As they turned into the after-school traffic, a streak of lightning danced through a cloud, then thunder rumbled over them. The scarecrow's phone lay on the seat between them.

"May I use your phone?" she asked.

Con had left his on the couch last night while he went to the kitchen, and Sofie had found Jade's number and memorized it. All day she'd been thinking about what to do. She really didn't want to share Connie with a girlfriend, but right now she was sharing him with a scary big black cloud, which was worse than a girlfriend.

"What for?" the scarecrow asked.

"We need to cheer Connie up."

He nodded his head in agreement. "What have you got in mind?"

"Getting him and Jade back together."

The scarecrow was quiet, paying attention to traffic. Did that mean she could use his phone? He hadn't said she couldn't, so she picked it up.

"Con may not like you getting in his business."

"I know."

But Connie didn't like anything these days. What difference would one more thing he didn't like make?

She called Jade's number. Of course, Jade wouldn't answer because she wouldn't recognize the scarecrow's number. But that was okay. Sofie had written out what she'd say to Jade's voice mail.

During afternoon recess—which had been inside because of the rain—Sofie had had a long talk with AnaMaria about brothers and girlfriends. Ana-Maria thought calling Jade was the best idea. "Do it, Sofie," she'd said, with her hands on Sofie's shoulders. "Give your handsome big brother happiness."

Even though she had practiced reading the message, Sofie felt nervous as Jade's phone rang.

"Hello?"

Sofie's heart jumped to her throat and panic choked her. Jade wasn't supposed to answer. Now what? Should she read what she had written? Or maybe she should hang up and call back later and hope Jade didn't answer.

"Hello?" Jade said again.

"Hi." Sofie's voice was squeaky. "Is this Jade?" Of course it was.

"Yes."

Sofie took a trembling breath and began to read. "Hi. This is Sofie Jones calling to let you know my brother Con is an excellent brother, and I think he would make an excellent boyfriend. He's smart and kind. And he's very nice. He bought me a pair of beautiful red shoes with his own money when my flip-flop broke on the way to Walmart. He has—"

"Sofie, why are you calling me?"

She wished Jade would let her finish. She had a few more well written, important sentences. "You and Connie have stopped talking and he's sad."

"He's the one who stopped answering my texts. He's done that twice now." Jade said *he* like *hay*. "I don't want to be friends with someone who keeps ghosting me."

Sofie heard voices in the background.

"He didn't want to ghost you," she said. "I know he didn't. Things got . . . really complicated."

Jade was silent.

"They really did. Connie likes you so much. He would never have ghosted you twice unless..."

Unless their mom had gone off and left them alone for three weeks. Unless she was on her way to prison.

"Unless what?" Jade sounded like she was about done talking.

Sofie couldn't tell Jade about their mom. That they were going to visit her in jail as soon as Connie got home.

"He didn't mean to hurt you." Sofie spoke faster because she felt Jade getting ready to hang up. Voices were louder in the background. "Ple—"

"Goodbye, Sofie." The call ended.

Sofie let the phone drop to her lap. She closed her eyes. If Jade had let her finish...

The scarecrow's voice was kind. "I guess that didn't go the way you hoped?"

She shook her head.

"You meant well, and you tried. That's all you can do."

She wasn't giving up. Connie looked after her. She was going to look after him.

At home, while the scarecrow changed clothes, Sofie peeled peaches for them. One for her, one for Con, one for the scarecrow. He had showed her how to use a peeler to scrape off the velvet part, then how to cut the bare peach in half in exactly the right place so the pit came out easily. Then to use a knife and cutting board to slice the peach.

Juice puddled on the cutting board, making the kitchen smell nice. She put each peach in its own little bowl and sprinkled it with brown sugar. She had never had a fresh peach until the scarecrow bought a box at the farmers' market. She wished she could take a peach to the jail for her mom.

They waited for Con, who didn't come. The clock on the stove kept moving closer to the end of jail visiting hours at 5:00 and it took at least fifteen minutes to get there. They tried to visit twice a week, but it was hard now that school had started and Connie was tutoring and the scarecrow was working at the car wash.

She stared at the colored-pencil drawing she was taking to her mom to brighten up her cell. It was a drawing AnaMaria had made last year and Sofie had taped to her wall. It was much better than any of Sofie's drawings would ever be. It showed a beautiful blond mama and daughter, and a beautiful dark-haired mama and daughter, all with big signature looks. Sofie had made a black paper frame for it.

What if her mom knew the picture made Sofie angry and she didn't like looking at it on her wall anymore? What if her mom knew Sofie sometimes wanted AnaMaria's mom? Sometimes AnaMaria's mom hugged Sofie and it made her cry.

Finally, the scarecrow gave Sofie his phone to text Con because she was a better texter than he was. Con didn't reply.

Had something bad happened? Or could he not face their mom and the stinky jail? Her heart ached for him, but she was also angry. It wasn't fair.

She saw the way the scarecrow was fidgeting. After they visited the jail, he would go to a meeting like he always did. He probably needed to go now.

She stared at the three bowls of peaches. To eat without Connie didn't feel right.

Both she and the scarecrow jumped when the phone finally dinged.

Sorry. I forgot. I'm tutoring.

She felt the scarecrow's breath of relief, and she was glad to stop worrying. But she didn't believe he'd forgotten.

That night, she lay on her mattress in her bedroom trying to fall asleep, but her bedding was knotted and lumpy from her tossing and turning.

Her mom complained about the mattress in her jail cell. Maybe she was tossing and turning too.

The scarecrow had put the back-and-forth fan in her room, but the hum made it impossible to hear small sounds. Connie might be climbing off the roof and she wouldn't know. She turned off the fan to listen.

Her ears ached with trying to hear him. She heard the scarecrow go in the bathroom. She didn't know how late it was. Maybe it would get daylight soon and she could stop worrying.

She went into the kitchen to look at the clock on the stove. It wasn't even midnight.

Back in her room, she did not hear one creak, squeak, or bump from upstairs. Maybe Connie had already left.

She had to check.

But she'd promised the scarecrow tonight she'd do her very, very, *very* best to stay in her own bed. She told herself she'd try as hard to stay as she was trying to win the Student Explorer globe. She would be clever and make herself stay.

When she heard the scarecrow come out of the bathroom, she called, "Hey!"

She turned on her lamp and squinted at his big, bony shape in the doorway.

"Would you like to listen to a good book?" she asked. "It has a skinny old man in it."

She saw the smile in his eyes. He nodded and sat down on the floor, leaning against the door frame.

She'd read a few chapters of the book a couple of months ago, but she'd start at the beginning. She sat cross-legged, the book resting on the bed. She pushed her hair back and began.

"There is nothing lonelier than a cat who has been loved, at least for a while, and then abandoned at the side of the road," she began.

She'd read those words earlier and they hadn't felt like they were about her. And now they did. Totally.

She took a breath and went on.

At the end of the first chapter, she looked at the scarecrow. He looked happy.

The second chapter was about an old loblolly pine. The scarecrow's smile said he too thought *loblolly* was a nice word. And the tree seemed to be more than a tree. It was almost like a person.

And there was a hissing creature trapped in a huge jar beneath the roots of the old loblolly pine. Sofie was pretty sure it was the snake she'd seen in the illustrations, the snake that looked right into her eyes. But she wouldn't tell the scarecrow that.

She read the bluesy notes of the redbone hound and showed the scarecrow the first illustration of the calico cat who had been loved for a while and then abandoned.

The scarecrow looked at the illustration of the cat standing on the roots of the loblolly pine and nodded.

"Go on," he said. "This is a fine story."

She was reading about the boy in the mean streets of South Houston when she couldn't go on. Her eyes needed to shut.

The scarecrow turned off the lamp and she felt the fan blowing over her again.

chapter 28

"Sof, wake up. School."

She felt heavy, waking from deep sleep.

Slowly, she realized she'd made it through the night without checking on Connie, and he hadn't disappeared. She had done it. She had tricked herself. She smiled.

Connie was smiling too. He was wearing the pink T-shirt he looked so nice in. His hair was gelled and his dark eyes shone. It took her a minute to figure out what that might mean. She opened her mouth to ask if he'd heard from Jade, then closed it. The scarecrow was right, Con wouldn't want her in his business.

But she felt like singing as she got dressed with the fan blowing over her. She took her beautiful, perfectly clean shoes out of their box and slipped them on. Today called for one of her best signature looks because Con was happy plus today was the field trip to the Science Center. She wore a pair of baggy black shorts and the T-shirt AnaMaria had brought her from Arizona that she'd been saving. It was white, with the shape of Arizona drawn in grass green on the front. Lots of desert flowers were blooming, and some of them matched her shoes. She pulled her hair to the side so it hung over one shoulder, and fastened it with a twisty. And, of course, the sparkly little studs her mom had stolen with love in her heart.

In the kitchen, Con was talking more than she'd heard him talk in days, telling the scarecrow his superpower was not falling off the roof, because he'd been there half the night.

"What were you doing out there?" the scarecrow asked with the tiniest glance at Sofie.

"Nothing. Talking."

Were they supposed to say *Who to?*

"Who to?" she asked.

Con's face turned pink. He shrugged. "Just Jade."

"Oh yeah?" the scarecrow said.

Connie looked at her. "She asked me to tell you she hopes you're enjoying school."

Sofie smiled. She would really enjoy school today.

"Anyway," Con said, as he leaned against the counter eating the eggs the scarecrow had scrambled, "I'm going to meet her at Tommy's Place at 4:30. She's taking the bus across town, and we'll hang out."

"When will you be home?" the scarecrow asked.

Sofie thought it was good he didn't try to boss Con around. It wouldn't have worked.

"I'll be home by dark."

The scarecrow nodded. "Want a ride to school?"

"Yeah, sure. Why not." After another bite of eggs, he said, "Jade says she likes me because I'm complicated. What do you think that means?"

The scarecrow shrugged and shook his head.

Con was looking at her.

"I think it means you're not like all the other boys she knows. I think it means you're truly special, Connie."

His face turned red, but his eyes said he was glad.

At her school, Con got out of the truck to let her out. It was the first time he'd ridden with her and the scarecrow. Until the scarecrow came, Connie had always walked her to school and picked her up every afternoon.

Maybe he felt like she didn't need him anymore. But she did. More than ever. Nobody was watching, so she threw her arms around him.

In Mr. Bloom's classroom, AnaMaria was waiting. She wore a matching Arizona T-shirt, and had tied her hair over one shoulder.

She put her hands on Sofie's shoulders. "Dressing alike was the *best* idea," she said. "Everybody will know we're besties."

Sofie nodded and smiled, but she wondered if AnaMaria would be so proud of their friendship if she knew about Sofie's mom.

Sofie hadn't been able to take AnaMaria's drawing through security yesterday. At least the guard had been nice, not like the grumpy guard the day Sofie set off the alarm.

This guard looked at the drawing and said, "I'll bet two of these pretty ladies are you and your mom. Am I right?"

Sofie nodded.

"I wish you could take it in, hon, but it's not allowed. I'll keep it and give it back to you when you come out."

Sofie felt bad. They were late for the visit because they'd waited for Con, and now she couldn't give her mom the drawing.

"If you ask when you get in the visiting room, they'll bring you paper and crayons. Maybe you can make your mom a drawing while you're here."

But it hadn't worked. They only had a few minutes before visiting hours ended, and Sofie couldn't draw nearly as well as she wanted to. At the last minute, she drew a heart in red and wrote *I love you* in the middle. It was true, but she was still mad at her mom for ruining their triangle.

chapter 29

Sofie stepped out of the house into a cool morning. She sat on the step and twisted up her hair to let the breeze dry the sweat on her neck.

Somebody in the neighborhood was hammering. It sounded like it might be coming from the chicken lady's place. She'd gotten a box of chicks in the mail a couple of weeks ago. Adorable, fuzzy, peeping creatures she'd let Con, Sofie, and Jade pet last weekend. Maybe she was building more cages for them.

Or the hammering might be something getting knocked down. Lots of things were getting knocked down. The landlord told the scarecrow they had to be out in six months because their place was coming down too.

Tommy called it *gentrification,* which was an interesting long word. Con said it meant rich people were moving in so they had to move out.

"So it's a bad thing?" she'd asked Con. "Why would Tommy like a bad thing?"

Con had shrugged.

The smell of burning toast told her he was probably texting Jade and forgetting everything else. Sofie tried not to like Jade, but she made Con so much happier, and she was nice to Sofie too. And the scarecrow. With all her expensive clothes and her snooty-wooty aunt and uncle in the rich part of town, Jade might not have been so nice.

The scarecrow came out with his tea and sat beside Sofie.

"Cooled off last night," he said. "Fall's in the air."

She nodded and searched his face to see if he looked tired, but he was so old she couldn't tell. She'd called out to him last night for the first time in a long time. Usually she could make it through without the awful urge to check on Con, but last night she hadn't been able to. And instead of just calling back *All's well* like he usually did, he'd come to her door and said he couldn't sleep either. Would she read to him?

So the scarecrow had sat on the floor, leaned against the wall, and she'd picked up where they'd left off in *The Underneath*. It had become their book. And although Sofie sometimes longed to know what happened next, she never read ahead.

Until this story, she hadn't known trees had memories and kept secrets and knew what was happening in the forest. She felt like the old loblolly pine had become a friend. The tree reminded her of the scarecrow because it was so old and broken but still kept watch and tried to look out for the lost kitten, Puck. The old man in the story, Gar Face, was nothing like the scarecrow. Gar Face had been hurt when he was a child. By his dad. And now he was evil. Sofie hated him, but she had a secret, tiny bit of understanding.

"It's going to be a hard morning, Sofie," the scarecrow said.

She didn't want to think about it.

"I better check on the toast," she said, getting up and hurrying inside. But then she turned and looked at him through the screen door. Had she hurt his feelings?

It was going to be a hard morning for him too. And for Connie. They were going to the garden after the jail, and Sofie was glad for that. She'd exhaust herself yanking up weeds.

She went back and sat beside the scarecrow. A big black ant worked its way through the grass at her feet, going up and down, appearing and disappearing.

After this morning, they wouldn't be able to see her mom for a month. Tonight she'd be sleeping in a federal prison, hours away. New prisoners couldn't have family visits for thirty days.

"Whatever happens when you say goodbye to Ashley this morning, it's all right, Sofie."

What would happen? Would she be nice to her mom? Or would she get upset and lash out? Would her mom cry? Would Sofie get to hug her mom?

"None of this is your doing, Sofie. It's your mom's doing. She made bad choices." She heard the strain in his voice when he said, "Believe me, I know."

"Sometimes I've hated going to see her," she blurted out, hoping that didn't make him mad. He really loved her mom.

He squeezed her foot. "County jails are awful places. Probably everybody hates going, deep down."

In the last three months, her mom had faded, wilted, dried up, and wrinkled. And she cried out against everything. It was like she was in a trap. It made Sofie think of the awful trap in *The Underneath*.

Silent tears streamed down her face, but the scarecrow noticed and squeezed her bare foot again with his warm, callused hand.

When they got there, they weren't sent to the regular visitor's room with lots of other people. This morning, they were in a small room with her mom looking very scared surrounded by people in uniform. The advocate was there and gave the scarecrow an envelope with information about the federal prison. He explained that if there was an emergency at home or in the prison during the next thirty days, communication would go through him. And if all went well, after that they'd be able to email their mom and talk to her on the phone and visit her when they were able.

He was very matter-of-fact, as if this were like ordering a box of chicks—which was how Sofie felt. Like she was a helpless chick being put in a box and sent away, even though it was her mom that was being sent away. The point was, it hurt Sofie so much she couldn't even see or hear or think or feel when she told her mom goodbye.

As she yanked at the weeds around the tomatoes, all she remembered was walking out of the jail with the advocate. His glasses had twinkled as he shook all their hands and said he'd be in touch. Or they could call him if they needed anything.

She didn't want to remember actually telling her mom goodbye. It was on the other side of the curtain. Maybe sometime she'd look there, but not now.

The scarecrow had taught her the best way to pull a weed was to grip it at the soil level, then twist and pull. She worked her way down the row on her hands and knees, stirring up the sharp smell of the tomato plants. Grip. Twist and pull. Grip. Twist and pull.

The sun soaking through her T-shirt felt nice because it was a coolish day. The sky was a brilliant blue, and crows were carrying on in the woods by the river.

The scarecrow was using a hoe to ruffle up the soil. It was supposed to rain tonight and the water would soak in better.

Close by where Sofie was weeding, Con and Jade were planting radish seeds.

Sofie heard Jade say, "Get a good nap. You're going to wake up to become a plump little red ball of yum."

Sofie mentally rolled her eyes. But if Connie was going to have a girlfriend, a seed-and-plant talker was probably the best kind. In *The Underneath*, the forest could hear, so maybe a radish seed could too.

Jade said quietly, "I'm sorry you won't get to see your mom for a long time, Sofie."

Sofie sat back on her heels and stared at Jade. Then she glared at Con. How much had he told her? Sofie hadn't told *anybody*—not even AnaMaria—that her mom was in a federal prison.

Jade's expression was kind, but Sofie didn't want Jade's sympathy. Secretly, Jade probably looked down her nose at Sofie for not having a regular mom.

"It's fine," Sofie said. So not.

Jade went back to planting, but she didn't talk to the seeds anymore. Con looked at Sofie like *Sorry* and shrugged.

"The reason I was sent to live with my aunt and uncle was because I got in trouble back home," Jade said. She looked Sofie in the eyes as she said it, but her face turned pink. "My best friend had an older brother and we loved to hang out with him and his friends because they seemed so cool. I got caught doing some stuff."

Sofie looked at Con. That's not the kind of girl she'd thought Jade was. Would she get him in trouble?

As if he'd read her mind, he shook his head.

"It wasn't that big of a deal," he said. "Jade's parents are . . . strange."

What did that mean? Did the scarecrow know all this? Was he listening?

Yes. He was looking at them.

Jade stared into space as she said, talking fast, "My parents are big-deal doctors. Everybody in Nashville knows them. They're on TV and stuff. My dad is running for the legislature." She rushed on. "And they don't really have time for me so they thought I'd be better off coming to stay with my aunt until the twins came. And now they think I'll be better staying for the whole school year. Who knows? I may be here until I'm eighteen. And I don't care that they don't want me around, but I miss my dog." With the last, her face crumpled.

Who would send their kid away? That was awful. No matter what she or Con did, their mom would *never* send them away. Sofie suddenly felt more than equal with Jade.

"You're always welcome at our place, such as it is," the scarecrow said. "And you're a good worker in the garden."

Jade smiled at the scarecrow. "Thanks, Mr. Jones."

Sofie thought the scarecrow stood a little taller at being called Mr. Jones. The young guys at the car wash called him Gunnie, which, to Sofie, was even worse than Gunner.

"Would you like to see a picture of my dog? His name is Bach."

Without waiting for an answer, she pulled up the picture on her phone and showed it to Sofie. Bach was *huge*.

"He's a German shepherd," Jade said. "He's a total marshmallow."

He looked like he'd eat a lot. That was why she and Con didn't have a dog. They didn't have money for dog food and stuff. Jade's parents must be really rich. But they weren't very nice.

Jade showed the picture to the scarecrow and he looked impressed. "Nice looking animal," he said.

When they were done in the garden and walking back to the truck, Connie and Jade were way ahead of them.

"I don't think that girl's going to break Con's heart anytime soon," the scarecrow said.

If she did, Sofie would take revenge.

The house felt stuffy after she'd been outside for a couple of hours. It also felt a tiny bit different somehow. In the kitchen, everything looked the same as when they'd left to go to the jail. Was there a different smell? The four of them smelled like dirt and sweat. She could hardly wait to get in the shower, but they always let the scarecrow go first because he was old.

"You look like you really need a shower," Con said. "Gunner won't care if you go first."

She looked at the scarecrow and he nodded. He had kind of an odd look on his face.

Okay. She wouldn't wait to be invited twice.

She went to her room for clean clothes. For a minute she thought she'd done a time slip or something. Her books weren't lined up around the baseboard. They were neatly shelved in two beautiful bookcases. And.

There was a bed in her room.

She'd never had a bed in her room.

Had new people moved in while they were gone? People with a fancy bed and bookshelves? Was this gentrification?

The scarecrow and Con and Jade crowded in behind her.

"Look," she said. "Something's wrong."

Connie laughed and hugged her shoulders. "Nothing's wrong. It's all good. Tommy's mom is downsizing and getting rid of a lot of stuff and Tommy thought you might like to have a few things she won't have room for."

"But..."

Bookshelves. Like in a library. In her bedroom.

"But..."

And the bed. She pointed at it, wordless.

"It's a daybed," Jade said. "I have one at home in Nashville. See, it looks like a couch with a back and arms." She curled up on it to demonstrate. "But at night"—she turned back the corner of the coverlet to show pretty sheets——"you slip right into bed."

Sofie had never seen such a thing.

"A daybed?"

"This will make that social worker stand up and take notice," the scarecrow said.

It sure would.

And her pink lamp wasn't on the floor anymore. It was on a small, round wooden table.

She approached the bookshelves slowly. Maybe this was a dream.

There was an envelope with her name on it.

Sofie,
Tom tells me that this morning you had to say goodbye to your mom for a while. I'm sorry.

My son also tells me you have quite a library and might have a use for these bookshelves which I won't have room for in the little condo I'm moving into soon. The daybed won't fit either, so I'd appreciate you giving it a good home. And your exquisite pink lamp needs a table, don't you think?

"What does *exquisite* mean?" she asked Con.

"Really fine," Jade said, her eyes sparkling. "Beautiful."

Sofie smiled, pleased that Tommy's mom thought her lamp was as splendid as all that. And she said she would *appreciate* Sofie giving the bed a good home. That's what she said. *Appreciate. Good home.* The words warmed Sofie clear through.

Tommy's mom signed the note *DCD.* Sometime Sofie would like to know what those initials stood for. The last D was for Donovan, of course. Tommy Donovan was Tommy's name.

There was a second note in the envelope.

Princess,

I hope the surprise delivery of Mom's stuff was okay. Gunner and Con and Jade helped us plan it. I know you had a rough morning, and I hope the rest of your day is much better. Keep punching above your weight.

Tommy

And he had drawn a bear below his name because she'd told him he made her think of a nice bear.

That night, as she lay on a real bed between soft sheets that smelled good, but strange, Mrs. Donovan's words played in her head. *Appreciate you giving the bed a good home.* Why did she love those words?

The next morning, she wrote her own notes, remembering what she had learned last year in language arts.

Dear Mrs. Donovan,
I will give your daybed a good home. I promise. I have slept in it one time, and will sleep in it many more times. I left my exquisite lamp on all night, and I tried not to go to sleep. (But I did.) I love looking at the bookshelves. I never thought I would have bookshelves until I was a librarian. Thank you.

Your friend,
SJ

Should she call her own lamp exquisite? Was that bragging? But she longed to use the word, so she went on to her next note.

Dear Tommy,
Your surprise delivery was <u>way</u> okay. Thank you!
Your mom sounds really nice. Is that why you're so nice? (Because you are.)

Your friend,
Princess SJ

And although it wasn't very good, she drew a small picture of a girl with a lot of hair wearing a tiara, boxing gloves, and garden boots.

chapter 30

Sofie opened her eyes and looked around. Because the leaves were falling off the trees, streetlights shone through the thin curtains and she could make out her bookcases. Maybe they were what had waked her. Although they'd been hers for a month, they were still wondrous. She loved to pet the golden wood and rounded corners.

In the darkness, she could make out the shape of the papier-mâché pumpkin she'd made in art class. She was giving it to Tommy's mom to say thank you for the bookcases, bed, and table.

What had waked her? She didn't hear Con stirring in the attic. She didn't hear the scarecrow getting up to use the bathroom. He did that a lot at night, he explained, because he was old and that was what old people did. It didn't bother her. His moving around meant he was there.

She didn't hear sirens or gunshots or people yelling. She didn't hear tomcats fighting. So why had she come suddenly awake?

Because her stomach hurt.

They were going to visit her mom for the first time in prison tomorrow. Because the prison was three and a half hours away and the truck was ancient, Tommy was taking them.

Sofie needed to see her mom so much. So why did she want to lock herself in her room and not go?

"Hey!" she called into the darkness.

The scarecrow said old people didn't really sleep, so he didn't mind if she yelled for him in the night.

Just *Hey!* felt rude, but calling out *Delbert*, his real name, felt silly. And she would never call him *Gunner*. It was a terrible name, and he was such a kind person.

A few seconds passed and she heard "All's well."

Sofie smiled. That was what he always said. She had never heard anyone else say that.

"All's well here too," she called, the way she always did unless she needed to read to him for a while.

She fluffed her pillow and turned over, letting the words ride on her breath. *All's well.* The ache in her stomach eased a little. *All's well.*

Because Con got carsick in the back, he and Tommy rode in front. Everybody was quiet in the car. They were going to a faraway prison where people who had done very bad things were punished for a long time. And deep in their bones, they loved one of those people who had done the bad things. It felt too complicated to talk about—like they should be quiet because it was that complicated.

And of course, Tommy didn't love their mom, but he seemed to kind of love her and Con and the scarecrow, because he was always looking out for them when they would let him. He loved them like a friend.

As they drove north on the interstate, she saw farm fields, trees turning beautiful colors. Cows, farm buildings, edges of towns, giant wind turbines, and puffs of white clouds in a blue October sky.

She had her book to read and the scarecrow seemed happy staring out the window. Mr. Bloom had recommended *Wonder* to Sofie. Somehow the word was getting around that her mom was in prison. And some days, it felt like AnaMaria was being too nice, like she felt sorry for Sofie. And one day, she found a piece of paper in her locker with *Prison girl* written on it. And another day, somebody had written *killer* on her desk in lipstick. She wanted to punch whoever wrote that, because her mom was *not* a killer.

Maybe that was why Mr. Bloom had recommended the book. Like Auggie, Sofie was a freak. She wasn't a movie star's granddaughter anymore. She was a criminal's daughter. So she was going to read *Wonder,* tell Mr. Bloom thank you for the recommendation, and destroy the competition for the Student Explorer Award.

At first, sun spread across the backseat, warming her. But gradually, as the sun moved, she felt warmth only on one shoulder. She pulled her feet onto the seat and read with her book braced against her bent knees. Every now and then, the scarecrow reached over and squeezed her foot and gave it a little shake. It made her smile every time.

When they pulled off at a rest stop, she saw a girl in a red hoodie walking with her mom. The mom pulled her daughter close and kissed her head. She kept her arm around the girl's shoulders as they walked. The girl's arm went around her mom's waist.

No one folded Sofie into long hugs. No one kissed her head, or braided her hair, or touched her fingers and toes to stroke on polish. She felt like a fallen leaf, curling around the edges, likely to get blown away.

The scarecrow stretched his legs for a few minutes, and Sofie tagged along, the breeze blowing her hoodie open. She zipped it. In the shade, it was chilly.

The scarecrow stooped and picked up the biggest leaf she had ever seen and handed it to her.

"There's a sycamore tree around here somewhere," he said, looking. "But I don't see any. Who knows where this leaf blew in from."

She looked for more because they were extremely large and pretty, and by the time the scarecrow's legs were stretched, she had four, one for each of them. Then she remembered she wouldn't be able to take anything into the prison, so she gave the fourth one to Tommy.

"Well thanks, Princess SJ."

He'd been calling her that ever since the thank-you note. And a smile always danced over his face as if he'd discovered something nice. Calling her

Princess had been a habit since she was a little girl. Lots of little girls got called that. But *Princess SJ* felt like someone she had become.

She smiled and bumped his arm with her shoulder.

Con looked a little embarrassed when she gave him his leaf. He was annoying these days, with his music, his tutoring, and the attic all to himself. And Jade.

Con and Jade had been peanut butter and jelly for the last two months. Connie brought her to the house and showed her the attic and took her out on the roof, which Sofie didn't much like. Jade went to the garden with them all the time.

At the exit for the prison, the scarecrow seemed to shrink into himself.

She caught his eye and mouthed *All's well.*

He nodded.

They followed a long drive with offshoots. DELIVERIES. PRISON INDUS-TRIES. EMPLOYEE PARKING. And finally, VISITOR PARKING.

"Wow," Con said. "Lots of people."

"Sunday is always the biggest visiting day in prison," the scarecrow said.

Sofie wondered if many people had visited him. He had been in prison in Pennsylvania the last time.

Tommy drove up and down two long rows before he found an empty space.

The air smelled clean and sweet when she got out of the car.

"This place is in the middle of nowhere," Tommy said.

Except for the low buildings inside the tall wire fence, all Sofie saw were trees and hilly fields and lots of sky.

"Doesn't look so bad from the outside," Tommy said.

They knew the rules from the prison website. Visits couldn't last more than an hour. They couldn't wear certain kinds of clothing. Everything except Tommy's keys had to be locked in the car.

She didn't make the mistake of barrettes again. She held her hair back with a forget-me-not-blue headband she'd found in her mom's room. She hoped it would make her mom smile.

Months ago, when they were cleaning for the social worker's visit, she and Con had crammed away their mom's things. Yesterday, when she opened drawers looking for the headband, familiar smells made her breath catch in her throat.

Con and the scarecrow walked ahead, and she and Tommy followed. She saw how much alike Con and the scarecrow were. Tall and skinny, with the same walk. The same thick hair, though the scarecrow's was a beautiful silvery color.

If she and her mom were walking together, people would probably say they were alike. Her mom's thirtieth birthday had been two weeks ago. Sofie hadn't been able to wish her happy birthday, which felt so sad.

"How are you doing?" Tommy asked quietly.

While she was thinking about her answer, he said, "Mom really likes the papier-mâché pumpkin. I stopped by her house the other day and she had it on a table in the entryway."

As they walked toward the visitor's entrance, they met a family leaving. A girl about her own age held the hand of a screaming toddler. The red-faced little boy was stomping his feet and trying to throw himself down on the sidewalk. His shrieks hurt her ears. The grown-ups walked ahead as if they'd forgotten the two kids. The girl didn't look up as they met on the sidewalk, she just clung to the hand of the flailing child. Sofie wished she could help.

She looked up at Tommy.

He gave a tiny shrug, but his eyes were kind. "Maybe it helps that you and Con are older than that poor little guy."

"Maybe. But he's too young to understand why his mom has to be here." He didn't have to think about it like she did. "I still see the gun," Sofie said, and felt her cheeks flush. She couldn't tell Con or the scarecrow that, but Tommy was just a friend. "I see it a lot."

She and Con were supposed to talk to a counselor about everything, but their first appointment wasn't for a long time.

He put his hand on her shoulder as they walked. "You're safe, Sofie. Trust me."

He didn't know that. Not for sure.

But she was glad he'd said it.

chapter 31

Nobody set off the security alarm. They put on their shoes and followed the signs to the Visiting Room.

The rules said offenders—which was what people locked up here were called—could share a brief hug at the beginning and end of the visit. Sofie ran the last few steps to her mom, who wrapped Sofie so tightly she could hardly breathe. But who needed to breathe? Being inside that hug was like drinking when she was really thirsty. She was gulping love, filling up.

Her mom finally held her away. "I'm so, so glad to see you," she said, tears rolling down her face.

Then she hugged Con, who had to bend down to hug back, which made them both laugh.

Then her mom took the scarecrow's hands and kissed his cheek. She did the same with Tommy.

Her mom looked so much healthier than the last time they'd seen her. And she was smiling.

This visiting room was a lot nicer than the jail's, though it was crowded. The tables and chairs could be moved, and there were shelves with games and puzzles and a bench piled with picture books for little kids. Their mom took Sofie and Con's hands and led them to the bank of windows that ran the length of the room.

She pointed. "See Building 4? That's where I live."

Halfway up the hill on the right, Sofie saw a big green 4 on a two-story, tan brick building, but she really wanted to look at her mom. She wore khaki pants and a khaki shirt open to show a green T-shirt underneath. All the offenders wore similar clothes. Khaki and green. Everybody wore brown boots that made Sofie think of her garden boots.

In the bright light from the windows, she saw tiny lines on her mother's face. She had on lip gloss, but no makeup. Her mom looked pale, but beautiful again.

"What's Building 4 like?" Con asked.

Sofie leaned against her mom's side, wondering if that was against the rules and not caring. Her mother's arm slipped around her. Sofie shut her eyes and sank into the feeling of being where she belonged. In the loving arms of her mom, a criminal.

Her mom was talking about Building 4. "It's where all the new offenders are housed at first. Until we get classified."

"What does that mean?" Con asked.

She didn't listen. She didn't want anything to take away from the joy of her mom's soft, warm body.

When it was time to leave, her mom walked with them to the sign that said NO OFFENDERS BEYOND THIS POINT. She thanked the scarecrow for coming and Tommy especially for bringing her family. Her voice broke but she didn't cry. Then she hugged Con, and then Sofie.

Sofie's throat ached with held-back tears as her mom kissed her face quickly and lightly over and over again. Sofie wanted to stomp and wail and throw herself down. It wasn't right her mom had to stay here so long. Years and years. She hadn't meant to be bad, she just didn't know how to get good boyfriends. This was so wrong.

On the way home, she stared out the window and wept, wiping her face and blowing her nose with tissues from a packet Tommy gave her from the glove compartment.

At first, Con and Tommy said things to try to make her feel better, but finally they gave up. She didn't want anybody to make her feel better ever again.

She kicked the back of Con's seat.

He turned and spoke over his shoulder. "Cut it out, Meerkat. Read your book."

She wanted to stick her tongue out, but the urge was so childish and bratty it shamed her. But she didn't know what to do with her misery. It sat on top of her like a huge, heavy, squishy thing. Gray and grungy. And the setting sun in her swollen eyes gave her a headache. She didn't want to read her book.

The scarecrow spoke quietly so the conversation was just for them. "When Summer was about your age, her mom brought her to prison to visit me. I remember it like yesterday. Summer wore a white headband. And a bright yellow sweater that was too big. Her hands kept disappearing up the sleeves." He smiled at the memory. "They were there, and then they weren't. Then after a while, her fingers would come out like they were little critters testing the air. Then they'd go back in."

The scarecrow was a good storyteller.

"That prison had an outdoor area where inmates could visit with their kids. You could toss a Frisbee back and forth. There were picnic tables. The day was kind of cool to be outside, but we were sheltered from the wind and had it to ourselves—Donna, Summer, and me. That was a remarkable and precious thing. In prison, you don't get many chances to be by yourself. The sky was clear blue, like today. We were sitting at a picnic table and Summer was working on a picture to leave with me. And what would you guess dropped out of a tree and landed on Summer's paper?"

"A leaf?"

"A buckeye."

"What's that?"

He looked at her. "You don't know what a lucky buckeye is?"

She shook her head no.

He gave her his cell phone. "I'll bet you can find a buckeye somewhere in there. Look for a California buckeye."

She searched and found images of a big shiny brown seed with a light patch, which she recognized. She showed the picture to the scarecrow.

He nodded.

"Mom has a buckeye in her keepsake box from her mom."

The scarecrow gazed at the fading light. Two jet trails made a huge X across the sky.

"Do you suppose it's the same one?" he finally asked.

She wanted it to be the same one, because it would make a kind of circle. And a triangle needed a circle for safety.

"I'm sure it's the same one," she said.

After a while, she said, "Would you like me to read to you?" She had brought *The Underneath* in case.

"You bet."

She kicked off her shoes and pulled her legs up onto the seat. They were getting close to the end of the book. The ancient redbone hound, Ranger, was injured and chained and in a bad way. The kitten Puck was trying to find his way home, but the forest was huge and scary. And Sabine, Puck's twin sister, was trying to comfort Ranger.

Sofie read until it was getting too dark to see, but she managed one last passage.

She turned toward the dark corner where Ranger lay, asleep, and rubbed against her old friend, tucked herself under his big ear and started to purr. Ranger stirred. His stomach was empty and he was thirsty, too. But Sabine was curled next to him, her soft purrs filling his head.

Little Sabine. She was the only one left for him. Faithful Sabine. How could he ever tell her how much he loved her, how much she meant to him?

She felt tears on her face and was glad it was too dark for the scarecrow to see. She closed the book.

chapter 32

After school, they'd all three gone to the garden to *put it to bed*. When Sofie asked the scarecrow why he talked about a garden that way, he said it couldn't wake up in the spring if they didn't put it to bed in the fall. Connie said it was an extended metaphor. She said they should hurry up and put it to bed then, because she wanted to get home to work on her costume.

Now the house smelled wonderful from something the scarecrow was cooking. They had brought home the last of the snap beans, carrots, and chard. Sofie hoped it wasn't the chard she smelled cooking. True, it had turned out to be a very beautiful plant—all red and green and white—but she didn't want to *eat* it.

She stripped off her clothes and pulled on the brown pirate pants, which were regular boring pants she'd found at the clothing pantry, but she'd cut them off all raggedy below the knee to make them pirate pants. And because they were pirate pants they made her garden boots look exactly like pirate boots.

Next, she slipped into the big white shirt from the clothing pantry that she and the scarecrow, with the help of a video last night, had turned into a proper girl-pirate's blouse. She cinched it at the waist with a huge beat-up leather belt that wrapped around her twice. She hoped it would be the perfect touch. She looked in the mirror and it was.

She tied one of the scarecrow's red bandanas around her neck and added three of her mom's necklaces that looked like pirate booty. She had emailed her mom asking if she could use her jewelry, and her mom had sounded thrilled Sofie was going to have a good Halloween.

Tomorrow night, she and Beth would trick-or-treat at the rich people's houses across town. She knew it was mostly an excuse for Connie and Jade to be together. The only dressing up Con was doing was a patch over one eye, and he said he wasn't going up on the porches with her. He'd probably stay in the shadows and kiss Jade. *Eww.* But Sofie would get a lot of loot. Plenty to share with the scarecrow.

There was only one more part to her costume. The real, true reason she'd decided to be a pirate.

With her hands shaking a little, she took a rainbow stud out of one ear and put in a big silver hoop of her mom's. She looked in the mirror and caught her breath. She moved her head, making the hoop swing and catch the light. She felt her mom smiling.

The costume was almost perfect. But before they went out trick-or-treating tomorrow night, she would make a few ratty braids to give her a Jack Sparrow look.

"What do you think?" she asked the scarecrow, who turned away from what he was stirring in the big iron skillet to look at her.

His face broke into a huge smile. He nodded.

She called up the attic stairs. "Come and see my costume. Take a picture and send it to Mom."

The next morning, when Con got out of the truck to let her out, she said, "Don't forget about tonight."

He rolled his eyes.

She didn't care. She gave him a quick hug whether he liked it or not.

"'Bye," she called to the scarecrow, and ran toward the door.

It was a beautiful day.

At lunch, she had given AnaMaria a short, fat carrot from the garden that Sofie thought looked kind of like a gnome, and AnaMaria had given her some chips, which looked like chips, when the office lady touched Sofie's shoulder and said she should come to the office. It was probably the advocate, who stopped by now and then.

But it wasn't the advocate. In a little room off the office there were a man and a woman she didn't know and Mr. Bloom. They were all standing staring at her. For a second, she thought maybe she was going to get the Student Explorer Award early.

But Mr. Bloom didn't look proud or happy. A knot tightened in her throat.

"I'm a social worker, Sofie," the woman said. "Your regular one is on vacation this week, so I'll be helping you."

She hadn't asked for help with anything. And if she needed help, she would have called the advocate. They had his phone number on the refrigerator.

"This is a Juvenile Court officer," the social worker said, gesturing to the man. "He has a judge's order to remove you from the home where you live, at"—she looked at a piece of paper and read Sofie's address out loud—"and place you in foster care. That's my job today. I'll be taking you to your new home." She smiled like it would be a big treat for her and Sofie both.

Wait. This was not right.

"I've already gotten your things out of your locker," the social worker said. She smiled and motioned toward the door. "So shall we go?"

This person was very confused. "You've got me mixed up with somebody else," Sofie said.

The social worker shook her head.

The walls of the room began moving closer and making the people taller. Sofie was being squeezed. She had to push back. What would Connie and the scarecrow do if she went to a foster home? The idea was ridiculous.

"I have a good home," she said. "Our granddad buys fresh eggs from a neighbor and grows food in the garden. He goes to meetings all the time to stay sober. And he's doing great. I read to him at night and he brings me to school each day in his truck and picks me up when school is out. We go to the garden most days. We put the garden to bed after school yesterday."

Her voice was threatening to break, but she would not let it. She looked at Mr. Bloom, whose face seemed blurry.

"Mr. Bloom knows my brother is the best brother in the world and he has always looked after me."

Connie might die if she got taken into foster care. So might the scarecrow.

"I can't go into foster care. It would ruin everything. I have a real bed now. And two bookcases. Two." She held up two fingers to make the point. Her eyes moved from the social worker to the other person. Didn't they understand what it meant to have two bookcases? People with two bookcases did not belong in foster care.

"Tell them, Mr. Bloom. I'm going to win the Student Explorer Award so I have to stay here."

"I can't possibly see how it's in Sofie's best interest to be taken out of her home," Mr. Bloom said. "She comes to school every day. She's my strongest fifth grader. I've known her and her brother for years. They're very responsible kids. Very resilient kids. Everybody should have kids like them."

His face was deep red like he was about to punch somebody. "I protest."

The man said, "You're free to contact the Juvenile Court office to register your protest. But the order is for immediate removal for the child's safety."

He nodded to the social worker, who reached her hand out to Sofie.

Sofie shook her head no. "I'm going trick-or-treating with my brother tonight. I have a pirate costume all ready. You're mixed up or something. There's nothing bad going on at our house. Our granddad is our guardian. The advocate said."

Connie would be furious if she went with the social worker. If he were here, he'd fight for her. And he'd expect her to fight for herself. These people were like the man on the bus who had stared at her bare feet that day. They thought they knew something about her and her family. But they didn't. They were stupid. And mean.

She bolted, but the man was quick and blocked the door. Sofie stared at him. He was big and there was no friendliness in his eyes.

"Why right now? What happened?" She tried to make her voice big and demanding.

Then she had an awful thought. Connie was always saying the scarecrow was too old to be working at that car wash.

Horror froze her. Barely breathing, she asked, "Is my granddad okay?"

The man glanced behind her at Mr. Bloom. "There's a need for confidentiality."

What did that mean?

But she understood now that something had happened to the scarecrow. Had he started drinking or using drugs again? Was he in jail? Had he hurt somebody? Was he hurt? Was he...

When they left, AnaMaria was at the water fountain. She looked scared as she watched Sofie and the social worker pass. Sofie wanted to speak to Ana-Maria, or touch her. But she was clammy and her tongue was tied by terror.

chapter 33

Sofie sat at the kitchen table wearing her jacket and holding her backpack on her lap. A row of action figures on the windowsill made weird shadows on the floor. The lady, who said to call her Cindy, offered a snack. Sofie said no thanks. The lady asked Sofie if she'd like to see her bedroom. Sofie got a book out of her backpack and said she'd rather read. She was not going to be sleeping here.

She pretended for what felt like a long time, turning the pages. Once, a little boy stuck his head around the door and watched her. She looked at him through her lashes, but kept her head down, turning the page. Eventually he went away. A kid's TV show was on in another room.

The lady kept coming into the kitchen to stir something in a pot.

"Do you like sloppy joes? That's what we're having for dinner."

She wouldn't be here for dinner.

"Judd and Marie will be home soon," the lady said.

Sofie had seen shoes and jackets of other kids by the door. She needed to make her move before there were more people in the house.

The lady talked about Judd and Marie. Sofie didn't listen. She had to find out what had happened to everybody. All the social worker would tell her about Con was that he was safe. But he hadn't been *unsafe*. And safe where? Was he in another foster home? The social worker said she was just covering for the week and didn't know about Sofie's granddad. The advocate would be in touch.

If only she'd memorized the advocate's number, but she hadn't known she'd have an emergency. Her heart was jumping like a frog. It was so hard to sit here until she got her chance.

She'd asked Cindy if she could call her brother, and Cindy said not until they heard from the advocate. When would that be? Soon, Cindy said.

Sofie startled at the long, loud buzz coming from the basement.

"That's the dryer," Cindy said, turning to go down the stairs.

Sofie gave her time to get there and then she crammed her book into her backpack and slipped out the kitchen door. She ran through the backyard, fought through a scratchy hedge where she had to turn and yank her bookbag free. She ran through another backyard, through a front yard, onto a sidewalk.

She ran for as long as she could, zigzagging a few blocks. A dog barked. A lady raking leaves called, "You okay, honey?"

Sofie raised her hand in a wave. "In a hurry!" she called breathlessly.

Around the corner, she slowed to a walk until she was able to run again. Finally, after a few more blocks of houses, she came to a wide street. She saw a bus stop in the next block and hurried toward it.

In the empty shelter, she made herself as small as she could. She prickled with sweat even though the day was cool. Wind carried a piece of paper along, bumping against the sidewalk, until it rolled into the shelter and hit her ankle.

When she saw a bus coming she stood, and the minute the door opened she ran up the steps and showed her pass. She moved to the back and sat down like she rode this bus every day. She looked out the window. She had no idea where she was. Except on a bus that stopped and started a lot and was taking forever.

She was afraid she was going the wrong way. But all buses eventually ended up at the bus barn south of downtown, and she could walk home from there.

She gripped her backpack and willed the scarecrow or Con to be there. And wherever the scarecrow was, she willed him to be sober. If he was at a meeting, that was okay. That was good.

From watching the shadows, she decided the bus was moving east toward downtown. She loosened her grip on her backpack a little.

The bus was on the freeway, going fast. There wouldn't be many stops before the bus barn.

A police car, siren blaring, whizzed by. The lady, Cindy, might have called the cops. She might have described Sofie. Ten years old. Curly blond hair.

Her heart raced as she dug around in her backpack. They had to bring hats and gloves to school now in case it was cold at recess. Sofie tried to cram as much of her hair as she could up under her hat. She felt the orange knit stretching, getting tighter and tighter as she poked and stuffed.

The lady across from her was staring. Sofie probably looked like a pumpkin head, and that was fine. She just couldn't look like herself.

She scrambled off the bus the second the back door opened at the bus barn and ran, leaving the stink of buses behind. After several blocks, she was in familiar surroundings.

If the cops were looking for her, where would they look? At first, probably in the neighborhood around Cindy's house. When they didn't find her, would they wonder if she had the street smarts to take a bus? If she did, where would she go?

Duh.

She slowed to a casual walk, her head down, most of her hair hopefully hidden. She cut through alleys and parking lots—always watching for a police car. Dogs barked from inside fences. Kids on bikes were doing wheelies in a vacant lot.

Even if nobody was home, she knew where a secret key was in the shed. She'd go in the house and call the advocate. The thought of an empty house stole her breath.

As she finally got close to their alley, her heart was in her throat, hoping so much . . .

And there was the scarecrow's truck.

And there was the scarecrow! Sitting on the back steps in the late afternoon sun, his head in his hands.

"Gunner!" she cried.

He looked up, taking a few seconds to spot her. "Sofie?"

She ran and hugged him and felt his arms go around her. He smelled like his tea. She clung to him, crying.

"Oh Gunner, I was so scared."

She was calling him by his name. It flooded her with a feeling of safety and love.

"Gunner," she said. It felt like a purr. Like tiny Sabine's purr. Why had she not known it would?

"You're shaking, poor girl," he said.

He held her back, his hands on her shoulders. His eyes were red rimmed. "They shouldn't have done it like that," he said. "It scared everybody half to death worrying about each other."

"Do you know where Connie is?"

Then she heard feet on the stairs and Con charged out the back door. He crushed her in a hug, then stepped back. "How did you get here?"

"I ran away. On the bus."

Her cap was so tight it was giving her a headache. She pulled it off. Her hair falling free felt wonderful. They were together and she could tell Gunner was sober. The people might come and try to take her away, but Gunner would never let them. If he could get rid of the stupid boyfriend with the gun, he could save her from foster care.

She was asking Con how he'd gotten there when she saw the advocate come around the corner of the house. His glasses caught the low sun and he twinkled.

"Sofia," the advocate said. "Conrad. Mr. Jones."

Gunner nodded. Con glared.

To Sofie, the advocate said, "I had a feeling I'd find you here. Did your granddad pick you up?"

She caught her breath. Had she gotten Gunner in trouble?

She shook her head hard enough to scramble her brain. "No, no, no. I ran away. He didn't know anything about it until I showed up. I just got here."

"How did you get here?"

"On a bus. And I walked. And ran."

He looked at her. She wasn't sure what to make of the look. Maybe it was friendly. Or maybe she was wrong.

"Well, you can't stay here," he finally said gently.

She moved closer to Gunner. He put his hand on her shoulder.

"Tell me why it had to be done the way it was," Gunner said, his voice shaking. "All of a sudden. Scaring Sofie and Con. I would have told those people about my record if they'd asked. I figured they could check on their own, and probably had, and that it was okay for me to be the kids' temporary guardian."

The advocate looked pained. "They did run a background check when the children's mother was arrested and you became their temporary guardian. And the background check showed your felonies and recent incarceration. But the report got misplaced and didn't surface until this morning."

He cleared his throat. "You have to understand. Social Services and Juvenile Court are short on staff. There's a lot of turnover. People have caseloads that are too heavy.

"When your background report surfaced this morning, alarms went off. If something happened to the children in your care, the state would have all kinds of liability. That's why they swooped in and took Sofie out of school. If I'd been available, things might have turned out differently." He sighed. "But I couldn't be reached. By the time I got off the plane, it was too late." He looked embarrassed. "You didn't do anything wrong," he told Gunner.

Sofie saw Gunner's lips tremble.

"The judge is fairly comfortable with Conrad being here for now, but it's different with Sofia. She's younger and a girl. We can schedule a hearing before the Juvenile Court judge and request a full waiver of the felony requirement. But that will probably take weeks."

Wait. Con could stay, but she couldn't?

The unfairness of it opened like a huge crack in the earth, and she teetered on the edge.

"That's not fair!"

Con looked miserable, and Gunner looked ashamed.

She would die in that foster home.

"I *don't want* to be in foster care," she said. "Gunner, Connie, tell him."

They had to save her. So they could be together, a triangle in a circle. She needed her books and her bookshelves. She needed to cut up fruit for breakfast and ride to school with Gunner every morning. She needed to hang out with AnaMaria. She needed to go trick-or-treating tonight.

"*I don't want to be in foster care,*" she wailed.

Why didn't Gunner or Con do something?

chapter 34

That lady—Cindy—had taken the other two kids trick-or-treating. Cindy said they could work out a costume for Sofie. And be a tag-along makeshift princess? No thanks. The memory of her splendid pirate costume spread out on her bed made her heart ache.

She was supposed to be with Con and Jade and Beth. Gunner was supposed to be waiting at home for her to return with lots of candy to share.

The doorbell chimed, and the little boy who kept trying to make friends with her raced to the door, screaming, *"Trick or treat, Papa. Trick or treat!"*

That had happened so many times Sofie wanted to put a pillow over her ears. After each batch of goblins left, the little boy came and stood by Sofie. She felt him looking at her. Waiting. She couldn't be nice to him or she'd break down and bawl.

"Is it okay if I take a shower and go to bed?" she asked the dad, whose name was Brian.

He looked doubtful. "It's awfully early."

"I'm tired."

"Sure you are," he said after a second. "Go ahead."

Downstairs, where her room was, Cindy had left pajamas on the bed. They were probably clean, but they smelled funny.

So did the shampoo when Sofie squirted it into her palm. She needed watermelon shampoo. Did her mom miss the watermelon shampoo? They were both away from home now. She jerked away from that thought as fast as she could. She would not start crying.

She dried with the red towel the lady had left on her bed, which wasn't really her bed. She didn't want to sleep in it. But she was a little bit glad the towel was red.

Cindy had placed a comb and brush and a handful of hair twisties and barrettes in a basket in the bathroom. But she needed her special brush for curly hair. She wiped steam off the mirror. She looked like a wild bush.

Overhead, she heard the doorbell and the little boy's feet pounding. She heard muted voices. Probably kids telling stupid jokes and riddles. Her riddle was *How do you hide an elephant in a strawberry patch?* The answer was *Paint his toenails red.*

Connie didn't think it was a very good pirate riddle, but it suited her. She would have been a powerful pirate. A cute pirate. People would have smiled at her with her single flashing hoop earring the same way they smiled at her mom.

Did her mom know what had happened to Sofie? Sofie tried to smother the thought that this was her mom's fault. If her mom hadn't gone off with the stupid boyfriend with the gun, she wouldn't be in prison. And if she hadn't gone to prison, then Sofie wouldn't be in foster care. Still, Sofie hoped her mom didn't know what had happened. She would so afraid for Sofie.

Now that she had started thinking about her mom, she couldn't stop. She brushed her teeth, but the toothpaste didn't taste right. It tasted evil. She needed her mom to take care of her. Her mouth hurt as she moved the toothbrush. Everything hurt. Her head, her hands, her shoulders, her knees, her back, her feet. Her stomach really, *really* hurt. She needed her mom.

She barely made it to the toilet before the sloppy joe the lady had insisted she eat came up. And Connie wasn't there to hold back her hair. She was alone.

She buried her face in her dirty T-shirt, which at least smelled right, and sobbed.

Eventually she wiped her face on her T-shirt and drank a glass of water. She would call Connie.

Earlier, she had pitched such a hissy fit about going back to the foster home that the advocate had bought her a prepaid phone so she could call Gunner or Connie anytime. And the advocate had said he'd push for the earliest possible hearing date before a judge to see if Gunner could be her legal guardian. In exchange, Sofie had promised not to run away from the foster home again. So she was stuck here.

She blew her nose and cleared her throat and drank another glass of water so there wouldn't be any tears left in her voice. She didn't want Connie to know she'd been crying.

When he answered, his voice wrapped around her. She shut her eyes and told herself she was there with him. She could smell Gunner's tea.

"What are you doing?" she asked.

"I'm hiding in the dark so no trick-or-treaters ring the bell. I'm eating the candy Gunner bought to hand out. I think I'm eating too much. I don't feel great."

"Where's Gunner?"

"At a meeting."

Good.

"What did you tell Jade? Is she mad?"

After what felt like a long time, he said, "I told her something really serious had happened. I asked her to call me later when we could talk as long as we wanted and I would explain everything."

Sofie squeezed her eyes tight, sending Jade a message all the way across town. *Call my brother. Be a good friend. Please.*

"Gunner blames himself for what's happened to you."

Her voice caught on tears. "Tell him not to, okay?"

"Yeah."

She couldn't quite shake the feeling of unfairness that Con could be at home and she couldn't.

"What's it like there?" he asked. "Is it okay? Do you feel safe?"

Only a week ago, Tommy had told her she was safe. She hadn't been. She wasn't. She was separated from everyone she loved. But she couldn't say that to Con right now.

"The dad seems nice. There's the cutest little boy. I can't tell if he's a foster kid or a regular kid. The two older ones are brother and sister. They hope to go home soon. The lady, Cindy, told me they've had twenty-one foster kids in all."

"Wow," Con said.

"Yeah. I have my own bedroom and share a bathroom with the other girl. It's okay. But I'm so homesick, Connie."

He didn't say anything. Time stretched between them. Then she heard a tiny explosive noise.

"Maybe I'll call later and talk to Gunner," she said in a rush. "But let's stop talking now."

"Okay." His voice was hoarse.

Hot tears rolled down her cheek.

"'Bye, Connie."

"'Bye."

She couldn't sleep. She lay in the dark listening to the kids come in from trick-or-treating. They were trying to be quiet, and finally they were quiet. The house was so still she heard her own breathing.

She ached to go home. She wished she hadn't promised the advocate she wouldn't run away again. Maybe she should call Gunner to come and get her and take her home for the night and bring her back before anybody was awake in the morning. But it probably wouldn't work, and she'd get him in more trouble.

She wished he didn't feel guilty. Maybe he was right and he had passed his weakness for drugs and alcohol on to Summer and to Sofie's mom. But if he hadn't gotten sent to prison when Summer was young, Summer might not have gotten pregnant with Sofie's mom when she was sixteen. And Sofie's mom might not have gotten pregnant with Con and Sofie so young. The people most precious to her wouldn't exist if Gunner hadn't messed up big-time way back in the day. She and her mom and Gunner and Connie wouldn't have each other. And how terrible would that be?

She was suddenly too tired and sleepy to call Gunner and explain that, but she would tell him sometime.

chapter 35

Sofie stared out the window. It was her eighth day in this school. Everything was so new. The playground. The trees. Even the sky looked like it had a fresh coat of bright blue paint. She didn't belong here.

Cindy gave her clothes to wear that were random stuff she had gotten from somewhere. Maybe foster kids before Sofie had worn them. So Sofie went to school looking random, instead of like herself.

She didn't like this teacher. She wanted a teacher who understood her like Mr. Bloom did. Who knew she was Con's little sister and could punch above her weight. This new teacher was kind and helpful, but in a way that said *Poor little foster child.* It made Sofie furious.

And a few of the kids went out of their way to be nice to the new girl who appeared one day from nowhere and was a—whisper—*foster child.* But their kindness felt like it was more about them than her.

Sofie needed to be with a real friend. When the advocate gave her the cell phone she had called AnaMaria and told her what had happened. AnaMaria had cried, then tried to explain to her mom what was wrong. Ana-Maria didn't really understand foster care, but she got that Sofie had been taken away from her family and sent to live with people she didn't know on the other side of town. AnaMaria said her mama said Sofie could come and live with them. They had room. The kindness made Sofie's heart ache and tears stream down her face. She had been able to whisper "Your mom is the best" before the sobs came and she had to get off the phone.

The teacher was saying her name.

The teacher smiled and pointed to the office lady at the door, who motioned to Sofie.

She felt her face blaze as she crossed the room in front of the entire class, everyone watching her. *Foster child business.*

As they walked down the hall lined with lockers and through a space where sunlight painted stripes on the floor, the lady said, "Mr. Stanley is here to see you."

She took Sofie into a room where the advocate was waiting. The room had a couch with a comfy-looking cover thrown over the back, a couple of chairs, a little table with a box of tissues on it, a crate of toys in the corner, and kind of weird-looking dolls on a shelf. A bad-news room, if she'd ever seen one.

A knot cinched in her stomach as her lunch tried to come up.

"Sofie..."

The advocate's owlish eyes behind his shiny round glasses frightened her with their kindness.

"There was a hearing this morning. The judge decided not to waive the rule about recent felons acting as guardians as it pertains to you. So your removal from Mr. Jones's care stands permanently. Con is allowed to stay with Mr. Jones. I'm sorry."

Dancing speckles appeared around the edges of her vision and gnawed to the center as things slowly disappeared. She'd been so sure....

The advocate's arms went around her shoulders and he said something, but the terrible words in her head were *Ashes, ashes, we all fall down.*

She found herself sitting in one of the chairs, so deep her legs stuck out, her boots a long way off. The advocate brought her a paper cup of water from the blue dispenser in the corner. She held the cup, which wouldn't stop shaking.

"Sofie," he said, pulling up another chair close to her. "I know this isn't what you wanted. Or what your family wanted."

She wished he would shut up. He didn't know anything.

She let the trembling paper cup tip forward. It was like peeing on Cindy's random clothes. On this awful wrong. She poured slowly, watching the wet patch spread, turning the purple pants dark. As the water soaked through it was cold and calming.

She handed the cup to the advocate and he put it on the table.

"For what it's worth, it wasn't what I recommended. I know your granddad is elderly and an addict with a serious criminal record. And the truth is, as you're moving into greater need for a parent, he is getting older and perhaps less able to parent." He took a breath and sighed. "But I was there when your mom was arrested, and I was there when you found your way across the city on your own to get to your granddad—probably because you were afraid of what he might do." He raised an eyebrow. "Am I right?"

She nodded. Not that it mattered now. Gunner was so proud to be her guardian. They were snatching his best thing away from him. It was cruel.

"So I strongly recommended taking a chance on Mr. Jones to the judge. But I was outnumbered. You can have visits with your brother and grandfather. For now, they need to be supervised, but I imagine that can change over time if all goes well."

It was quiet in the room. Each time the minute changed on the wall clock, she heard a little click saying *next*. Before, she'd always known she and Con would manage whatever was next together. Now she didn't know what next was. She was losing everything. She was being erased.

The advocate said, "Have you ever heard the saying *When one door closes, another door opens?*"

She shook her head.

"Sofie, possibly your dad has come forward."

"I don't have a dad."

The advocate smiled a little. "Everybody has a dad."

"I don't."

"You may," he said.

She had seen her birth certificate. *Father* was blank. She had a mom, a brother, and a great-granddad.

"My mom says I don't."

"Mr. Donovan thinks he might be your dad."

"*Tommy?*" The advocate had gotten really mixed up. "Tommy isn't my dad. He's our friend."

"He could be both."

That was so embarrassing she couldn't even begin to think about it. She wanted Tommy to be a wonderful friend. Not . . . the other thing. Not one of her mom's stupid boyfriends.

"Then why would my mom say I don't have a dad?"

"She might not know whether or not Mr. Donovan is your dad," the advocate said. "There are ways to find out for sure. There's an easy test to match up parents and their kids. So even if your mom didn't know, it could still be true. Mr. Donovan would like for the two of you to have the test."

He seemed to be waiting for her to say something.

But this would change her whole world. She would lose her good friend Tommy. She would have a dad but Connie wouldn't, and that didn't feel right at all. It might push them apart. Stupid boyfriends had been bad enough in their lives. But a *dad*? *Now?*

Tommy was so kind and reliable.

"Maybe Tommy is Con's dad too." That would be wonderful, like a fairy tale. But then what about Gunner? He'd get left out.

"No," the advocate said. "Mr. Donovan isn't Con's dad." He sounded certain. "To make sure he's your dad, we'd go to a laboratory and they'd put a Q-tip in your mouth and rub it on the inside of your cheek. And they'd do the same to Mr. Donovan. And if the tests match up, well . . ." He opened his palms in a *That's the end of that story* gesture.

She felt like a kite on the end of a string, diving and swooping. She couldn't imagine what she'd do with a dad. She was fine without one. Except she wasn't. She was sitting here in soaked pants away from everybody she loved.

But having a dad would be so weird.

Why did Tommy even *think* he was her dad?

She felt her face burning at the answer to why he *could* be her dad. But why did he think it *now*, when she was ten years old?

Or had he always thought it and not owned up to it? That's what one of her mom's stupid boyfriends would have done.

But Tommy was not a stupid boyfriend. She felt that in her bones. He was smart and kind and funny and cared about other people. And he had a really nice mom.

If Tommy was her dad, Mrs. Donovan would be her grandmother. Did Mrs. Donovan know she was Sofie's grandmother? Was that why she gave Sofie the bookshelves and daybed and little table for her lamp? Maybe she wasn't downsizing at all.

She wished she could talk to Con or Gunner about this. But Con was in school and Gunner was at work. And she could never talk to Connie about this anyway. It would crush him if she had a dad, because then she wouldn't need him so much.

Anger filled her. "Then why didn't Tommy say he was my dad a long time ago?"

Everything could have been different. She felt herself clutching the arms of the chair as a wave of all that could have been different hit her. Maybe their mom wouldn't have gone off and left them. Maybe she and Connie could have been more like other kids, without so many secrets.

But maybe dear Gunner wouldn't have worked his way into her heart. Maybe she and Connie wouldn't have meant so much to each other. Maybe she wouldn't have loved her mom so much.

Everything was spinning.

"Maybe you should talk to Mr. Donovan about this. Would you like to? I know he would like to talk to you."

"No!" The word sprang out of her mouth as almost a shout, but it wasn't exactly what she meant.

"Maybe we could all get together and talk about this," the advocate said.

She was not giving up on her and Con and Gunner staying together. They were a triangle inside a circle now because of the lucky buckeye.

"I need dry clothes," she said.

The nurse would have something she could wear for the rest of the day. Whatever it was, it couldn't be less *her* that what she had on.

She looked at her boots. She loved them, but someday she would outgrow them. She held back tears.

"Let me tell Connie and Gunner," she said.

chapter 36

She sat on the floor in front of her closed bedroom door and called Con about an hour before Gunner would be going to a meeting. She could imagine them in the kitchen. Con with his hair flopping in his eyes and the table covered with his homework and whatever Gunner had made for dinner.

Gunner would be starting to clean up, then he would make a cup of tea and drink it before his meeting. She could see his junky old truck waiting in the alley in the shadows cast by the streetlight.

When Con put her on speaker so Gunner could hear, she told them. She was shaking a little because she knew she was telling them terrible news. A dad would change their lives—and not in a good way. But she had to admit she was telling them wonderful news too because if Tommy *was* her dad and wanted to *be* her dad, she'd never have to worry about foster care again.

They let her talk without saying anything. Not a sound.

"So the advocate thinks we should all get together and talk about things. Soon. And when we do, I'll get to see you," she said, her voice trying not to break in the silence. Tears filled her eyes.

She heard the rasp of the scarecrow clearing his throat.

"Gunner," she said, making her voice stay steady though it hurt to do so, "I told him I would rather you be my guardian forever, but the court won't let you be."

"Tommy is a good man," Gunner said. "And a young man."

"And Connie," she said, "we won't have to worry about foster care anymore."

That monster under the bed would be dead.

"Yeah," he said.

She needed her brother to say more. She waited. She could see Gunner watching Connie, telling Con to step up and say something good about Tommy being her dad.

"We'll be okay, Sof," he finally said, his voice deep.

A few days later, on a Sunday because Tommy's Place and the car wash closed on Sunday, the advocate picked Sofie up at the foster home. The sky was gray and the trees were bare, but the advocate, in his long coat, still seemed to twinkle a little.

"Scared?" he asked.

"Kind of." But she was also thrilled to be seeing Con and Gunner for the first time in two weeks.

"The paternity test is scheduled for tomorrow," the advocate said. "So the suspense will be over soon."

That soon? The two weeks in foster care had felt like two years. But suddenly tomorrow felt like only a minute.

"The quicker Mr. Donovan can prove paternity, Sofie, the quicker the court can decide whether or not he's capable of parenting you. And the sooner you can get out of foster care."

Of course, she wanted out of foster care this very instant, but she'd rather go home to Con and Gunner.

Gunner was supposed to bring her the special brush for curly hair. She hoped he wouldn't forget. Today, her hair made her look like Annie from the movie, only blond. And her clothes looked like some other kid's. Or several other kids'. And she wouldn't smell right. Con and Gunner might not recognize her.

The parking lot at Tommy's was empty except for two cars and Gunner's truck. Gunner and Con got out of the truck as Sofie and the advocate arrived.

Sofie jumped out of the car and flew to Con, her boots crunching in the gravel. She threw her arms around him and held on, her head buried in his puffer coat, which was so slick it was hard to hang on. She felt his hands smoothing her hair.

"Oh, Connie, I miss you."

She turned loose of him, then flung herself at Gunner. "Gunner!"

She hugged him too, then stood back. How could she ever have thought of him as a scarecrow? He was tall and strong with beautiful silver hair and a loving face.

"I brought you something," he said.

"My hairbrush." He hadn't forgotten.

"Yes," he said, taking it out of his pocket and giving it to her. "But something else."

"What?"

He handed her a small brown paper sack. Inside was a cluster of grapes.

"They're special," he said. "They're called holiday grapes."

She looked more closely. They were large and perfectly round. She had never seen perfectly round grapes before.

"They're sweet and crisp," Gunner said. "Try one."

The flavor exploded in her mouth. She smiled and nodded. "They're delicious. Thank you."

"They're for you to take to that foster home."

Why did that make her feel so well loved?

"Would you like to try one?" she asked the advocate.

He smiled and took one. "Thank you."

She held the grapes out to Connie, but he shook his head no, which really hurt for some reason.

"Do you want to leave them in my car?" the advocate said.

She nodded. The wonderful gift and the taste and the sad angry look on Con's face and Gunner's love made her feel like her skin had been peeled off and the whole world was rubbing against her bare heart.

She saw Gunner give Con's shoulder a quick squeeze. It reminded her of the way he used to squeeze her foot and wiggle it.

The lights around the door to Tommy's Place weren't on, but the door was open. There was clatter from the kitchen and Tommy came out.

He greeted them, calling Con *Professor* as always.

"Hey, Princess SJ." But he seemed a little embarrassed and almost shy.

"Hi." That didn't feel like enough, but she didn't know what to add.

He was looking at her like he didn't know what else to say either but would really like to say something.

She suddenly wanted to run and hide and never be found. She couldn't suddenly get a dad when she was ten years old. Who did that? And if he *was* really her dad...she'd never be able to call him that. That would be truly weird. *Dad*... No.

They sat at a long table covered with a red tablecloth, Sofie between Con and Gunner on one side, the advocate and Mrs. Donovan on the other side.

Tommy introduced Mrs. Donovan to everybody. She was pretty for an old person. She wore a colorful scarf and had a nice smile.

Sofie couldn't help smiling back when Mrs. Donovan held out her hand.

Sofie shook it. "Thank you for the nice things. I'm not home now, and I really miss them. Especially the bookshelves."

"I hope this whole problem will be over soon," Mrs. Donovan said. "And we can get to know each other."

Tommy turned on the twinkling fairy lights around the bar, kind of like they were having a party. She felt Con stiffen. She leaned against him, trying to say the fairy lights were wrong. She was so happy to see him, but not to be with this new maybe family. Her stomach felt wavy.

Mrs. Donovan looked at her. "Sofie, Tom tells me you plan to be a librarian when you're older?"

"A head librarian." She sat up straight. "And Connie is going to be a doctor."

Mrs. Donovan smiled at Con. "A helping profession."

"Maybe I'll be a teacher instead."

He sounded like he was cornered and might have to fight his way out.

"You taught me to read," she reminded him.

In the closet, remember? While what's-his-name beat Mom and banged her into the wall. The magic of sounding out words saved us. Jack and Annie. Nobody but us will ever really know. Nothing can separate us, ever, no matter what happens. No matter who my dad is.

"And Con is a great algebra tutor," Tommy said.

Mrs. Donovan's face was kind, and so was Tommy's as they looked at her and Con and Gunner. But this was so hard.

If only they could go back to last spring when school was out and their only worry was their mom's partying. That was such a long time ago. She had been a little girl then.

Tommy stood. "I'll put the finishing touches on lunch."

While he was in the kitchen, Mrs. Donovan talked about him, and Sofie heard the pride in Mrs. Donovan's voice. It was like the pride her mom took in her and Con.

Her mom knew what they were doing today. Connie had told her. Sofie wished she knew how her mom felt about all this. She wished she could sit on the floor between her mom's knees, with her mom brushing the tangles out of her hair, and talk to her about so many things. Her mom wasn't perfect, but she loved her kids. And Gunner.

Mrs. Donovan got Gunner talking about the garden and growing strawberries. And Con was texting with Jade. His face looked more relaxed.

"I'm going to go help Tommy," Sofie said, so quietly only the advocate heard.

He nodded.

She remembered rushing through the loud, crowded kitchen the night of the gun. Today it felt huge and empty except for the spot where Tommy was stirring a pot of something that smelled really good. She didn't want the food to smell good, but it did.

"White bean and kale soup," he said, looking only a little surprised to see her. "I made it yesterday. It's always better on the second day. I thought Gunner would like it, especially. And I know Mom likes it, and I hope you and Con do."

"How long have you thought you were my dad?"

That was something she liked about the advocate. He said things the way they were and asked what he needed to know.

Tommy's eyes looked right into hers. He didn't seem surprised.

"Since the first time I brought you and Con food after Ashley left. In your kitchen that night, I saw family similarities I'd never noticed before."

She didn't look a thing like Tommy or Mrs. Donovan.

"It shocked me into thinking about things I'd put behind me years ago. Those dark months after my wife and Summer were killed."

He shook his head. "I remembered stuff I hadn't thought about in years. And I realized you could possibly be a precious jewel that came from that terrible time. And I felt so happy about it, Princess SJ."

His face turned a little pink. "I went to visit your mom in jail and we talked about those days. It was strange and hard to stir up all that again. We both lost so much. And Ashley was in a bad place in jail. Maybe I should have waited, but I just couldn't."

"So were you Mama's boyfriend?"

He didn't say anything for a while, but he kept looking at her. "Not really," he finally said. "But we were friends who went through something terrible together. And I'm still pretty sure I'm your dad."

She didn't know how she felt about that. She guessed she liked the idea of her mom having a good person to go through something terrible with.

He ladled soup into a bright bowl and handed it to her. "Want to put this on the cart?"

When the cart was filled with six bowls of soup, a tray of sandwiches, a big basket of fries, and six little dipping cups of sauce, Tommy rolled it out and she followed.

Grown-ups were strange. She did not personally ever want to be one.

As they ate, Tommy and the advocate talked about college wrestling. Gunner and Mrs. Donovan talked about how to make easy strawberry preserves.

Mrs. Donovan picked up a french fry with her fingers, dipped it in sauce, and popped it in her mouth. Sofie tried not to stare, but the way Mrs. Donovan ate felt spookily familiar.

And her hands.

Sofie looked at her own. Like Mrs. Donovan's thumbs, Sofie's curved up at the end in a little ski-jump swoop. Connie used to tease her about her thumbs, saying she could use them as spoons.

She remembered the first night Tommy brought food to the house. He had stared at her with that odd look on his face.

She was probably his daughter.

She shivered. She had the urge to grab Gunner's and Connie's hands and run.

After they finished eating, the advocate said he'd pick her up at school tomorrow and meet Tommy at the DNA Diagnostic Center.

"Because this is a legal paternity test, I'll sign an affidavit that you are both who you say you are, I'll witness the cheek swabs being taken and sealed, and there will be a record of chain of custody of the swabs until the results come back. It'll be at least a couple of days. Maybe as long as a week."

He looked around the table. "Does that work for everybody?"

"I want Con and Gunner to go along," she said.

"There's no need," the advocate said.

"Wait," Tommy said. "If Sofie wants that, I'm for it."

"Me too," Gunner said.

Con nodded. "Me too."

That meant she would get to see them again tomorrow. She hugged them both.

In the advocate's car, she shut her eyes and leaned her head back, the little bag of holiday grapes in her lap.

"It's a lot, Sofie," the advocate said.

She let out a deep breath. Yes.

"Do you talk to your mom?" he asked after a while.

"We mainly email. There's a computer I can use in the foster home."

"How is that going?"

Her throat caught fire with held-back tears. "She worries about us. We worry about her."

Yesterday, her mom had said she had no idea if Tommy was Sofie's dad, but she always knew Sofie's dad was somebody special because Sofie was a great kid. That's what her mom had always said. Maybe it was true.

"If the paternity test tomorrow shows Mr. Donovan is your dad—"

It would. Sofie knew it in her bones. In her thumbs. She needed to get used to the idea.

"—the court will move quickly. They don't like kids in foster care a minute longer than they need to be. They'll assess his suitability to parent, and if he passes, which I'm almost certain he will, the court will no longer act in the place of a parent, because you'll have a parent who can be responsible for you."

She ate a grape. She pulled another one off the stem and looked at it, turning it between her finger and her thumb like her grandmother's.

If the circle couldn't hold all the triangles—her, her mom, and Connie—her, Connie, and Gunner—her, Tommy, and Mrs. Donovan—her, Connie, and Jade—maybe a sphere could.

chapter 37

A week later, Sofie still didn't know for sure, but she believed Tommy was her dad. Every time she touched that belief, she felt a whirly swirl of hope, fear, relief, and plain weirdness that almost knocked her down.

Tonight she lay in bed wide awake, feeling so whirly swirly she knew she would never sleep. She listened to the quiet house. The brother and sister foster kids had gone back to their real family, and the little boy, Sam, had been in bed for hours. All she heard was sleet tapping gently on her window.

Maybe they'd have a big blizzard and school would be canceled all next week. She hated her foster school. She'd rather stay home with Sam. She had given in and liked him a little.

Yesterday, she'd been at the kitchen table doing homework and he'd handed her a board book, *Good Dog, Carl*, and climbed into her lap. She'd kind of wanted to push him off and kind of wanted to smell his hair.

He'd turned the pages, which had hardly any words—a few at the beginning and the end. He'd said the words as if he could read, and looked at her very proudly. When he was done, he got off her lap and went away. But later he came back with a book with a lot more words in it and climbed in her lap. That time she'd smelled his hair and read to him.

Her thoughts swooped back to probably having a dad.

At eleven thirty, she called Gunner. The rasp in his voice said she'd waked him, but he sounded glad to hear from her.

"Can't sleep?" he asked.

"No."

"All's well," he said.

"All's well here too, but I still can't sleep."

"I'm needing to know how *The Underneath* ends. You think that old hound is going to die chained up?"

He wasn't supposed to if the book followed the rules.

"It's on my mind, Sofie. Let's find out."

She turned on a light. It wasn't cozy like her pink lamp. It made her squint.

"Gunner, is my pink lamp okay?"

"You bet. Con and I look out for it."

She folded a pillow behind her back and began to read. She could hear Gunner listening because every now and then he made little sounds of surprise or tenderness.

The sleet had turned to rain that streaked the windows. No snow day tomorrow.

As the turned the pages, she felt more and more certain the book was going to end badly.

☆

Terrifyingly close to the end, Grandmother, the giant cottonmouth snake, loomed, hissing, over Ranger and the kittens.

Sofie couldn't keep the surprise and horror out of her voice when she read "...she opened her steel-trap jaws and struck!"

She heard Gunner gasp, and she cried out.

The dear old blues-singing hound and the brave brother-and-sister kittens were dead.

No! She felt utter betrayal as tears came. But there were still a few pages to go.

On the next page, her heart melted when she understood that Grandmother cottonmouth hadn't *killed* Sofie's friends, she'd *snapped the chain* that bound Ranger!

A hoarse cheer burst out of Gunner.

Sofie's tears were so happy when she read

Grandmother who had spent a thousand years in a jar had finally chosen love. She had seen it, pure and simple and clean, seen it in the small beings of two gray cats and an old dog. Love in all its complexity and honor made a circle around them all.

A circle around them all. The old hound and two kittens were a triangle safe inside a circle. Maybe it was a sign something wonderful was going to happen to her and Con and Gunner that she couldn't see yet.

As she read on to the very, very end, she wished she could show Gunner the final illustration of the redbone hound and the pair of kittens as they walked off the page and into their future. They had become so dear to her and they would always live on in the piney forest.

There was quiet on the phone. She could hear Gunner breathing, she could feel her heart beating, she could smell the piney woods, she could hear the old hound singing the blues.

She wondered if Gunner was crying too. It didn't seem right to talk.

But after a while she said, "Good night, Gunner."

"Good night, Sofie. All's well."

Yes, it was.

The next morning, Cindy and the little boy were at church, and Brian was watching football. Sofie was in her room holding *The Higher Power of Lucky* and thinking about giving it another chance. Since she abandoned it, she had become a ward of the state like Lucky.

But most of all, Sofie was considering a second chance because Lucky punched above her weight too. Maybe Lucky was going to find a happy ending *even if* she had a dead mom, a weird dad, and a strange guardian. Surely the gold sticker didn't lie.

She jumped when her phone rang. It was a weird number. Not Con's or Gunner's or the advocate's or AnaMaria's—who were the only people who called her.

"Hello?"

"Sofie."

"Mama?"

They couldn't call their mom in prison, but she could call them. But it was so expensive she almost never did.

Her mom made a choking-laughing sound. "Sofie," she said again. "I can't talk long. I don't have much money in my account."

They had put some in when they visited her, but that was a month ago. She rushed on. "Sofie, the test shows you're Tommy's daughter."

Even though she'd known almost for sure, hearing it all official was like having a house fall on her. She shut her eyes.

"I found out from the advocate yesterday. He wanted to know how I'd feel about you being in Tom's—in your dad's—care. I said I'd feel good about it and asked if I could be the one to tell you. Sofie, you may hate me sometimes for the way I've done terrible things."

She paused for a second.

"I'm so sorry I messed up so bad. But Tommy is a good man. Maybe the best man I've ever known. If I didn't think that, I'd fight to keep you from going to him. Tommy has told me how much he wants to be your parent. And how much his mom wants to be your grandmother."

Sofie heard her mom suck a fast breath.

"So, Sofie . . ." There was a long pause, then Sofie heard tears in her mom's voice. "I want you to really be Tommy Donovan's daughter. Let him take care of you. I'm stuck in here forever. My time will be more bearable if I know you're safe with the Donovans. Not just safe. Happy." He mom's voice flooded with tears. "Be happy, Sofie."

Sofie had to say it. "But I want to be with Connie and Gunner."

"I know. But you can't. So please put your heart into this, okay? Really have a life with your dad. If you can do that...oh, Sofie, if you can do that...please."

Her mom was really crying now. "Have to go. 'Bye. Love you."

And she was gone.

Sofie didn't even take time to breathe. Her heart was beating fast and her hands were shaking as she called Con.

She heard the hum of the microwave.

"Is Gunner there?"

"Yeah."

She could smell his tea.

"Put me on speaker, Connie. I need to talk to him too."

Con said something to Gunner in a muffled voice, then Gunner said, "I'm here, Sofie."

"Mom called. Tommy is my dad. For sure."

They were quiet. She heard a football crowd cheering on the TV upstairs.

Her most precious people were being swept away. Or was she the one being swept away, even though she was hanging on?

"That's good news, Sofie," Gunner said. "It's good he wants to be your dad. What does your mom say?"

"She's happy about it."

"Well, she's right," Gunner said. "It's what's best for you."

She knew his face looked old and sad. She wished Connie would say something.

She heard the garage door go up. Cindy and Sam were back from church.

Finally, Con said, "That's cool, Sof. Tommy's a good guy."

She *hated* her brother being hurt. It was her mom's fault. Everything was her mom's fault. She covered her face with her hands and cried.

"Oh, Sofie," Con said, "It will be all right."

Her brave brother.

chapter 38

During the almost two weeks it took to get the court's approval for Sofie to live with Tommy as her official dad, she tried to get ready for the move. The advocate came to the foster home with Tommy to talk to her. Tommy asked what he could do to make the change easier.

That was a no-brainer. Let her go back to her old school where Mr. Bloom and AnaMaria were. Let her stay with Connie and Gunner sometimes. Let her have her own clothes. And watermelon shampoo.

He had listened, nodding, and when she finally finished, he said, "You've got it, Princess SJ."

The advocate said soon she would have a new birth certificate with her dad's name on it. Tommy asked if she would like to have the new name of Sofia Donovan. Not really. But she didn't want to hurt his feelings, so she said she'd like her new name to be Sofia Jones Donovan. He nodded.

That morning, she'd said goodbye to her foster parents and Sam after a month with them. She'd miss Sam a little, and he might miss her a little. But he was used to foster kids coming and going. He'd be fine.

She wanted to give him something because the way he'd sat on her lap and read books with her meant a lot. She'd asked the advocate to please get one of her old Magic Tree House books from her room and bring it when he picked her up.

And he'd remembered.

Last night, she'd snuck a quick kiss onto Sam's head. And this morning, she'd left *Dinosaurs Before Dark* on the kitchen table along with a note.

*Thank you for reading Good Dog, Carl to me. Soon you'll be able to read
this book, and I think you'll love it.*

'Bye. Sofie

The day was a cold and sunny Monday. The restaurant was closed, so Sofie
would skip school today and go back to her old one tomorrow. The brightness made the advocate very twinkly. A gust of wind rocked the car as they
got on the freeway. Sofie gripped the armrest.

"Excited?" the advocate asked. "Nervous?"

She nodded.

"How did the visit with your mom go yesterday?"

"Okay, I guess."

Her mom had been *so* glad to see them. She even had on a little makeup.
After the phone call a week ago when their mom was almost totally out of
money, Sofie had asked her dad if he could send some, and he had. That was
the first time she'd called him her *dad* in her head. Her mom had bought
lipstick at the commissary. It wasn't the clear, bright red she wore before,
but it looked cheerful.

The way a couple of the other prisoners in the VR, as her mom called
the visitor's room, looked at Tommy made Sofie wonder if their mom had
told them Tommy was her newly discovered dad.

Sofie felt her cheeks turning pink. For some reason, it was embarrassing.
But if Tommy noticed he didn't show it. Although Sofie saw sadness in Tommy's
eyes sometimes, around people he always seemed so comfortable and easy.

Sofie stayed close to her mom the whole hour. To hold her hand, to nes-
tle against her side, to touch her hair. It soothed Sofie, even if she was still
angry deep down.

In a few minutes they got off the freeway, and after several blocks they
turned into the driveway of Tommy's condo.

It was clean and bright and new, like everything in this part of town. She wished it was in the same part of town where Gunner and Connie lived. But Tommy promised he'd get her to and from her old school every day. They'd work it out, he said. Sofie hadn't told AnaMaria for sure she was coming. She wanted it to be a surprise.

"Your new home, Sofie," the advocate said. "And I know your dad has a nice new phone for you, so you can give me back the one you've been using."

She took it out of her bookbag and handed it to him. She shivered inside. She was cutting a lifeline and dropping off the edge into a new world.

"Are we going to see each other again?" she asked. "Or is this it?"

The twinkly advocate had been there for the worst moment of her life—when her mom was arrested. And he'd told her the most unfair news of all: Connie could stay with Gunner, but she couldn't. And he'd broken the news that the judge said Gunner wasn't a fit guardian for her. So why did she like him?

He smiled. "We're done in an official capacity because you're not under the court's jurisdiction anymore. But Con will be for a few more years, so you'll see me around, I imagine."

Tommy's door was red, which was a good sign. In the sun, the door was very bright. A leafy green Christmas wreath hung on it.

Tommy startled her by answering the door immediately, as if he'd been waiting on the other side. Sofie wasn't ready.

Squinting in the sun, he looked almost as worried as she felt.

"Princess SJ," he said, smiling.

Mrs. Donovan was right behind him.

"Sofie, we're so glad to see you," she said, clasping both Sofie's shoulders the way AnaMaria did when she had the best idea.

Sofie felt a rush of happiness for a moment that almost lifted her off the ground. Tomorrow she was going to see AnaMaria. She was truly free of foster care. And Mrs. Donovan was nice.

The advocate offered her his hand to shake goodbye. She took a deep breath and kind of wanted to hug him, but she shook his hand.

"Good luck, Sofie," he said. Then he shook hands with Tommy and Mrs. Donovan.

After he was gone, Sofie felt her eyes getting wide because it was so hard to believe where she was. There was the orange leather chair Con had sat in when they were here before, when Gunner was trying to get rid of the horrible boyfriend.

"Let's have milk and cookies," Tommy said.

Milk and cookies? Why? Sofie didn't much like milk. Though she sometimes got chocolate milk at school.

She tried to look as if she liked that idea very much.

"I'll get them," he said. "Mom can show you your room."

"I don't live here," Mrs. Donovan explained as they walked through the living room and down the hall. "But my townhouse is not very far away. I didn't have to go to the office today, so I thought I'd help Tommy welcome you."

She lowered her voice almost to a whisper. "I know it's going to feel very strange at first. We can take it slow. Tom is so glad you're here, but it's very strange for him too—as much as he wants this." She shrugged and smiled. "We'll find our way."

Sofie nodded. She'd try.

"And milk and cookies is a comfort ritual Tommy never grew out of. It came from his grandparents' home. And he only does it with people he cares about."

"So," she said in a normal voice. "This is your room. We thought you might like to decide how you want it. That's why it's so blah."

Was this the same room she'd awakened in the night of the gun? That night had been so terrifying, she didn't remember much.

The room was very blah, but it was *big*. She and AnaMaria could have a wonderful time in this room. The ceiling was high and a pretty white fan turned slowly overhead. It stirred the air in a nice way even though it was very cold outside. But cozy warm in the room.

There were big windows across from the door. The carpet soaked up the sounds of her feet as she crossed the room to look out. She saw winter-brown grass, two small trees inside cages, and a birdbath that looked kind of surprised to be there. The yard was enclosed by brick walls. She could see the top of a house on the other side.

Raised beds ran around the edges of the yard. Sofie saw a few brown lumps of dead plants. They hadn't been put to bed.

"Does Tommy like to garden?" she asked.

"He doesn't have time to know if he likes to garden or not," Mrs. Donovan said. "But I'll bet he'd be glad for you to do some gardening."

Gunner could help her. He would love this backyard.

"Here's your bathroom," Mrs. Donovan said, gesturing.

Mrs. Donovan explained that the weird short-but-deep tub flooded with sunlight from a high window was a soaking tub. Sofie could probably sit chin deep in that tub if she filled it to the brim. There was a sink and a toilet, and in a little ell there was like a shower room with no curtain, only a sheet of pretty glass she'd stand behind. But what she loved most was the floor. It was made of small, colorful bit of green and brown stones that made her think of the piney forest floor in *The Underneath*.

Why did some people have so many things, and other people have so few things? The people she loved and who loved her didn't have much. Would she ever be able to love these people? Really love them, as much as she loved her mom and Con and Gunner?

Tommy had said *milk and cookies* like it was a thing that might have rules. So she planned to watch closely as they sat on stools at an island between the kitchen and the other room.

The other room was big and open and had a lot of different things in it. Furniture for reading or watching TV, office-y stuff in one corner, a large table at one end with six chairs around it. There was a game table set with chess pieces. None of the large pretty rugs on the floor matched, but they looked nice together. Kind of signature. She wondered who had chosen them.

But *milk and cookies* didn't seem to have rules. They passed a bag of cookies around and ate them and drank the milk. Tommy really liked milk. Every bite of cookie required a drink of milk.

It was kind of weird, but okay. She tried not to watch too closely.

When he glanced at her, his eyes were warm.

She drank most of her milk to get it over with, then enjoyed the cookies.

Mrs. Donovan talked about whether Sofie was ready to start choosing stuff to make her room truly hers—if she was, they could go shopping, or shop online. Or they could browse online, then go out shopping too.

Tomorrow she would get to see Mr. Bloom and AnaMaria, her real people. She wished today were shorter.

She didn't really want to shop because she wasn't used to shopping the way Mrs. Donovan was talking about. The thought of doing it made her feel very small and her heart beat fast in her throat.

"I like to play chess," she said.

Tommy looked surprised, then he beamed at her. "Of course you do, Princess SJ."

"Connie taught me."

He nodded.

"He doesn't let me win," she said.

He shook his head no as if to say *Of course not.*

He looked so pleased it made her hopeful for these people. And this person was actually her dad and was planning to raise her like a real dad.

It took over an hour, but Tommy eventually checkmated her and she laid down her white king. He extended his hand across the board. She shook it. He looked so happy. And proud.

Mrs. Donovan didn't enjoy chess, but she loved Scrabble, which Sofie sometimes played during rainy-day recesses.

The day passed. Slowly sometimes, but not when she was caught up in a game. Tommy made lunch and dinner and she and Mrs. Donovan cleaned up the kitchen. It was so gleaming compared to the kitchen at home. Sofie didn't even know what some of the stuff on the counter was.

Mrs. Donovan went home after dinner, saying she hoped Sofie would have a great day at her old school tomorrow, and Sofie and Tommy watched a movie and then, thank goodness, it was time to go in her room and shut the door.

She flopped down on the bed with the blah coverlet and stared at the bare wall. She was worn out. And so glad to be alone. She thought about calling Gunner or Con, but she couldn't. Becoming Tommy's daughter and Mrs. Donovan's granddaughter was going to be hard work. But her mom had told her to do it and be happy, and Sofie had said she would. But she still wished with all her heart they could turn back time to the night her mom went off and left them.

chapter 39

Sofie's new birth certificate said her father was Thomas Emory Donovan. He wasn't her dad like her mom was her mom. Tommy was more like her boots. She felt strong in her boots, and she felt strong having Tommy for a dad because she'd didn't have to worry about foster care ever again. She was glad he didn't know she compared him to her boots.

She saw his car stop in front of the house and him get out.

"Con," she yelled from the bottom of the stairs, "Tommy's here. I'm leaving."

He came down in sweats and a hoodie and bed hair, looking half-asleep. He'd probably stayed up all night talking to Jade.

"You okay?" he asked, rubbing his eyes.

She nodded.

"I'll see you Tuesday," she said, then whispered, "Hang out with Gunner."

"Okay."

This was the second weekend of the new arrangement. Since the restaurant was closed Sunday and Monday, Tommy picked her up on Sunday morning and kept her until Tuesday. Gunner picked her up at school on Tuesday afternoon, and she was at home until Sunday morning, when Tommy picked her up again.

She heard Gunner letting Tommy in.

She hugged Gunner goodbye and picked up her backpack. Gunner gave Tommy a half carton of fresh eggs and a plastic sack of fruit.

"He knows I own a restaurant, right?" Tommy said on the way down the sidewalk.

"Gunner thinks eating fruit is important. And fresh eggs are really good." And she didn't like him suggesting Gunner was doing something silly when he was showing he loved her.

The freeway across town was slushy as snow tumbled out of the sky. Wipers kept half circles clear on the windshield, but snow piled up around the edges and on the side windows, which made the car feel dim and cozy.

"When I was a kid, we went to this park with a great sledding hill. It's still there. Does that sound like fun?" Tommy asked. "Would you like to go sledding?"

They could have a good time without being weird. "Sure."

"Okay." Tommy smiled. "We'll stop at the mall and pick up a snowsuit and boots for you."

She had those. Every year a church provided stuff like that to the kids at her school who couldn't afford it. But she knew Tommy wanted to buy her nice new things. After last weekend, Monday and Tuesday she'd gone to school looking like Tommy Donovan's daughter, and the rest of the week she looked like Sofie Jones.

The mall was huge and beautiful, with giant murals and Christmas decorations and skylights. And it was crowded. Much worse than last weekend. What if she and Tommy got separated? She stopped gawking at stuff and paid attention, staying close at his side.

"Do you know what you want for Christmas? I know it's only two weeks away, but I'm a last-minute guy. I get busy, you know."

She shook her head. He'd bought her so much stuff already. She didn't need more.

The sporting-goods store they went into had two levels. Sofie felt small and hot the minute they stepped inside.

She didn't like to ride escalators. Rising above the swarm of shoppers on the lower level made her feel a little sick. She looked straight ahead.

When they got off, Tommy touched her shoulder to steer her. "Over there."

There were so many snowsuits, boots, hats, scarves, gloves, goggles, and helmets. She'd never worn goggles and a helmet for sledding before.

Tommy waited for her to pick out stuff. The forget-me-not-blue snowsuit was very pretty, but it didn't feel like a good choice. Maybe the red snowsuit with the fancy stitching on the jacket. She loved red. Maybe the silvery one with fur trim on the hood?

Tommy's expression said *Pick whatever you want.* She didn't really want any of them. But she stroked the fur trim on the silvery one, and it felt nice, so she chose it.

When they walked out the doors to the parking lot, cold air cupped her face. It was still snowing. She felt the flakes landing in her hair as they found Tommy's car. She wondered what Gunner and Con were doing without her.

They stopped by Tommy's mom's house to pick up the sled. It was actually a toboggan, Tommy explained, with a big curling front end.

She didn't know what to call Mrs. Donovan. She didn't want to call her Grandma because she didn't call Gunner Grandpa. But calling her Mrs. Donovan made her sound like a teacher.

"What should I call you?" she asked.

She got the idea Mrs. Donovan had been thinking about that because she answered so quickly.

"My full name is Dora Claire Donovan. I go by Claire. Dora was my grandmother's name. My grandpa called her Dorie, so it's a special sound to me. One I like to hear. One that carries nice memories. Would you like to call me Dorie? It would be a name for only you to use."

Gunner sounded like a purr, and *Dorie* had a ring to it. Like a doorbell. Doorbells caused doors to open.

"Dorie," she said. It felt right. "Hi, Dorie."

Her grandmother smiled. "Hi, Sofie."

Even though Halloween and Thanksgiving were over, Mrs. Donovan—Dorie—still had the papier-mâché pumpkin on a table in the entryway. She'd taken off the stemmed top and filled the pumpkin with a bundle of pretty dried grasses.

"Come back here after you sled if you want to," she told them. "We can order pizza."

At Tommy's condo, they cut off tags and Sofie took her stuff to her room to put on. Her room still didn't have any personality. But it would gradually get her signature look. Actually, the first thing it needed was a nice cozy lamp, but she wasn't going to tell Tommy that or he'd take her shopping for one.

She pulled on the snowsuit and looked at herself in the mirror. She looked like a princess. She truly did. All silvery and furry. Her boots were the kind Tommy said you didn't wear socks with because they were sheepskin inside. When she slid her bare feet into them, it felt so wonderful she wiggled her toes.

Tommy had asked her what she wanted for Christmas. And now she knew. She wanted boots like these for Gunner and Con. She could see their smiles when their bare feet slid into all that softness.

By the time they got to the sledding hill, the snow had stopped and the gray sky was breaking into patches of blue. The sledding hill was big and there were a lot of people in bright clothing streaking down and climbing back up, yelling and laughing and flinging themselves into the snow. The little kids and their parents stayed on one side. Bigger kids and teenagers took the middle. And a few tobogganers were on the other side, which was where she and Tommy went.

He helped her adjust her goggles and helmet. She felt like a princess from outer space. And Tommy looked funny, kind of like a bear in goggles. She tried not to smile, but Tommy said, "What?"

She shrugged, letting her smile break free.

He was grinning.

"We should probably make a couple of runs together, then you can go on your own if you want to."

He sat at the back and motioned her to the front. "Okay, on this run, you're the passenger and I'm the driver," he said. "So you keep your feet in. I'll steer with my heels in the snow. Always use only your heels—otherwise you could break a foot. We won't go full speed."

She sat with Tommy's legs on either side and the curl of the toboggan in front, her knees bent. He shoved them off with his hands and they sailed down the hill.

"Now if I want to slow down, I really dig in both heels." Which he did. "And if I want to curve left, I use my left heel." They snaked down the hill that way—left, right, left, right. "Got it?" he said when he braked them to a stop at the bottom.

She nodded. It didn't seem hard.

They got off and walked up the hill, taking turns pulling the toboggan. She was breathless when they got to the top. The sun was fully out now and she understood why she needed goggles. Otherwise, she'd be snow-blind.

"Okay," Tommy said, taking the driver's seat again. "Hop on and we'll make a real run. Remember, keep your feet inside."

When she was on, he said, "Ready?"

She nodded.

He shoved them off. At first they didn't go all that fast, but then it was like the toboggan wasn't even touching the snow. Wind scoured her cheeks and she felt a scream come out and sail away behind her.

At what felt like the last moment, Tommy made a braking left curve and they came to a stop in an explosion of snow that left them looking like they'd been dusted in glitter.

Tommy got off and offered her his hand. She took it and he hoisted her up. She didn't know whether to laugh or cry or dance. She bumped against him and he squeezed her shoulder.

"Fun, huh?" he said.

She nodded. She didn't have a word for how much fun that had been.

At the top, she was tired and breathless. She lay down and made a snow angel. Tommy reached out a hand and helped her up so it was a perfect angel.

"Well," he said. "Do you want to try a run by yourself?"

"No. Let's go together."

It was more fun with him.

On the ride home, her face tingled in the warmth of the car and she was worn out. She wondered if it had snowed at the prison today. She could email her mom and ask. Maybe she would later.

chapter 40

The heater in the truck hardly worked, so Sofie's nose was numb with cold as she and Con and Gunner stomped the snow off their boots on the back porch. Inside, Sofie leaned against the wall and pulled hers off. Her bare feet were summertime pink and warm. She *loved* her boots. She glanced at Con and Gunner and hid a smile.

When her dad had taken her back to buy the boots for Con and Gunner yesterday after school, she'd thrown her arms around him and said, "Thank you so much, Tommy!"

He'd held her face in his hands and grinned. "You are welcome so much, Princess SJ!"

"A package came today," Gunner said, nodding at the box on the kitchen table. A box like that had arrived from California every Christmas of Sofie's life. The money inside would be nice. Maybe Gunner wouldn't have to work so much for a while. But what would they do with the other stuff without their mom to sell it online? Though the box wasn't as large as usual.

"Why don't you open it?" Gunner said.

"Go ahead, Sof," Con said with a shrug. "If there's anything good you can tell me."

"Connie. Help me."

She didn't need help, but she wanted her brother to do something with her. She didn't get to see him all that much.

He used scissors to cut the tape, then pushed the box toward her. "You open it."

When she pulled back the flaps, there was a red-and-white-striped card with Con's name on it. Beside it was a book with a beautiful cover. A fox was standing in the snow.

She picked it up and flashed it at Gunner, pointing to one of the names. "Look! This is the person who wrote *The Underneath*."

"I see that."

A bookmark poked out from between the pages with something written on it: *A signed copy from the personal library of your great-grandmother, the librarian.*

"She's a *librarian*?" she said to Gunner. Her mean great-grandmother?

"*Was.* She's been retired for many years. But like you, Sofie, she has lots of books."

"Is she mean?" She'd learned from the advocate to ask what you needed to know.

"She was probably mean sometimes. She had to raise and educate two boys all by herself. But Donna is a good person."

"But she was mean to Summer, right? Mom said."

Gunner's eyes were sad. "Summer blamed her mom because I ended up in trouble. For some reason, she thought it was Donna's fault I couldn't keep my act together. I wouldn't be surprised if Donna got a little testy." He sighed. "Summer and I were two of a kind. Summer and her mom were always a storm brewing."

Con was looking inside his envelope. He held up two gift cards for video games he and Jade liked to play. He looked so pleased.

This year, the California Christmas box had presents *for them* in it.

"Gunner, this must be for you." She handed him a pretty metal box of tea.

His face looked almost young and a laugh exploded. "Lapsang souchong. We drank this the summer we met." He shook his head. "Kids."

Under the tea was a green envelope with *For everybody—Merry Christmas*. Sofie assumed that was the usual money, which would be welcome. And under that, the very last thing, was a large manila envelope with the words *California Family*.

"Go ahead," Gunner said. "Let's see."

Sofie slid out a color photo of people looking kind of windblown. Sand and rocks were in the background, and shallow waves rolled up on a beach.

There was a tiny old lady, as old as Gunner, as short as he was tall, in the group.

"What?" Con said, coming to look.

Gunner leaned over to point. "That boy on Donna's right is Jess, our older son."

He wasn't a boy. He was old.

"He's a professor at Berkeley. Never married. Always been good to Donna. Has no use for me. Which I understand. The boy on the other side is Matt. He's a psychiatrist. Probably because somebody in the family needed to be. It's hard growing up with a dad who's an addict and a criminal and can't stay out of prison longer than a minute."

Sofie looked up at him. "You're not like that now."

He shrugged and shook his head.

"Those three grown kids around Matt are his daughter Ari, his son Chris, and his youngest daughter Molly. The girl beside Ari is her daughter. She's your age, Sofie."

Sofie stared. She was looking at her cousin. All these people were her family. They didn't look at all mean—not even her great-grandmother. The girl her age looked Hispanic like AnaMaria. The names Gunner was saying were running together, but there was a little boy who made Sofie think of Sam from the foster home. And one of her cousins was holding a sweet bundled baby.

"Holy cow," Con said. "Who knew?"

"My name is mud with all of them, of course," Gunner said. "But I'm trying to make amends."

He opened the little can of tea and sniffed it. Sofie saw his eyes tear, but he smiled.

"Donna started sending these boxes a year after Summer died. I was the one who told her about the accident. Your mom thought Donna wouldn't care. And she did care. She never had the chance to get to know you kids, but she always wished you and your mom well. And she worried. But she didn't know what to do."

Sofie could feel Con staring at the photo. Gunner wasn't their only blood kin. That was good to know.

Sofie lifted the beautiful book to her face and smelled it. It had belonged to the little old lady in the picture, who had given it to her. She was the great-granddaughter of a librarian.

chapter 41

A rustle, a squeak, a thud, and then more soft shuffling tried to tug Sofie awake to a Christmas day as scary and exciting as the dark side of the moon. She curled down deeper into the soft sheets and covered her head.

Last Christmas, they had stayed in pajamas and played spa all day. Con had even let them style his hair. And she and her mom had given each other mani-pedis.

They watched the movie DVDs they'd asked for on the angel tree at the Y. They watched *Moulin Rouge* twice. And Christmas night they used money from the California box to order pizza delivery to their door like rich people.

Sofie wiped away tears. Last year she hadn't known Gunner existed, and this morning she felt sure he was the one making noises, and he was doing something he hoped would make her and Con happy.

When she pushed the covers away from her face, a weird smell drew her out of bed.

It was still dark except for the streetlights, but a glow came from the living room. Was it even morning? The icy floor under her bare feet made her think of her cushy new boots. The best part of Christmas would be at her dad's later, watching Gunner and Con try on their boots for the first time.

The glow in the living room, she saw as she peeked around, was coming from a rope of tiny lights. They were mainly puddled on the floor, but Gunner had already draped a few on the tree. He kept working, not seeing her in the dark doorway.

Was it the tree she smelled? Could it be a real tree? One year her mom had brought home a little Christmas tree, but it was plastic. The ornaments were glued on and the whole thing had been sprinkled with glitter. This tree smelled like the floor of the piney forest in *The Underneath*. Gunner was the skinny redbone hound, and she and Con were the kittens who had once been loved. And were again.

She slipped through the kitchen and very quietly up to the attic.

Con was snoring as she knelt beside him. "Connie," she whispered. "Connie."

He sat up. "Sof?"

"Shhhhh! You need to come and see what Gunner is doing."

He was quiet. "Is it something bad?" She heard sick dread in his voice.

"No! He's putting up a real tree. One you can smell. And he's wrapping it with tiny lights. He doesn't know I saw. What time is it?"

He looked at his phone. "Five thirty?" He groaned.

"Shhhh!"

"I've not been asleep that long," he whispered. "I need more sleep." He rolled away from her and fluffed his pillow.

But fairly quickly he rolled back toward her. "The old guy is putting up a real tree?"

"Yes."

He got up wearing his long underwear, and wrapped a blanket around his shoulders. "Take me to your leader."

Sofie smiled in the darkness.

Later, as the sun was rising, they took their plates of eggs and cinnamon buns and sliced oranges to the couch and sat staring at the beautiful lit-up cedar tree. Turned out, Gunner had bought it for almost nothing as the tree stand was closing last night.

"At home, we always had a cedar tree," he said. After a while he added, "I wish it wasn't too late for making amends to my parents and brother."

He had been spending hours at the table writing letters to his California family, telling them he was sorry for letting them down and hurting them.

"You could still write to your parents and brother," she said.

"They've been gone for years, Sofie."

She knew that.

After a while, he patted her knee. "But I will write to them."

When Con finished, he took his plate to the kitchen and came back with a piece of foil and began tearing and crumpling it into a star shape, which he placed in the treetop. When she and Gunner were finished, Con took a selfie of them in front of the tree—all of them with wild hair, Con seeming to be wearing a crooked star on his head. He was in the middle, and he had stretched his blanket like wings and wrapped Sofie and Gunner close.

"Send it to Mom," Sofie said.

She saw the looks on Gunner and Con's faces. Maybe she shouldn't have mentioned her. But what Sofie wouldn't give for a hug.

Dorie's cheeks were flushed and her eyes sparkled with happy tears as she flung open the door and hugged first Sofie, then Con, then Gunner. "Never *ever* did Tom and I think we would have a family to celebrate Christmas with."

Gunner took a glistening jar of strawberry preserves he and Sofie had made last summer out of his pocket. "Merry Christmas, Claire," he said, giving it to her.

Her dad rushed from the kitchen. His face was flushed and he had a smear of something at the corner of his mouth.

"Princess SJ," he said, putting both warm hands on her cold cheeks.

"Merry Christmas," she said.

Christmas would be here from now on. Forever. A swell of feeling made her throat tight.

Her dad and Gunner shook hands, and Gunner gave him a jar of strawberry preserves from his other pocket.

Sofie couldn't resist the urge to hug Gunner.

"Professor," her dad said, pulling Con into a back-pounding hug. Con pounded back, but Sofie caught the almost eye roll.

Con smiled. "Thanks for inviting us over."

"Yeah, of course," her dad said. "The kitchen can run itself for a while. Come and see what Santa brought."

They unbundled from their coats and boots and scarves and followed her dad to a corner of the huge room bright with sunny afternoon snow light.

"Oh man!" Con said, reaching for a pool cue.

"What about you, Gunner?" her dad asked. "Do you play?"

Gunner raised an eyebrow and nodded.

Later, the *tok tok* of the balls from the pool table mixed with the clatter of Dorie and Sofie cleaning up.

Dorie was packing leftovers into containers for Con and Gunner. Sofie would spend tonight here, and her dad would take her home on his way to work tomorrow.

Sofie and Dorie stood close as Sofie held the container for Dorie to spoon the sweet, sticky, tart cranberry relish into. From years of food pantry holiday donations, Sofie thought cranberries were nasty. But her dad's cranberry relish, chunky with big toasted walnuts and striped with bits of orange peel, was better than...a book. She kind of hated to see it be spooned into a container for Con and Gunner. But not really.

"You smell good," she said to Dorie.

Dorie laughed. "Shampoo and soap."

Sofie didn't try to explain.

When Jade's uncle dropped her off at Tommy's it was dark. Sofie's dad had turned on the electric fireplace. And the tree, covered with all kinds of ornaments and lights of many colors, made the room beautiful.

"Wow!" Jade said, looking around.

Con introduced her to Dorie. He looked so happy when he said "This is my girlfriend, Jade."

When he brushed snow gently out of Jade's hair, Sofie fought tears.

The best moment, as she'd known it would be, was when Gunner opened the big box that said *To Gunner from Sofie.*

"Put them on," Sofie said. "No socks."

He looked a little embarrassed by his socks with holes, but he pulled them off and stepped into the fleece-lined boots.

She watched his face as he stood. She saw in his eyes what a nice feeling it was. He nodded.

"Thank you, Sofie."

He didn't look at her dad, which made her happy. He seemed to know that while the money was Tommy's, the love was hers.

With excitement, Con was ripping open his own big box from her, knowing now what was inside.

"Picture, picture," Jade said.

And Con and Gunner stood in front of the tree wearing their cushy boots.

The best part of the day was over.

chapter 42

The wind whistling under the back door sounded like a ghost moaning.

Gunner raised his bushy gray eyebrows at Sofie. "Hear that? Old Man Winter trying to sneak in."

But near the stove, where Gunner was making popcorn over a burner in a pan with the lid on, and Sofie was keeping close watch, the space was toasty warm. Sofie hadn't known popcorn could be popped in a skillet by just anybody. And she still thought possibly Gunner was wrong.

Con was at a party at Jade's house, and because it would be so late by the time the new year came in, Jade's aunt and uncle had invited him to spend the night. He and Jade would probably kiss when everybody jumped up and down and cried *Happy New Year!* Sofie had never been to a New Year's Eve party, but that's what they did on TV. The kissing part looked gross. Maybe Connie wouldn't do it.

Gunner was shaking the pan over the burner with one hand, clamping the lid down with the other hand, but nothing was happening.

She knew this wasn't going to work.

Pop. Pop, pop, POP, pop. Pop, pop. Pop, POP, POP.

"See," he said, as the shaking pan sounded like there was a hailstorm going on inside. "An old dog knows a few tricks."

She smiled. Wait until she told Connie.

Gradually the popping slowed. Gunner kept shaking the pan until it was quiet except for a couple of last pings against the lid. Then he took it off the heat and lifted the lid. A smell billowed out—nothing like the smell of regular popcorn. This was a fresh kind of woody smell.

Gunner poured a thin stream of melted butter over the popcorn, sprinkled a little salt, and shook the pan a few times, then he dumped it into two big white bowls.

"Wow," Sofie said, as the first bite dissolved against her tongue. "This is magic, Gunner."

He laughed. "You know what's magic? Magic is spending a New Year's Eve sober outside the fence. I don't think I've done that since I was about fourteen, Sofie. In twelve more days, I'll have been sober for seven months."

"Is it still hard?"

When he looked at her, she saw the truth in his eyes. He nodded.

They had to leave this house in March. Con and Gunner would get their own place and she'd begin living with her dad full time. That was going to be so hard on Gunner.

"We'll still be together almost every day," she said, knowing he could read her mind.

To let her finish the year in Mr. Bloom's class, her dad or grandmother would drive her across town to school every morning, and Gunner would pick her up after school and she'd stay with him until Tommy got off work.

"We can make popcorn after school," she said.

"You bet," he said. "Every day if we want to."

They took their popcorn into the living room and sat on the couch to watch the movie Gunner had picked at the library, *The Right Stuff*—what he called an oldie but goodie—which Sofie really liked. And the movie she'd watched a million times—*Coco*—which she wanted Gunner to see so he'd know he'd always be alive in her heart.

Sofie had a big cry at the end, like always, and Gunner said, "Wasn't that a fine movie?" in a thick voice.

Then they switched to regular TV to wait for the countdown, and Gunner went into the kitchen, telling her to stay put.

She hoped Connie was having fun at Jade's party and Tommy's Place was very busy the way it should be on New Year's Eve. Her dad would sleep late tomorrow, probably. Then he'd pick her up.

Gunner came back balancing a plate of little red balls skewered by toothpicks. The toothpicks had festive ruffled ends.

"Maraschino cherries!" he said. "Voilà!"

She'd had them on top of treats a few times, but she always took them off because she thought they tasted nasty.

"I used the whole bottle!" Gunner looked so happy as he set them on the table in front of the couch. "We had these at home when I was a kid. Only on New Year's Eve."

Sofie smiled.

On the TV, they were beginning the countdown.

When midnight struck, Gunner beamed and clasped her foot. "Happy New Year, Sofie!"

She scooted over and hugged him, catching the smell of tea and the car wash and...maraschino cherries. "Happy new year, Gunner." Tears came to her eyes.

He offered the plate to her. She smiled and took two.

"They're really pretty," she said. And they were. Red was her favorite color. But she wished she didn't need to eat them.

When Con called, she was surprised. She thought he'd be having so much fun he wouldn't think about her and Gunner.

"Happy New Year, Sof." His voice sounded weird, and she didn't hear any background noise.

"Connie," she said. She wished she could hug him. They had never spent New Year's Eve apart.

Sofie remembered how her mom had looked that night exactly four years ago when she went out to party. She'd worn a beautiful forget-me-not-blue dress that had one bare shoulder with a skirt that kind of twirled out at the bottom. And her signature dangle earring. Sofie remembered her warmth and perfume as she hugged Sofie close and kissed her.

Sofie shivered. "I love you, Connie," she said.

"Love you too, Sof," he mumbled.

Shortly, her phone buzzed again. There was her dad's face. He looked very busy and delighted. She could see waiters moving behind him and the noise of celebration almost drowned him out.

"Happy New Year, my girl," he said.

His eyes were so warm. He'd started calling her *my girl* instead of Princess SJ. *There's my girl. How's my girl? What does my girl want for breakfast?*

It was nice.

"Happy New Year," she said. She could think of him as *my dad* and she could say *my dad* when she was talking about him. But she couldn't call him *Dad*. But *Tommy* was starting to feel really wrong.

In bed with socks and two extra blankets because the furnace wouldn't be able to keep up with Old Man Winter, Sofie read *The Higher Power of Lucky*. This was the second time through. She was starting to feel like Lucky could be her best friend if AnaMaria wasn't already.

Tommy should meet Lucky. That girl *really* punched above her weight. She had an actual job tidying up after AA meetings at Hard Pan's Found Object Wind Chime Museum and Visitor Center.

Hard Pan, the little town in the Mojave Desert where Lucky lived, reminded Sofie of her neighborhood. She didn't live in a desert, of course, but it was a place where addicts looking for their higher power lived. It was a place where people needed help getting food. Where grandparents raised a kid whose mom was in prison. It was a place where people lived in makeshift places.

Lucky was cozy in her canned-ham part of the house, which wasn't exactly a house, but definitely a home. And Sofie had been cozy in the hot, cramped attic with Con.

And they both had guardians, although Sofie didn't have one anymore. At the end of the book, Lucky was getting an adoptive mom who loved her. Sofie was getting a real dad who loved her.

Lucky didn't like to think about the shiny metal vase on a high shelf and what was in the vase. Sofie didn't like to think about the terrible New Year's Eve when her mom had abandoned her. Sofie wished she could rip that memory out like a page in a bad book. She wanted to wad it up and throw it away. But it was always there, hanging tight.

Lucky found her higher power at the end of the book, and Sofie was still looking for hers. She hadn't known she needed one until she read this book, but now she knew it was *exactly* what she needed.

She wasn't sure what a higher power was. And at the beginning of the book, Lucky hadn't been sure either. That's why she was always eavesdropping on a bunch of old alcoholics at their meetings.

Lucky did understand she had to hit rock bottom first to get her higher power. That's why Sofie was reading the book again. She *felt* Lucky hit rock and find her higher power. That's why, at the end, Lucky was able, finally— after two years—to dip into the beautiful metal vase and fling her mother's ashes into the desert breeze while her friends sang "Amazing Grace" and a big moon roared up into the sky.

Sofie longed to do something that beautiful and wonderful and free and full of love, but she had to find her higher power.

chapter 43

The March morning was foggy when Sofie held the screen door open for the couch. Gunner and Con wrestled it into the yard. Carrying the cushions, Sofie followed them to the truck. The bare branches of the big oak dripped fog drops on them.

Nobody else would ever live in this house again because the bulldozers were coming. Sofie was used to the rumble of the big machines in the neighborhood. This block and four others were being knocked down for new buildings. Connie and Gunner were moving into a tiny, cozy place on the second floor of an apartment building not very far away, and Sofie was moving in with her dad *for real and forever* as he liked to say.

A ding came from Connie's hip pocket. Sofie knew it was Jade. She was going home to Tennessee for spring break, which began this week. Jade hadn't seen her parents in almost a year. What kind of family lived that way? It should be easy for rich people to live, but Jade's parents made it look very hard.

In the fall, Jade would go home to Tennessee, to a different school—not to the one where she'd gotten in trouble. Her leaving would be hard on Connie. He had invited her into their family the same way he'd invited his friend Dylan years ago. Connie was brave.

As soon as the couch was settled into the back of the truck, Connie grabbed his phone. He was still the best brother in the world when Sofie needed him, but now he bent over the phone as if he and Jade were the only people on the planet.

"She has landed in Nashville."

Sofie caught Gunner's eye and she could tell they both had the same thought. Even though she'd be away for a week, she'd still be here. But that was okay. Con wasn't the only one who liked her. So did Gunner. And so did Sofie.

Inside, they worked at packing the kitchen and carrying more boxes to the truck. Con brought down his few things from the attic.

The bedrooms in the little apartment didn't have room for a regular-size bed, so Gunner was selling her mom's bed to a guy he worked with. Gunner would sleep on the daybed Mrs. Donovan had given Sofie—something he seemed a little embarrassed about. Con would have his mattress on the floor, which he said was fine with him.

A couple of months ago, they had taken one of Sofie's bookshelves to Tommy's so she could keep half her books there. Her room was starting to get a signature look. She now had two red beanbag chairs in front of the big windows. And a full-length mirror that stood on legs and could be tilted.

She and Gunner had found it at Goodwill with a damaged hinge so the tilt part didn't work right. But Gunner fixed it. The mirror was fun and kind of beat up. It reminded her of this neighborhood. And she could see all of herself at once, which was amazing.

Her dad helped her choose colorful rugs that fit in with the ones in what he called *the great room.* Her room had carpet, but it was very blah. Now the floor looked like something she and AnaMaria would dance on.

AnaMaria wasn't allowed to come to this house anymore. Not since everybody in the world had found out about her mom and Sofie had landed in foster care. Now when Sofie asked her over, AnaMaria said they could go to her house instead.

It was hard for Sofie to like AnaMaria's mom after she'd decided that, so Sofie and AnaMaria were friends mainly at school. AnaMaria's mom would probably let AnaMaria go to Tommy's condo because it was fancy schmancy.

But that wasn't fair to Gunner, who was kind and loyal and had control over his life. Maybe had even found his higher power.

She went into her mom's room. That day the cops took her away was the last time their mom saw her forget-me-not-blue walls, but she hadn't known it was her last time until it was too late. Sofie stared at the walls. She didn't want to ever forget them.

In science, she was learning about animals that could regrow parts of their bodies. The cute little axolotl could regrow even its heart if it needed to. Mr. Bloom had a poster of an axolotl on the classroom wall and Sofie liked to look at it. Sometimes she felt like she was regrowing her heart.

She jumped when Con spoke to ask if she wanted help in their mom's room.

She could tell by the look on his face he didn't want to help. Con was so angry at their mom.

She hoped he could regrow his heart. Jade would help with that. And Gunner. And her.

Later, they ate oranges and peanut butter sandwiches on paper towels. The sun had come out, and the bright light showed the shabbiness of the kitchen.

"Remember how we used to play Uno with mom before she went to work?" she asked Con.

It had only been nine months ago, but it felt like forever. Sofie hadn't thought about it in a long time, and it used to be so important to her. She'd believed playing Uno could save them.

"What happened to the deck?" she asked.

Con looked surprised. "Don't you remember throwing it in the trash one night?"

"No. Why did I do that?"

He shrugged.

How weird that she wouldn't remember throwing away the Uno cards.

She had taught Gunner to play chess at this table. The chess set was packed with Con and Gunner's stuff to go to their apartment.

"Sometimes can I come to the apartment and play chess with you?" she asked Gunner.

"You bet," he said.

She would always call him in the night and read to him when she couldn't sleep.

Jade's plant was on the table waiting to go to the apartment with Con. He was caring for it while she was in Nashville.

"Don't forget Jade's plant," she said.

He rolled his eyes.

Con had thought it would be fun to give Jade a jade plant for Christmas. When Jade brought it over yesterday, Sofie heard her telling it goodbye, that she'd only be gone a week. And she'd heard Jade tell Connie all he needed to do was keep it in a sunny place and talk to it a lot. And absolutely not to water it.

"Remember not to water it. And to talk to it."

Con blushed. "I know."

After everything else was packed, they still had to face their mom's bedroom. Sofie had sorted things into throw away, give away, and keep. The three of them stood looking at the small keep pile on the bed.

Sofie had a knot in her throat. She picked up the green velvet keepsake box.

"Would you like to see what's in here?" she asked Gunner.

Gunner shook his head. "Not right now."

Sofie could see he was fighting to stay steady. He needed a meeting.

"It's mainly pictures and cards and our hospital bracelets. Stuff like that," she said.

"You take the keepsake box, Sof," Con said. "Mom would want you to have it."

"I think you should have this back, Gunner." She took the glossy buckeye out of the box. "To close the circle."

"Con and I will keep it on the kitchen table. For luck," Gunner said, taking the buckeye.

To a place where she would be only a visitor.

They were down to her mom's favorite forget-me-not-blue T-shirt, her mom's big purse, and her jewelry. Sofie could see her mom in that shirt, the purse over her shoulder, her dangle earring catching the light as she went wherever she was going. People looking at her because she was the tall, beautiful mom with the dimpled smile.

Gunner said, "Sofie, why don't you put everything in the purse and save it for her."

Save it for her? It would be such a long time. Years. She thought of the metal vase that had held Lucky's mother's ashes.

But she opened the purse, crammed the things inside.

Then they turned to the little table with the green candle and the photo of Summer Jones. What had it been like for Gunner every night to see this picture of his beautiful young daughter?

"Was she really a movie star?" Sofie asked.

She hoped Gunner would say yes. Con always thought their mom made that up, but Sofie kind of believed it.

"She was an extra in a movie," Gunner said, picking up the photo and looking at it. "Right here in Iowa."

"Right here?" Sofie didn't know movies were made here.

He nodded. "When she was a teenager, she wasn't getting along very well with her mom, so she came here thinking to get to know my family. And they were shooting a movie nearby. She was in some of the crowd scenes. It was pretty exciting for her. She wrote to me in prison about it." He paused. "And then there was that boyfriend. He didn't stick around long enough to be helpful after Summer was expecting." He paused again. "Summer and Ashley kind of raised each other."

Sofie understood why her mom said Summer Jones had been a movie star. It's the kind of thing you did when you loved your mom.

Gunner's voice was hoarse. "You kids didn't know Summer, so I'll take all this." He gestured to the little altar table with its picture and candle, and was quiet for a moment. "I don't know what I'll do with it. Is whatever I decide okay?"

"You should save it for Mom until she gets home," Sofie said.

That would mean Gunner couldn't die for a long time.

Finally, everything was loaded except her mom's bed, which the man at the car wash was coming to get tomorrow.

When they got in the truck and settled themselves—Sofie holding her lamp and Connie holding Jade's plant—she wanted to turn and take a last look at the house.

Con held up his hand to block her view. "Don't look back. Right, Gunner?"

"Right," Gunner said. "Bad luck."

As they rattled down the alley, she remembered how relieved she'd been to see Gunner on the back step the afternoon she ran away from the foster home. She wouldn't look back at the house, but she'd never forget how happy she'd been to see him. Sober.

She'd really like to know if he'd found his higher power, but it seemed rude to ask.

Maybe the foster home had been rock bottom for her. Now she had to get her life in order like the addicts talked about in their meetings at the Found Object Wind Chime Museum and Visitor Center in Hard Pan. And then she'd find her higher power.

Sofie sometimes wondered what Lucky and her friend Lincoln might be doing—if he'd really grow up to be president. Lucky would probably lead insect safaris. The only part of the book Sofie thought was silly was the way Lucky tried to glisten her eyebrows so Lincoln would think she was pretty, and how she put on her guardian's red silk dress to run away.

As they turned onto the street that ran in front of their house, Sofie snuck a look. She wasn't looking back, she was saying goodbye.

chapter 44

After her dad helped unload Sofie's stuff, he followed Gunner back across town to help them unload at the apartment. Then he'd go back to work, and Dorie would stay with Sofie until he got home.

Dorie was taking the baking sheet of blossom cookies out of the oven.

"Now for the fun part," she said, carefully pressing a chocolate kiss into each piece of hot cookie dough firmly enough to make the dough take the shape of a blossom.

Sofie found it was tricky to get the kiss in the exact middle and to press hard enough, but not too hard. And to work quickly. As they turned all the little circles of dough into blossoms, Sofie saw again how similar their hands were.

"My grandmother taught me to make these," Dorie said. "When Tom was young, I tried to teach him." She laughed. "But even as a child he sensed these are totally girl cookies."

Exactly. She didn't think Con or Gunner would appreciate them. But maybe someday AnaMaria would enjoy coming over to make them. If Sofie invited her. Sofie would be going to a new school next year. One closer to this home. So she and AnaMaria wouldn't see each other every day. Staying friends might be hard. Maybe she and Dorie could invite Jade to make them.

They slid the blossoms back into the oven for three more minutes, then took them out and lined them up on a cooling rack, where they looked like something in a fancy bakery.

"A watched cookie never cools," Dorie said.

Sofie didn't understand what that meant. With this new family, things that didn't make sense worried her. Maybe it was a saying of some kind that was supposed to make her laugh. Or smile.

She smiled, hoping it was what Dorie expected.

Dorie smiled back, and Sofie felt she'd gotten it right.

"Maybe we should taste test a couple," Dorie said. "What do you think?"

"Sure."

She expected the chocolate kiss to be firm, but to her surprise her teeth went right through it and she ended up with a smeary blob of soft chocolate almost up her nose. But it was so good. The chocolate and the peanut butter and the granules of sugar they'd rolled the dough ball in. Connie and Gunner might appreciate these cookies, after all.

"Methey, but gou," she said, wiping chocolate off her face with her finger, then licking her finger.

Dorie laughed. "I agree."

Sofie wet a paper towel and wiped her face and said, "I'm going to unpack my books now."

She was afraid it sounded rude, but she needed a while by herself.

Dorie nodded at her laptop open on the table. "You unpack and I'll do a little work."

Sofie eyed the two bookshelves lined up along the wall and decided. She had books from the Community Center, she had the new book from her great-grandmother and books that Tommy and Dorie had bought her. And Jade's family had given her books for Christmas which she was pretty sure Con had helped pick out because they were perfectly her. *Blended* was about a girl like Sofie, a girl who had to keep switching households. And Con must have told them how much she loved *Orbiting Jupiter*, because they gave her three books by Gary Schmidt.

She'd been keeping the shabby books she loved separate from the new ones that smelled good and made little welcome sounds the first time she opened them. But now that she was going to be sleeping here every night, probably all her books—new and old—should be blended together by author's last name.

As she worked, she found herself wondering what Con and Gunner were doing. Maybe Gunner was making his first cup of tea in the new place.

After a while, Dorie came in and said, "Would you like help?"

She felt she should say yes.

So they sat cross-legged on the floor. She took *A* through *L*, and Dorie took *M* through *Z*. As they worked, Sofie promised herself she would always take time to alphabetize books, even when she was a head librarian with the keys to the building.

This place was so quiet. Sometimes she felt like she was floating, because she couldn't hear her own footsteps. And it felt weirdly like there was nothing outside because she didn't hear mufflers or music or roosters. But now she realized she was hearing rain patter the windows.

Gunner would be happy about the rain. Last week, they had spread compost over their plots at the Community Garden. It had been cold and miserable at first, but as she worked she got warmed up and felt very happy and cheerful by the end.

"Until you entered our lives," Dorie said, "I was afraid my son was going to end up all alone. He's an only child because my husband was killed in a military training exercise right before Tom was born, and I'm an only child. Tom and his wife planned to have kids, but she died so young. And I won't live forever. I'm so glad he found you, Sofie."

She sensed Dorie looking at her, and she knew she should make eye contact and say she was glad to be found. And she was. But packing up the house today had been awful. She wanted to look at Dorie, who was very nice. But she couldn't help the tears that flooded her eyes. She kept her head down, but a tear rolled off and plopped onto the book she was holding.

"Oh, sweetie," Dorie said, scooting over and putting her arms around Sofie. "You poor sweetie."

For a second, Sofie almost pushed her away.

Dorie smoothed Sofie's hair and kissed her forehead. "You go ahead and cry. You have a lot to cry about."

They sat there for quite a while, Dorie messing with Sofie's hair. Stroking it and twisting and lifting it in a way Sofie liked.

Dorie finally got up and came back with tissues. She put them in Sofie's hands, then went back to messing with her hair.

"That tiny mole on your shoulder?" Dorie said. "My Tom has one in the exact same spot."

"Really?"

"Really. It appeared when he was about four. Just that single one."

That was about the time Connie had noticed hers and tried to scrub it off.

"My mom said an angel put mine there to mark me as special."

Dorie smiled, but didn't say anything. She probably thought Sofie's mom was a huge loser.

"I know that's not true," Sofie said. "But it's the kind of thing moms say."

Dorie nodded. "Exactly."

Sofie took a deep breath and let it out. The little dark spot wasn't put there by an angel, but now it wasn't just a mole either. It connected her to her dad.

"The first night Tom took food to your house, he saw it. He came straight to my house and woke me. At first, I thought something terrible had happened, but it wasn't terrible," Dorie said. "It was wonderful."

Later, after Sofie had her shower, she went into the great room to tell Dorie good night. Dorie was on the couch with her laptop.

"Good night," Sofie said.

"Good night. Maybe I'll see you and your dad tomorrow."

Tomorrow was Sunday. Tommy's Place was closed.

"Okay."

In her bedroom, she started to email her mom. But she thought about the day and couldn't.

In bed, she mounded her pillows—she *loved* her down pillows—around her and got comfy with *Hatchet,* the book she was reading to Gunner. She'd chosen it because she thought he'd like it, and she really liked it too—so much she wanted to peek ahead. Actually, she wanted to rip right through to the end. But she didn't. It was fun to ride the roller coaster of the story with him.

She called him. She would read to him until she got sleepy.

chapter 45

On Mr. Bloom's Room Awards Day, which was also the last day of school, Sofie stood at the classroom windows watching for her dad. He said he was eager to meet this Mr. Bloom he'd heard so much about. Sofie thought her dad was a little jealous.

She watched from the window as he turned into the school parking lot, got out, and disappeared through the front doors. He would go through the sunny entrance area, up the twisting stairs, down the hall, around the corner, and into Mr. Bloom's room. Except for the five weeks she'd been in foster care, Sofie had made that journey every school day. She would miss it so.

Sometimes her mom had embarrassed her when she came to the school. She always looked beautiful, but the way she dressed was more movie star than mom. And Sofie sometimes heard words she hated from kids. She pretended she didn't know or care what they meant. She made those mean kids invisible by not seeing or hearing them.

Her dad was in one of the black T-shirts he always wore to work—Sofie had discovered he ordered them by the dozen—and Levi's jeans. He looked like a very friendly sandy brown bear. He looked like a dad.

"This is my dad," Sofie told Mr. Bloom, feeling her cheeks turn pink.

"Tom Donovan," her dad said, offering his hand.

Mr. Bloom shook hands and said how much he was going to miss Sofie. And he said other nice things about her and Con that were kind of embarrassing but made her secretly happy.

As Mr. Bloom talked, her dad rested his hand on her shoulder. She looked up at him. There was a tiny patch of sandy whiskers he'd missed under his chin.

She really liked having a dad. And a grandmother. Really, really liked it. But her old world was precious to her, and sometimes she felt like it was being demolished by big lovable bulldozers who wanted to take care of her and encourage her and cherish her. But she wouldn't be *her*—she wouldn't be signature Sofie—if she let herself be bulldozed.

Gunner wanted to be there for Mr. Bloom's Room Awards Day too, but his work supervisor said no. Most of the kids' parents weren't there. But AnaMaria's mom was. She smiled and waved at Sofie, who waved back.

Mr. Bloom signaled for the kids to sit at their desks and the parents to sit in chairs around the room. He stood in a patch of sunlight coming through the windows and Sofie saw he had flecks of gray in his black hair.

She didn't want Mr. Bloom to get older, to someday be as old as Gunner. But she thought of the family in *Tuck Everlasting* who *didn't* get older. And that didn't work out well either.

"So," Mr. Bloom said. "How do we define *school*?"

"As the place that's so much fun we don't want to leave," everybody answered together.

That's what the banner on the wall said. *School is the place that's so much fun we don't want to leave.*

"It's been a great year," Mr. Bloom said. "I'll miss every one of you."

Sofie would miss him too. He had a way of knowing what each kid needed, and he tried to open doors for them.

"Some of you I'll see at the Community Center this summer."

Sofie almost never went there anymore. Most of the regulars had vanished, and the new people looked at her like she'd wandered into the wrong place. The last time she'd gone with Connie, about a month ago on a Saturday, she hadn't seen either the mom with the sweet baby or the tattooed guy. She worried that the mom with the sweet baby might have gone off with the man Sofie had seen them with the last time, who made her think of her mom's stupid boyfriends.

Mr. Bloom was saying "Some of you I'll see in the hallway next year."

Somebody behind Sofie cheered. She would have cheered *and* thumped the table if she had been one of those lucky ones.

"But for all of you, this is the end of the great adventure of fifth grade as we explored the world—"

"And beyond!" a kid across the room said.

Mr. Bloom grinned. "—and I want to thank you for being my copilots."

He waggled a rolled-up piece of paper tied with a green ribbon. There was one for each of them in the basket on his desk.

"When you leave, I'll give you your Graduation from Mr. Bloom's Classroom diploma. Please don't unroll it until you get home."

Sofie nodded, as did others who knew this was what Mr. Bloom always did. Connie kept his Graduation from Mr. Bloom's Classroom diploma tied up with the green ribbon. Sofie wanted to know what it said, but Connie said some things were private.

When had Connie started to get into privacy? Was it at the end of fifth grade?

Was that going to happen to her?

She didn't think so.

Mr. Bloom opened the glass case where the beautiful globe had tantalized them all year. She had learned that word yesterday. *Tantalized*, meaning something teased you to want it, but you couldn't have it.

Only one kid would take home the globe, and deep down, Sofie knew it wouldn't be her. She hoped Connie and her mom and Gunner wouldn't be too disappointed.

Sofie had been in another school for over a month, not paying much attention to anything except how miserable she was. She'd been going back and forth between homes for six months up until now, and that wore her out. For a while, she'd kept trying to be the winner. Then Mr. Bloom had asked her to talk to the school counselor, who helped Sofie understand a person had only so much energy. It was okay not to win sometimes.

Although she'd longed for the Student Explorer Award ever since Con won it, Sofie felt like she'd been on a life-or-death exploration instead of a student exploration for the last year.

Mr. Bloom held the globe up briefly, but didn't keep them in suspense. He set it on the desk of the boy in front of her. The one who had the fly in his hair last August.

Mr. Bloom stuck out his hand. "Congratulations, Nate. Stand up and take a bow."

Nate did, his face glowing.

He bowed as everybody clapped, including Sofie.

Then Nate sat down and hugged the globe to his chest. "Thank you," he said.

Sofie thought she wasn't going to mind so much, but when Nate hugged the globe and said thanks, it stabbed her heart. She *could* have had it.

Anger at her mom flared. If her mom had stayed in the triangle in the circle, Sofie would be hugging that globe. Her picture would go on the wall with Connie's.

Mr. Bloom was explaining what everybody knew. The Student Explorer Award went to the student who started wherever he or she was, and was the most energetic explorer of anything and everything and tried to take others with them in their interest. A kind of class leader. Or head copilot.

Nate had been that person this year. She hadn't.

As they left the classroom, Mr. Bloom handed them their rolled-up diplomas. Sofie shook Mr. Bloom's hand.

"Goodbye," she said. She felt tears in her eyes she hoped her dad didn't see. "Thank you."

Mr. Bloom's very dark eyes seemed to look right into her. "You are going to have a good life, Sofie. I know you are."

She nodded. She wanted to wipe away the tears that were rolling down her cheeks, but she didn't want her dad to know.

As they walked down the hall to her locker, he kept his hand on her shoulder. "My girl will always punch above her weight," he said.

She nodded.

This was the last time. The last time she would make her way down the twisting stairway and out into the brightness at the bottom.

It was hot in the car. Her dad turned down the temperature and turned up the fan until it was whooshing cool air at them. She undid the green ribbon and unrolled the diploma. The paper was crisp. She sniffed it. It smelled like a book.

Mr. Bloom had written her a personal note at the bottom, the way he did for all the kids.

Sofie,

I will miss you in the neighborhood. You have been brave and strong through the storm this year. You are smart, imaginative, and determined. And you're one of the keenest readers I've ever had in my classroom. I know you will live your own story with energy and imagination and love. I feel very lucky to have had you as a student.

Godspeed. Mr. Bloom

Her dad was glancing her way with a curious look on his face, but he didn't ask.

She rolled the paper up and retied it with the ribbon. It did feel private. She would always cherish it.

She hung out on the patio waiting for Gunner to text her he was in the parking lot. He was getting better at texting.

When he did, she replied with a heart emoji and went inside to tell her dad goodbye.

"I'll see you." She thought about saying *at home*. But she smiled instead.

"Have fun, my girl. Tell Gunner I said hi."

She and Gunner were going to Tommy's condo to plant the raised beds. Tommy had told her to plant whatever she wanted, and she'd decided to plant flowers. And maybe watermelons.

Gunner patted her knee when she got in the truck. Did he notice she wasn't carrying the beautiful globe? Should she tell him she hadn't won?

As they started across town, she leaned her head back and let the May sun warm her face. Garden equipment rattled in a familiar, friendly way. She didn't think Gunner cared whether she'd won or not.

The seed packets were in an envelope between them. Sofie dumped them in her lap. Apricot Lemonade cosmos. She'd chosen that because Gunner loved fruit. Foxglove. She'd picked that because of the fox on the cover of the book her great-grandmother had sent her at Christmas. Raspberry Ripple poppies. Chosen because it sounded like ice cream.

She was also planting borage, with its tiny blue star-shaped flowers, because Gunner said the flowers were edible and good on ice cream.

And Sugar Baby watermelon. But she was torn about that. She'd always loved the summer lunches at the Community Center when they served watermelon. And the watermelon vines at the Community Garden had such fancy leaves. But she could still see the piece of watermelon falling from her mom's hands and smashing at her feet.

She shook the packet against her ear as if it might speak to her. Yes or no.

It didn't speak, but Gunner did.

"Sofie, the soil temperature isn't warm enough yet to plant those. We can do it later."

She was glad she didn't have to decide yet. Some things took time.

chapter 46

Sofie's room was filled with sunlight, and the condo was quiet.

She had dreamed about her mom. The details were melting away, but in the dream her mom was doing some ordinary thing with Sofie. She couldn't remember what exactly. The dream left her feeling sad, but also kind of... warmed. A year ago, almost exactly, was when their mom went off and left them. They were going to see her next weekend. Tommy, Gunner, Con, and her.

Her dad liked to sleep in on Sunday morning, so she stayed in bed reading until she heard sounds from the other side of the condo.

Then she went into the kitchen. After three months, the kitchen still felt like a place for extraterrestrials. She heard her dad running on the treadmill.

He had a shelf of wrestling trophies in the workout room and he was teaching her about baseball. For Christmas, he'd given her a book called *Belles of the Ballpark* about a women's professional baseball league in the old, old days. She hoped he didn't want her to be a ball player, because she was going to be a swimmer. She was on a swim team now.

Hanging beside the trophy shelf was a framed photo of a man who had her dad's coloring and smile. It was Tommy's dad who died before Tommy was born. Now that she knew and loved her dad, she felt sad for what he had missed.

In the fridge, she found the last few sugar snap peas from the garden in a little container with her name on it. Yesterday, she and Gunner had pulled up the sugar snap pea vines because they were through bearing, and planted bush beans in their place.

In the truck yesterday, coming back to Tommy's, she'd told Gunner about *The Higher Power of Lucky,* about how she was reading it for the third time, about how it was her favorite book ever. And she asked him if he'd found his higher power.

He didn't answer for so long she thought she'd offended him. Maybe a higher power was private unless the person himself brought it up.

Finally, he reached out his hand and squeezed her knee. "I do believe I have, Sofie."

She put her hand over his and said she was so glad.

"Me too," he said.

She got out the eggs, butter, cheese, and milk. The skillet and spatula. Their plates and placemats. Yesterday, she had picked the very first of the sweet-pea blossoms from the garden and put them on the island in a glass. When she held the little bouquet of pink and purple flowers to her nose, they smelled wonderful. Gunner told her sweet peas were poisonous—unlike sugar snap peas, which were delicious and nutritious. Why would something beautiful and nice-smelling be poisonous? It didn't make sense. But Gunner said some things didn't.

Today was Sunday and they were going to a ball game. But now that school was out, most days she went to work with her dad. From the restaurant, she could walk to Gunner and Con's apartment, but her dad didn't really like for her to. Usually Gunner would come and get her, or her dad would take a break and drive her. The restaurant was an okay place to hang out, especially when she could be on the patio. But she spent a lot of time with Gunner in the garden.

She saw Con when he was working at the restaurant. Sometimes she helped him. As they washed and dried pots and pans, or stood in the corner wrapping silverware, their arms brushed. They glanced at each other and away, the love and memories close between them.

While she waited for her dad to get off the treadmill, she texted Gunner a heart, took a selfie making a face and texted it to Connie, sent Dorie a good-morning text, then emailed her mom.

Her dad came into the kitchen wearing jeans and a T-shirt—but not a black one because this wasn't a workday—and smelling like soap and shampoo. Every morning, he looked at her like he'd discovered a planet or won the lottery.

"Morning," he said.

"Hey."

"Do you want more than eggs and fruit?" he asked. "Want me to make pancakes or biscuits?"

"That's okay. We can eat at the ballpark, right?"

"Sure."

She was planning to have a hot dog. Maybe two. Gunner was working this afternoon and wouldn't be with them, so she could eat all the trashy— as he called them—hot dogs she wanted.

Later, getting dressed, she put on a black skirt Dorie had bought her at the mall last week and a girly white top she'd had for a while. It was soft and so cute it made her smile. She looked in the mirror. She didn't see a girl who punched above her weight, and she didn't want to stop being that girl. She put on her new garden boots over red-and-white socks that showed at the top, and added a khaki baseball cap and the sparkle studs her mom stole.

"I'm ready," she told her dad.

They picked up Jade on the way. Then Con. Then they walked a hundred miles from where they parked to the stadium where the crowd streamed in.

Sofie smelled hot dogs and thought of the soft bun, the sharp mustard, the crispy stripes on the hot dog that burst with flavor.

The first time she'd been here was the day after the night of the gun. But now she'd been here several times. Today, under a soft blue sky, everything was fine, considering her mom was in prison and she didn't see as much of Connie and Gunner as she would like. She was beginning to understand baseball. She liked to talk to her dad about it and had learned to read box scores, which impressed Con.

She saw people in the crowd notice Con and Jade. Con being so tall, with his bush of thick, dark hair, and Jade with her red hair, made them noticeable. People smiled.

When they were in their seats—Con, Jade, Sofie, her dad—Jade took a small wrapped package out of her shoulder bag and gave it to Sofie.

"I know you're trying to give your room your signature look," she said, "and I thought you might like these."

The package was lumpy and interesting. Sofie peeled away the paper. It was a coiled string of fairy lights.

"Thank you," she said. "I know where I'm going to put them."

"Where?"

"Around a mirror. A tall one that stands on legs and tilts. These will be perfect."

She enjoyed the ball game. She ate lots of popcorn out of her dad's box. It was nowhere near as good as what Gunner popped fresh, because that was truly magical. But good enough that her hand kept reaching in the box and her arm kept touching his, and he kept smiling.

That night, she put up the fairy lights. After her shower, when she was in her pajamas and about ready to get into bed and call Gunner to see if he wanted to hear more of *Hatchet,* she turned on the fairy lights and turned off her pink lamp.

She stood in front of the mirror in the dark room. It still fascinated her to be able to see all of herself at once. Her button-like toes from her mom, her movie-star hair from Summer Jones. Seeing her whole self dimly, framed by the tiny lights, was very strange. She thought of Lucky putting on her guardian's silky red dress and glistening her eyebrows with a drop of oil to run away in a sandstorm.

The first time Sofie read the book, she thought that was very strange. A swaying red silk dress wasn't a good choice for running into the desert in a sandstorm. And Lucky herself had seemed puzzled by her decision.

But a few pages later, when Lucky finally felt her higher power and she could open the vase, reach in, and finally—after two years—*finally* cast her mom's ashes into the wind, the red silk dress was simply perfect.

Sofie could see it. Lucky in red as the moon rocketed into the purple sky. The silky, swaying comfort of the dress as her friends sang "Amazing Grace."

Somehow Lucky had known, although it seemed silly at the time, that the red dress would be part of finding her higher power.

Sofie stood, perfectly still, gazing in the mirror.

The next morning, the light in the kitchen made her squint, and her dad's white T-shirt seemed very white.

"Dad, I need a silky red dress. One that sways."

He was looking at her with an odd expression.

He liked to buy her stuff. What was wrong?

"Say that again."

"I need a silky red dress that sways."

He shook his head. "No. Say the whole thing."

Oh.

She smiled. "*Dad,* I need a silky red dress—"

His hug cut off the rest of her words. It was a bear hug. He kissed the top of her head, and Sofie felt something break loose inside. Something that had been blocking a big rush of something wonderful.